I0581831

COLD HEARTED
TOOTH & CLAW BOOK 1

HEATHER GUERRE

Copyright © 2020 by Heather Guerre

All rights reserved.

No part of this book may be reproduced in any form or by any electronic or mechanical means, including information storage and retrieval systems, without written permission from the author, except for the use of brief quotations in a book review.

AUTHOR'S NOTE

Cold Hearted touches on topics that may be difficult for some readers, including depression, anxiety, toxic past relationships, stalking, and parental emotional neglect. It also includes scenes of violence, including mild gore (vampire bites/attacks) and consensual pain/injury (werewolf bites).

CHAPTER 1

Grace gripped the edge of her seat as the plane touched down. Normally, she wasn't afraid of flying. But in this instance, she was strapped into a four-seater plane whose wingspan nearly clipped the spruce trees growing tight on one side of the gravel—yes, *gravel*—runway. A frozen river snaked alongside the other side. At the end of the runway, a corrugated metal shed served as Longtooth, Alaska's airport.

When the tiny plane had bumped and lurched its way to an idling stop, the pilot flicked switches across the instrument panel. He killed the engine and pulled his headset off. The sudden silence pressed on Grace's ears, thick and cottony. She pulled her headset off and looked over at the door handle beside her. It seemed very wrong that an airplane door should look like a car door from 1989, but she reached for the handle anyway, and let herself out.

It was only four in the afternoon and already pitch dark. The surrounding mountains formed jagged silhouettes against the night sky. The air was bitingly cold, but she was prepared for it. Sure, she was from the lower-48, but she'd grown up in northern Wisconsin and had been living in Chicago for the last four years. Her blood was good and thick from decades of lake-effect snow, winter winds out of the Canadian prairies, and polar vortexes. She already owned good winter gear, and knew how truly dangerous the cold could be. She wasn't going to embarrass herself on that front.

The pilot came around the body of the plane and opened the belly hatch where her bags had been stowed. He was a large man—tall and broad—with dark eyes, a perpetually furrowed brow, and a thick beard that hid his mouth. Despite the fact that he'd said less than a dozen words to her, Grace was certain he didn't like her. And yet, she just didn't care. The part of her that used to care about other people's opinions had shriveled to a rattling husk.

Over the course of their three-hour flight, he'd only spoken twice to her. First, to order her to buckle in and put on her headset. And then, a second time, when she'd asked him how long he'd been flying, and he'd tersely answered, "Long enough." She'd taken the hint and stopped trying to make conversation.

"Thanks," Grace told him as he hauled her massive, wheeled suitcase from the hatch. She moved to take it from him, but he held on, and with his other hand, pulled out her other bag—a large canvas duffel. Turning away from her, he carried both bags towards the metal pole building.

She followed awkwardly behind him. "You don't have to—"

"Get the door," he ordered.

She felt a flare of annoyance so strong, it froze her for a second. She hadn't felt *anything* strongly for such a long time. It was prickly and painful, like the feeling returning to frozen toes. When she realized the pilot was waiting, staring impatiently at her, she hurried past him and pulled open the heavy steel door on the pole building.

Inside, fluorescent lights hummed, starkly illuminating raw walls with exposed two-by-fours and yellow foam insulation. There was another airplane parked on the far side, a twin-prop plane larger than the single-engine plane she'd arrived in, but still a far cry from the commercial jets she was used to. Otherwise, the small building mostly housed maintenance equipment—a battered old pickup truck with a plow mounted on the front, a tractor with a wide rake attachment, a dusty brush hog, chain saws—all things she was used to seeing in the barns and garages of her childhood. Except for the transportation, Alaska was, so far, not the culture shock she'd been expecting—or, if she was being totally honest with herself, that she'd been hoping for.

She'd wanted a change. She'd wanted to get far, far away and start over in a place that was new and different. So far, it looked like all she'd done was move back to her rural Wisconsin hometown—conifer trees, snow, and farm implements included.

A woman stood just inside the door, bundled in a heavy down parka, an ushanka hat, and thick hide gloves. Though Grace had never seen her before, she knew it had to be Margaret Huditiltik, the superintendent of the Teekkonlit Valley School District, and principal of both the elementary and the secondary school. She looked to be in her mid-fifties, with a freckled brown face, lightly weathered in a healthy, frequently-outdoors kind of way. A long braid, silver threaded with black, emerged from her ushanka and lay over her shoulder. Her eyes were a surprisingly pale gray against her tawny brown skin. A smile stretched her cheeks and she stepped forward to intercept Grace with a handshake.

"She made it!" Margaret's gloved hand enclosed Grace's. "I hope Caleb didn't talk your ear off." She shot the pilot a teasing smile. He responded by dumping Grace's bags on the floor at her feet.

"No, he—" Grace glanced uncertainly at the taciturn pilot, glimpsing only his back as he pushed the door open and disappeared back into the cold. "Uh, he was an excellent pilot."

Margaret gave her an apologetic look. "He's the best there is, but he's not exactly a one-man welcome wagon. Anyways, you're here. I'm Margaret Huditiltik. It's nice to finally meet you, Grace."

"Thank you, it's good to finally meet you, too."

Margaret released her hand. "Alright. Let's get your bags loaded up and we'll get you set up at The Spruce. I'm sure you're tired after traveling all day."

"A little," She agreed politely. In truth, she was exhausted. But she was always exhausted. She could never seem to get enough sleep. And at the same time, could never fall entirely asleep either. She spent her days and nights caught in a half-conscious state of perpetual, mind-spinning fatigue.

Margaret helped her carry her things out another door to the other side of the building, where an old black Suburban sat idling.

Longtooth's airstrip was only a two minute drive from the center of the little town, visible from the main street.

"There are basically two main roads in Longtooth," Margaret explained. Towering snowbanks lined the gravel road. Both sides of the street were bordered by rows of weathered, metal-sided buildings, in a motley patchwork of faded blues, grays, and reds. There was a combination grocery-and-hardware store, a lawyer's office, a small medical clinic, a bank, and the post office. Archaic-looking power lines spidered out from each building, accumulating in a mass around a single, overburdened electrical transformer mounted high above the street.

The river curved close to the road on the eastern side, wide as a freeway. The ground sloped upward from the river. A few narrow streets spidered along the slopes. Small, boxy, log-sided houses sat at irregular distances and angles from each other, rising above the main road. Further up the slopes, the houses gave way to a thick forest of needled conifers. From there, the ground rose steeply, transitioning into rocky mountainsides, forming towering walls that cradled the city from the east and west. Grace could only see a narrow wedge of the night sky overhead, most of the view dominated by jagged mountain peaks.

At the end of the road, Longtooth's two schools faced each other from opposite sides. The secondary school, where she'd be teaching grades seven through twelve, was a one-story building, shingle-sided and topped with a steeply-pitched metal roof. The entire building would've fit in her last school's library. She'd already seen pictures of it online, but in person, it was even smaller than she'd expected.

"Teekkonlit Valley Secondary School," Margaret said, slowing to a stop. "One hundred and eighty-three students. Think you can handle it?"

Grace realized she was joking when the same teasing smile Margaret had directed at the pilot was now turned in her direction. At her last school, back in Chicago, there'd been nearly three thousand students.

Grace returned her smile with practiced ease. She knew it looked warm, genuine, natural. Nobody ever seemed to realize how hollow it was. "I'll see if I can manage," she told Margaret.

"Alright, my girl, let's get you to your new home." Margaret turned back the way they came and took a right at the intersection. "This is the other main road," Margaret explained. "The Spruce is at the end."

There were fewer buildings on this road, but they were constructed of more expensive materials—brick, stone, and timber. Rustic, log-sided buildings nestled up against classic brick storefronts. There was an outfitter, a wilderness guide service, a small office for dog sled tours wedged next to another office advertising chartered flights, a general store, and a tiny, two-pump gas station. Businesses were marked by hand-painted wooden signs hanging over their doors.

"And here's your home. The Spruce." Margaret pulled up to the curb alongside the largest building on the street. It was three stories tall, constructed of massive, ancient-looking dark logs.

As part of the terms of Grace's employment contract, the city of Longtooth provided her room and board at The Spruce, an eighteenth-century boardinghouse and hotel.

"This time of year, long-term tenants are the only residents. But in the spring, when hunting and fishing kick off, The Spruce is usually at full occupancy."

Margaret parked on the street in front of The Spruce and helped Grace haul her bags from the back of the Suburban. A recent snowfall still dusted the sidewalk, disturbed by one set of boot tracks, and the tracks of what had to be an absolutely *massive* dog. Grace stared at the paw prints as she followed Margaret to The Spruce's entry, and a thought occurred to her.

"Do a lot of wild animals come into town?" she asked. In the small town where she'd grown up, deer, black bears, and coyotes made regular forays into town.

"We get a bear or two every winter, a handful of moose." Margaret paused with her hand on The Spruce's heavy wooden front door. "The wolves are pretty frequent. If you don't bother them, they won't bother you."

With that ominous warning, she pulled the door open. Inside The Spruce, the lobby was dim. All the interior walls were made of the same massive logs as the exterior. The floors were wide wood planks, worn smooth from over a century of foot traffic. Thick timber beams crisscrossed the peaked ceiling. She could still see the gouges in the wood where they'd been hand-hewn by long-dead lumberjacks.

The front desk was empty, but Margaret waved Grace past it and led her into an expansive dining room. There was a long, diner-style counter at the head of the room, and the floor was filled with heavy wooden tables. A long bank of windows looked out on a thick copse of spruce trees, threaded through by a narrow, iced-over creek. Paper New Year's decorations hung from the ceiling.

It was getting close to dinner time, and a few of the tables were occupied. The diners glanced up at Margaret and Grace with curious expressions.

"Hey there, Maggie," an older man greeted her from the counter, swiveling on his stool to face them. He looked well into his sixties, but still hardy, with swarthy skin, acute gray eyes, and thick silver hair. "This our new teacher?"

"Grace, let me introduce you to the town's postmaster

and resident ne'er-do-well, Wade Evers. Wade, this is Grace Rossi. She is, indeed, the new English teacher."

"Don't listen to Maggie," Wade told her, rising from his seat. He offered his hand to Grace and she shook it. "I'm Longtooth's moral compass—"

Margaret snorted.

"—and it's a pleasure to have you here."

"Very nice to meet you, Mr. Evers," Grace told him with another one of those smiles that nobody ever saw past. It was strange how she could recognize that an interaction was going well, without *feeling* it. She knew what to say, how to act. She knew how to leave people feeling that she was charming and sweet and engaged. And all the while her mind was just a mess of white noise.

"It's Wade to you, sweetheart," he told her sternly.

"Wade," she complied, taking her hand back.

"Grace just flew in from Chicago," Margaret said.

Wade let out a low whistle. "Big city." He glanced around the dining room as if he were observing all of Longtooth. "Big change."

Grace shrugged. "Not entirely. I grew up in a pretty small town."

Behind the counter, the swinging kitchen door slapped open. A short, buxom, caucasian woman emerged. Like Margaret, she looked to be in her early fifties, with her hair dyed deep auburn, and her eyes expertly lined and heavily lashed. She was dressed in a utilitarian zippered fleece with The Spruce's logo on the chest, but she wore a clattering bracelet loaded with golden charms and big gold hoops hung from her ears.

"Tasha," Margaret greeted her.

"This is my new tenant?" the woman asked with a slight

Slavic accent. Pale blue eyes tracked over Grace. Bow-shaped lips pursed speculatively.

"Yep. Meet Grace Rossi. Grace, Natasha Freeman owns The Spruce with her husband, Arthur Freeman."

"Ms. Rossi wants dinner and sleep," Natasha pronounced.

Grace had no appetite, but Natasha's tone didn't allow for dissent.

Natasha gestured at the empty stools along the counter and commanded, "Sit. You like caribou? And bread?"

Before Grace could answer her, Natasha disappeared back into the kitchen.

"Well," Margaret said, giving her an assessing look. "I think Tasha's got the right of it. Enjoy your meal and get some sleep. Why don't I meet you here at eight tomorrow morning, and I can give you a better rundown of things? You can see the town in the daylight, I'll show you around the school, and we can get your vehicle sorted out."

Grace nodded. "Sure. That sounds good."

They shook hands once more, and then Margaret was gone. Grace's bags sat on the floor at her feet, taking up walking space in the dining room. She was working to tug them out of the way when Natasha burst through the kitchen door again, bearing a steaming bowl of stew with two thick slices of generously buttered bread.

"Leave those things," she commanded, setting the food in front of Grace. "Aleksandr!"

A few seconds later, a harried young man appeared around the doorway beside the front desk. He was tall and thin, with dark hair, honey-gold skin, and muddy green eyes. Though he towered over the pale, blue-eyed Natasha, there was something in his features that reflected hers. "Yeah, mom?"

"Alek. Take Ms. Rossi's bags up to her room."

"You can call me Grace," she told Natasha, watching as the reedy teenager hoisted her bags. He did so with less ease than the big, broad bush pilot had done, but he still managed better than she would have.

"Grace," Natasha acknowledged, nodding. "Now, eat." She disappeared back into the kitchen.

Grace slid onto the stool beside Wade. She pulled out her phone and sent a text to both of her parents. *Hey, arrived safely in Longtooth. Just getting settled into my new place.*

She got an immediate read receipt from dad—and no reply. A few minutes later, Mom texted, *ok.* She stared at the response until her phone went dark. She hadn't expected anything more than that. Honestly. Even so, the cold inside of her became a little more brittle.

She laid her phone facedown and picked up her spoon.

"How was the flight?" Wade asked.

"Uneventful," She told him. "Just how I like 'em."

Wade chuckled. "Can't argue with that."

She ate quietly while Wade chattered at her. He recounted the town's history for her, and she tried her best to feign interest. Long ago, the area was inhabited only by an Athabaskan people from whom the Teekkonlit Valley derived its name. European Russians and indigenous Siberians arrived a few centuries ago during Russian colonization. Then an influx of African-Americans following the Civil War. Then Anglo-Europeans during the tail end of the Klondike Gold Rush. As a permanent settlement, Longtooth was first a lumber camp, then a boomtown during the gold rush, then a ghost town, and now a moderately prosperous throughway for tourists and hunters headed for the Gates of the Arctic. After the town history, Wade gave her a crash course on the who's who of Longtooth. The endless stream of names went in one ear and out the other, but she nodded and pretended to be interested.

When her spoon scraped the bottom of her bowl, Natasha appeared again. "Grace needs to sleep," she told Wade. She turned imperious blue eyes on Grace. "Up you get. This way, please."

Natasha's commandeering brusqueness was softened somewhat by a maternal air. She guided Grace through the dining room to a creaking flight of wooden steps. Dark log walls hemmed them in tightly on either side. Natasha led her up one story, then another. The narrow hall at the top of the stairs was lined with heavy wooden doors, brass numbers affixed to the center of each one.

"You are number thirty-four," Natasha said, stopping in front of that particular door, at the end of the hall. She pulled a key from her pocket and unlocked it. She flicked the lights on. There was no overhead light, but a table lamp on the nightstand and a floor lamp in the opposite corner filled the room with a gentle, warm glow.

The room was extremely narrow, awkwardly L-shaped, with a low, sloping ceiling. There was a double bed on an old brass bedstead, made up with a beautiful cathedral window quilt. Tucked beneath the lowest point of the ceiling, the bed stood just next to the only window, overlooking Longtooth's main street. There was an old mission-style dresser across from the foot of the bed. Beside the dresser sat a mini-fridge with a microwave mounted on top. At the back of the room, another wooden door led to a full bathroom, complete with a cast-iron tub and a black and white penny tile floor. Grace's bags had been laid neatly on the bed.

"Breakfast is served from five a.m. to nine a.m. Supper from five p.m. to nine p.m." Natasha said, pacing around the room and inspecting its cleanliness as she spoke. "Your board includes both meals. The kitchen is closed for lunch, but you can buy packed lunches in the morning. Otherwise, you have a fridge that you can fill with whatever you like and a microwave. No hotplates. No pets. No overnight guests."

"No problem," Grace said, wishing she would just leave.

Natasha glanced at the bags on the bed. "You did not pack very many things." There was an unspoken judgment in her tone. Grace was too tired to unravel the what or why of it. But she didn't dare tell her that the bigger of the two bags was mostly filled with books.

"I got rid of a lot of things before I moved," Grace said, which was the truth. "There wasn't much to pack except for clothes and toiletries." The most significant lack was the little wooden chest that held all her sentimental keepsakes. After she'd broken up with her ex, the chest had gone missing.

Natasha gave her a searching look and then shrugged. "It's not my business."

Then why'd you ask? Grace swallowed the words and smiled blandly.

"Here." Natasha deposited her key on top of the dresser. "If you lose your key, you must come to the front desk for the spare. Now. Get some sleep."

Natasha bustled from the room, pulling the door shut behind her.

Grace began to undress for bed, moving slowly, disjointedly. Alone, without people and tasks and obligations to distract her, that old familiar void opened. The emptiness, the numbness, swallowed her and she sank into it without a fight.

She was always cold. No matter how warm the day, how high the furnace was cranked, her blood ran cold. It'd begun a few years ago, when the depression had started. She'd been to the doctor—it wasn't anemia, her blood pressure was fine. "Some people just run cold," he'd told her with a shrug.

She couldn't feel the heat, could never feel warm. But the cold could cut through her like a knife. She savored the way a harsh wind bit into her skin, reveling in the intensity of the sensation, the brief moments of *feeling*. She hadn't been able to savor it earlier, distracted by the pilot's surliness and the necessity of making a good impression with Margaret. But now... She crawled across the bed to look out the window. It was evening, the sky dark and moonless. There wasn't a soul on the street.

She pushed the window open. The cold hit her like a slap. She inhaled deeply, savoring the broken glass feeling in her lungs. In the distance, she heard the ululating howl of a wolf. The single howl was joined by another, and then another, forming a ghostly chorus that echoed off the mountains.

Grace stepped out onto the narrow Juliet balcony, dressed in only underpants and the worn cotton t-shirt. The cold ate at her exposed skin with a pain like fire. It was nega-tive-forty with the wind chill. Exposure would result in frostbite in less than 10 minutes. She was aware of the danger. She'd grown up with cold advisories. She just needed a couple minutes to feel...something. Anything. She meant to go inside before any real damage was done.

She'd been standing there for less than a minute when

the scuff of boots on ice caught her attention. She looked down at the road and saw the bush pilot—Caleb Kinoyit—staring up at her. Even standing three stories away, even with most of his face covered by a dense beard and a slouching toque, she could read him loud and clear. His eyes said *What in the ever-loving fuck are you doing?* more succinctly than words ever could.

Embarrassment spiked through her, a flush of sudden warmth. God, when was the last time she'd cared enough to feel anything so sharply? She stumbled back through the window and threw it shut.

Inside, her room was too warm. Sticky, nervous sweat prickled over her chest and back. She went to the bathroom, wet a towel with cold water, and mopped at herself until her skin cooled enough to feel the cold that had filled her room while she'd had the window open.

Idiot, she chided herself. Natasha wouldn't appreciate her driving up the heat bill. And what if the window had slid shut behind her? She would've been trapped. Her extremities could've been lost to frostbite before anyone responded to her humiliating cries for help. And now there was a witness to her idiocy.

She double-checked the latch on the window, then turned off the lights and crawled into bed. A few minutes later, she heard the tromp of boots in the stairwell. They came down the hall, passing her door. She lay frozen in place, listening as keys jingled at the door next to hers.

Oh, fuck. He's my neighbor, isn't he?

CHAPTER 2

Even when she couldn't make herself care about anything else, it was easy to care about teaching. There was actually something at stake—the minds and futures of hundreds of kids. Or, at Teekkonlit Valley Secondary, dozens.

Grace's teaching methods were not totally conventional. At her old school, the administration had often been on her case about it. But they'd been desperately understaffed and shamefully underfunded, so she'd been able to do what she wanted without too much interference. It helped that her students always outperformed their cohort on state testing.

When she'd interviewed for the position with Teekkonlit Valley, she'd been so despondent about her life or prospects that she hadn't cared enough to downplay her general disdain for following curriculum. To her surprise, they'd offered her the job.

On her first day, she waited at the front of the classroom, propped against the edge of her desk as students filed in. Several stacks of battered paperbacks sat next to her. The final bell rang, and the last few stragglers wandered in from the hall, slumping into their seats.

"Good morning," Grace said, her voice still rough with sleep. She cleared her throat. "I'm Ms. Rossi. I'm taking over from Mr. Hendricks. I understand you read *Great Expectations*, *The Scarlet Letter*, and *The Great Gatsby* last semester. Is that right?"

A few slow, dull nods in response.

"Did you guys like those books?"

Blank stares. A few bordered on hostile, startling a genuine laugh out of her.

She coughed, collecting herself. "Alright, here's the thing—the state requires us to learn certain skills and meet certain milestones. Traditionally, we do this by reading the classics of Western literature. Books like *Great Expectations*. The problem is that those books are super boring."

A few glazed looks sharpened with surprise.

"I didn't enjoy them when I was in high school, and I'm the kind of nerd who took advanced English classes and went on to get an English degree. I really love books, you guys. But the reason I love books and literature isn't because of Dickens or Hemingway or whatever long-dead, crusty old guy they want us to read. I loved the fun, weird books—gothics and sci-fi and fantasy. I loved ghosts and spaceships and witches and adventure.

"And it's okay if you don't like those things. Maybe you like murder mysteries. Or romances. Or political thrillers. Or historicals. Or really thoughtful, subtle character studies. Maybe you actually do like books like *Great Expectations*. That's great. I just want you guys, if nothing else, to find at least one book that you really enjoy reading. That's my goal for the rest of the school year."

The looks had turned wary. They'd probably heard plenty of *we can do this, guys!* from previous teachers. That wasn't Grace's angle, but words alone wouldn't make them believe it. She really, genuinely just wanted kids to enjoy reading. At her last school, a few of the more crotchety teachers in the English department had snidely referred to Grace's classes as "book club." She didn't mind. She'd rather run a book club than the psychological torture programs their mind-numbing classes had been.

"So, anyways, we're supposed to learn about things like characterization, and foreshadowing, and symbolism, and allusion—and we will. I'll make sure you guys know what those mean and how to identify them. But I hope you can enjoy the process. So, we're going to start with *Howl's Moving Castle* by Dianna Wynne Jones." She stood up, grabbed her stack, and began passing them around. "This is loaded with foreshadowing, allusion, characterization—all those terms we're supposed to learn about. But it's also just fun."

Grace spent the rest of class going around the room and having the students introduce themselves. They were all from the Valley, born and raised, and they interacted with each other with the easy familiarity of lifelong neighbors, even though some of them lived over an hour away from each other. It was clear they were skeptical of her, but they were polite enough, which was more than she could say for her first day of classes at her last school.

Class period after class period, Grace did her song and dance and passed out novels. Natasha's son, Alek, showed up in her fourth period class of juniors. He'd inherited slightly lighter hair and skin from his mother, but he still had what Grace was coming to think of as "the Valley look." Her students had the same ethnically ambiguous look that most of the townspeople did—tawny skin and dark, sleek hair along with hooded, often light-colored, eyes. High-bridged noses and wide cheekbones. Several generations of indigenous Alaskan, African-American, and Euro-immigrant intermarriages had homogenized into a distinct ethnicity, particular to the Teekkonlit Valley.

Compared to the rest of the valley's residents, Grace was a frizzy, goggle-eyed, ghost lady. Her thick, wavy, unmanageable hair was a drab shade somewhere in between blonde and brown. If there was even a single drop of moisture in the air, it expanded into a ragged lion's mane. Her eyes were heavily lidded—*Byzantine eyes*, her grandmother had always told her fondly—and an ordinary shade of brown. Her skin was naturally a pale olive tone, but the last few months of deepening depression had left her wan and sallow.

In the faculty bathroom at lunch, the sight of her reflection almost took her by surprise. Her skin looked thin and fragile, laying too close to the bone. Dark circles made hollows beneath her eyes. The severity of her cheekbones might have been attractive if the rest of her face weren't so gaunt.

She turned away from the mirror in dismay. Putting on the friendly mask, she made her way to the staff lounge to eat the lunch she'd bought from The Spruce. Margaret had called a brief staff meeting on her second day in Longtooth, so she'd already been introduced to all of the other teachers before she started classes.

They greeted her warmly now as she slid into an empty chair. Most of them had the same sable handsomeness as the rest of the Valley's locals. Roger Yidineeltot, the history teacher, Tamsyn Taaltsiyh, one of the math teachers, Alan

Evers, one of the science teachers, and Linnea Teague, the art teacher, had all been born and raised in the Teekkonlit Valley.

But a few others were clearly outsiders like Grace. Eric Hansen, the other science teacher, was a nordic blond who'd moved up here from Minnesota two years ago. Lucia Alvarez, one of the math teachers, originally from Texas, was a petite Latina woman who could be mistaken for a local at first glance. But upon closer inspection, her curling hair and large Spanish eyes set her apart from the locals as much as Grace's own hair and eyes did.

Grace spent lunch fielding more questions about herself —where she'd come from, how long she'd been teaching, why she'd decided to move to Alaska, and so on. After lunch, she went back to evangelizing for her lord and savior, books. By the end of the day, she was out of steam. After eight hours of performing a one-woman play about a mentally-engaged, emotionally functional human, she had nothing left in her.

She bid her final class goodbye and when the last student had filed from the room, she dropped into her desk chair and stared out the window. It was only three-thirty, but already dark outside. Her reflection stared back at her, haggard and apathetic. The coldness beneath her skin made her entire body ache.

CHAPTER 3

Pretty quickly, Grace learned that the locals of Teekkonlit Valley fell into two camps—those who were excited by the arrival of somebody new, and those who saw her as a trespasser.

"Not the big, fun adventure you expected, is it?" Harry Lance, the owner of Lance Outfitters, demanded scornfully one morning at breakfast. "Bit colder and darker than you were prepared for, I bet."

Grace took another methodical bite of oatmeal. "Nah," she said dismissively. "It's not that different from the upper Midwest."

Harry scowled, deprived of the opportunity for smugness. "Well, there aren't any grizzly bears in Chicago, are there?" he persisted.

"No. But I haven't seen any in Longtooth, either."

Behind her, Arthur Freeman—Natasha's husband—chuckled. "She's got you there, Harry."

Like Harry, Arthur was another Teekkonlit Valley local, as broad and strapping as the rest of the men. His hair had gone steel gray, still shot with threads of black, and his eyes were a muddied hazel. He kept a perfectly groomed, Sam Elliot-style mustache. The mustache somehow made him seem trustworthy and authoritative. Grace saw him on nearly a daily basis around The Spruce, usually doing some sort of maintenance—fixing a leaky sink, sealing drafty windows, taking apart and reassembling one of the coffee machines, nailing down a loose floorboard. He wasn't a talkative man, and she appreciated that about him.

Natasha, on the other hand, was anything but quiet. Every morning, she poured Grace's coffee and then forced her into conversations with anybody else who'd come to The Spruce for breakfast. She kept introducing Grace to single men with an unapologetic intensity that was somehow both amusing and exasperating.

Through a combination of assertive friendliness and maternal bossiness, Natasha subtly but persistently directed the seating arrangements every morning and evening. She had a clear directive—hook Grace up with a Teekkonlit Valley native. Like a determined collie, she kept the other lower-48ers away, shooing them towards local women while driving local men into Grace's orbit.

In her first week, Grace had eaten breakfast beside Maxim Freeman (Natasha's oldest son, and Longtooth's sheriff), Adam Toonikoh (owner of the Blue Moose tavern), and Connor Ankkonisdoy (a hunting guide). Natasha had twice chased away Eric Hansen, her fellow teacher, making sure the two of them sat at opposite ends of the dining counter, surrounded by locals.

Grace had managed to speak to Harlan Bennett, a doctor originally from Georgia, for all of a minute before Natasha intervened. Harlan was tall and handsome, with rich dark skin, a thick black beard, and the shoulders of a discus thrower. His deep voice was inflected with a gorgeous Southern accent that even Grace—numb as she was— couldn't help but be entranced by.

Andy Watanabe, a lawyer from Oregon, was whipcord lean, with a face composed entirely of blade-sharp angles. He managed to introduce himself one morning before Natasha herded him over to sit between Elena Morris and Jessica Taaltsiyh, both born-and-bred Teekkonlit Valley women.

Clearly, Teekkonlit Valley was looking for fresh blood, and they weren't going to let outsiders waste their shiny new genetic material on each other.

Grace's amusement with the situation was a detached feeling. She soldiered through breakfasts, making small talk with the ease of a born and bred Midwesterner, all the while wishing she could just be left in peace. Max was polite but seemed similarly amused by his mother's matchmaking, and didn't press his suit. Adam and Connor, though, were more than happy to accept Natasha's meddling. They watched Grace with bright, hungry eyes, asking what she liked to do for fun, what her plans were for the weekend, if she'd ever ridden a snowmobile—or "snowmachine," as they called them—and had she been to the tavern, and did she like hunting? (Nothing, nothing, yes, no, and no.) She managed to put them both off without an outright rejection, explaining that her first few weeks would be taken up with getting accustomed to her new job, et cetera.

"Well, when you're free," Connor had said, holding her gaze intently.

"Sure." She put on the smile that nobody ever saw through. "I'll let you know."

But she had no intention of doing that.

Just as in Chicago, Grace fell into a mindless routine. Every day felt the same. When she didn't have the distraction of teaching, exhaustion unraveled her like a cheap sweater. She could feel the pieces of her mind falling apart into disconnected chunks of thought. Her body seemed to do the same, clumsy and off-kilter. The cold beneath her skin was a constant ache.

Outside of school, she wanted nothing more than to lay in her bed in the dark until it was time to get up and go back to work. But, since she had to go to the dining room to get her meals, and Natasha insisted on serving her at the counter, Grace had no choice but to sit in the open, twice a day, fielding the social overtures of anybody and everybody who strolled through The Spruce.

It was probably good for her. But keeping up the pleasant mask she wore in public was exhausting. After supper each night, other Spruce residents often remained in the dining room, chatting, playing cards, arguing over what to put on the television mounted on the back wall. But as soon as her plate was empty, she returned to her room, alone, where she showered and collapsed into bed. Beneath a pile of blankets that never managed to warm her, she drifted in a shallow half-sleep until morning came.

Before leaving Chicago, she'd tried everything. She'd gone to the doctor, been diagnosed with depression. She'd cycled through a few prescriptions and dutifully attended therapy. Nothing seemed to break through the numb fog that dragged at her mind and body. Nothing banished the bone-deep cold.

She was still faithfully taking the most recently prescribed antidepressants. They seemed to work better than nothing at all, but she still didn't feel like a real person. The pills, combined with a steady intake of caffeine, gave her just enough energy to get through the basics of keeping herself alive.

The next week, Monday morning, Grace straightened her spine as she stepped into the dining room, preparing herself for another half-hour of forced socialization.

"Gracie!" Natasha spotted her immediately and waved her over to an open stool at the counter. The broad shoulders and dark heads of local men occupied the stools on either side of the open one. She'd already resigned herself to Natasha's maneuvering, so she took a breath and hung her parka over the back of the stool.

As she dropped into the seat, she glanced over and nearly jumped out of her skin when she found the bush pilot staring back at her. The last time she'd seen him, she'd been standing outside in negative-forty degrees wearing nothing but a t-shirt and underpants. His expression hardened at the sight of her, and he looked away.

Well. Now she knew what he thought of the view.

"Gracie, have you met Caleb Kinoyit?" Natasha asked with a smile as she poured a cup of coffee.

"Uh, yeah. He—" *witnessed the full extent of my mental detachment* "—flew me in from Anchorage."

"Caleb!" Natasha scolded. "You didn't tell me this."

Caleb shrugged, taking a drink of coffee. "You want a manifest every time I fly, Tasha?"

She swatted his arm. "Don't be dense on purpose."

His lips curled into a mild smile and he returned to his coffee, studiously ignoring Grace. She sat in awkward silence. All her midwestern small talk skills had completely deserted her. Out of the corner of her eye, she observed him.

He had the same sable-haired, tawny-skinned look as the other locals. His face was angular, rawboned, with hollow cheeks and a high-bridged, hawkish nose. His hooded eyes were as dark as the coffee he was drinking. The rest of his face was hidden by a thick black beard.

He wore a gray thermal shirt layered over a black t-shirt. The collar of the t-shirt was stretched and flecked with bleach while the thermal shirt had a hole on the shoulder. The cuffs, pushed up over his thick forearms, were frayed. His beard needed oil and a comb. His rumpled, shaggy hair was flattened on one side of his head and obviously hadn't been treated to a brush that morning.

Caleb's gaze flicked over to Grace. "What?" he demanded flatly. A muscle flexed in his cheek.

She realized she'd abandoned the corner-of-her-eye technique, and was just openly staring at him. "Nothing. Sorry." She turned away, and another span of excruciating silence stretched between them.

Mercifully, Natasha appeared with her food—an egg sandwich and stewed apples. Grace wrapped the sandwich in a napkin and stood up, shrugging into her coat.

"Thanks, Natasha. This looks great."

"Gracie," Natasha objected. "Sit. Eat."

"I have to take care of some things before class starts today. Sorry."

"You have to eat your fruit!" She gestured at the bowl of stewed apples.

Grace scooped up her bag. "Sorry. Let Caleb have them."

The man in question scowled at her as she strode from the dining room. She couldn't get away from him fast enough.

When she reached her truck, she disconnected the block

heater and started the ignition. She sat behind the wheel as it idled, waiting for the heat to defrost the windows, and tried to tamp down the anxiety fluttering in her chest. It was clear Caleb didn't like her, but why that should bother her was hard to explain.

It'd been a while since she'd cared much about anyone's opinion of her. She was self-aware enough to understand that she had to pretend, in order to get along with society at large. But she coasted through most days just going through the motions of social nicety, ambivalent to the people she interacted with. People who wanted nothing to do with her were generally a relief. That was one less audience member she had to perform for.

But Caleb's dislike unsettled her and made her angry in return. Anger was another emotion that had previously been beyond her range of feeling, and the return of it was an uncomfortable adjustment. Absurdly, tears burned at the backs of her eyes—all because some guy she barely knew had been sort of rude to her. It was ridiculous. She squeezed her eyes tightly shut, pressing the heels of her hands against them, willing the emotional turbulence away.

By the time Grace got to school, the anger had faded to a manageable simmer. She sat at her desk, eating the slightly-smashed egg sandwich and staring out the window at the dark sky. Beyond the low roofs of the town, dense spruce forest swept up rocky hills, giving way to the jagged peaks of snow-capped mountains. In mundane contrast, a line of school buses—vans, really—pulled up to the curb, spreading their doors and barfing out students.

"Grace?"

She turned to see Margaret Huditiltik standing in the doorway. Margaret was dressed as if she were about to chop wood—thermal-lined work pants, gore-tex boots, and a button-up flannel shirt. Grace glanced uncertainly at her knitted sweater and tapered wool trousers. She'd worn her snow boots to school, then stowed them under her desk and changed into leather oxfords. Was she overdressing? After a second's deliberation, she realized she didn't care.

"Hey Margaret," she said, swallowing the last of her sandwich and crumpling the napkin. "What's up?"

"Not much. Just coming by to see how you're doing." She walked into the room. "Settling in alright?"

"Everything's going well." Grace hesitated. It felt unnatural to purposely invite personal conversation, having avoided it for so long. But irritation was still prickling at her, and she needed an answer. "Can I ask you something?"

Margaret nodded, leaning her hip against the desk.

"Do you know if I did something to offend Caleb Kinoyit?"

Margaret's eyebrows shot up. "Caleb? No. Why?"

Grace shrugged. "I don't know. He likes me about as much as Harold Lance does—but Harry's kind of..." She trailed off, unable to think of a diplomatic word. "Anyway, Caleb seems to get along with everyone else just fine. So I was worried I did something." Well, there was that whole thing where he caught her standing half-naked on her balcony in deadly cold weather, but hating her for it was kind of unfair. She was only a threat to herself, not anybody else.

Margaret shifted, pursing her lips as she considered her words. Finally, she said, "You may have noticed some of the locals don't care for outsiders."

"Ah. He's one of those." Grace thought about it for a

second. "But wait—I've seen him talk to Eric and Harlan. And Andy. And Lucia."

Margaret shrugged. "Caleb takes a while to warm up to people. Don't take it personally."

Grace snorted. "Right."

Margaret pushed off of Grace's desk and squeezed her shoulder. "Caleb's not so bad. And for what it's worth, I'm very happy you're here, Grace. I saw Daniel Gray reading during lunch period. That's very...well. I had to pinch myself."

Grace pulled Daniel up in her memory—a stocky, stubborn-chinned, angry-eyed boy from her sophomore English class. He hadn't yet spoken up in class, but the fact that he was choosing to read the book on his downtime filled her with a flush of happiness. It was stronger than the anger Caleb had inspired, and she sat up straighter in her chair.

"Thanks, Margaret. That's really—" As unused to strong emotions as she was, the feeling nearly overwhelmed her. She felt her throat tighten. She swallowed hard, trying to play it off as a dry cough. "That's great."

Margaret left, and Grace threw herself into her classes, engaged by a vigor she hadn't felt in months. Each day a few more kids started speaking up, participating in discussions and asking good questions. Each day, the new-teacher-skepticism faded just a little more. Each day, even the quiet ones became more engaged—their expressions and postures shifting from bland disinterest to watchful listening.

The change thrilled her, but the high feelings didn't last long. By the end of the week, she was a shell again—living for class, just going through the motions during every other waking minute.

. . .

FRIDAY NIGHT, Grace trudged up the steps to her room and tried not to think about the two-day void opening up in front of her. Without work to occupy her mind, the hollowness would take over again. Last weekend, she'd managed to occupy herself with lesson planning and grading the first-week assignments she'd given out. Now, her lesson plans were squared for the next several weeks, and she'd caught up on all the grading. She had nothing to do. Once upon a time, that would've been a reason to jump for joy.

She dug in her bag for her key as she reached the top of the stairs. As she turned onto the third-floor landing, somebody else was emerging from their room at the end of the hall. Grace stiffened with recognition. Caleb Kinoyit.

He pocketed his key and strode towards her. The hallway was narrow, forcing her to shrink to the side so he could pass without touching her. He made no such accommodation for her, staring straight ahead and marching past as if she wasn't even there.

Annoyance flared like a struck match. How was it that the only person who made her feel anything beyond numb exhaustion was one who wanted nothing to do with her?

Margaret's assurances that he was just slow to warm up to people dissolved like smoke. His dislike was obviously personal. She had done something to piss him off, and she couldn't figure out what it was.

CHAPTER 4

Grace found that there really wasn't much she missed about Chicago. The lack of big-city conveniences didn't bother her. The extremely limited nightlife, the quietness, the lack of competition over things like the latest fashion and the latest tech, and all those other luxury possessions, were all a welcome change.

However...there was one thing she missed. The delicious, take-on-the-world rush that came from a double-shot macchiato.

As she sat down to breakfast on her third Monday in Longtooth, she caught Natasha before she poured her usual cup of coffee. "Hey, Natasha—I know this is a longshot, but is there anywhere in town to get espresso?"

Four seats down from her, Harry Lance scoffed so hard, Grace was surprised he didn't blow himself backwards off his stool. "*Espresso?*" he echoed, as if she'd asked for it in gold-plated bone china, with her portrait drawn in the foam. "Might have to go back to Chicago if you're going to need an espresso every morning, darling."

Next to him, Caleb Kinoyit chortled like an asshole.

Grace bristled and leaned over the counter so she could look Harry in the eye. "Well, *darling*, since Chicago's a long fucking way from here, I guess I'll have to learn how to do without. I sure hope I don't chip a nail hefting a regular old coffee mug like you tough Alaskans." She'd started speaking before she even realized what she was doing, and by the end of it, her heart was pounding in her throat.

She refused to play into their notions of the out-of-her-element city girl who couldn't hack it in whatever their idea of "the real world" was. Grace might have moved to Long-tooth from a big city, but she'd grown up in a place where cows outnumbered people. She knew how to drive a tractor, how to field dress a deer, and she could split a cord of wood with nothing but an ax and a can-do attitude. Meanwhile, Harry Lance would probably have an aneurysm if he had to drive through Chicago rush hour traffic.

"She's teaching our kids with that mouth?" Harry groused.

Behind him, Caleb was grinning down into his coffee. With a smile on his face, strong white teeth contrasted against thick black beard, he was alarmingly attractive. He looked up, caught Grace watching him, and his grin abruptly vanished. It took her a second to tear her gaze away.

"So...coffee, then?" Natasha asked. She had a carefully fixed expression that hinted at a suppressed smile.

"Yes, thank you."

"Cream? Sugar?"

"Black," Grace said firmly.

She drank her coffee without tasting it, wondering where that burst of outrage had come from. For the longest time, she hadn't cared enough about anything to feel self-righteous or angry. It was a strange feeling—and not a good one. Her heart was racing, her skin flushed. She ate quickly, a slight tremble in her hand.

Natasha hovered nearby, wiping down a coffee carafe. "Gracie."

She managed not to flinch, but adrenaline was still coursing through her. If anybody startled her, she was going to shoot through the roof like a cannonball. She looked up at Natasha with a calm expression. Or at least she hoped so.

"This Saturday, we are having a party for Roger Yidineel-tot's sixtieth birthday. Here at The Spruce."

"Oh." An inkling of dread bloomed. "That sounds nice."

"Everyone will be there. You should be there, too."

The dread pooled in her gut. *Everyone will be there.*

"You know Roger already, of course. But it will be a good chance for you to meet the rest of the town."

The rest of the town. So many strangers. "Oh. Uh." Her mind raced to find an excuse for not attending. The problem with small towns was that everybody knew your business. Not only did everyone know Grace's business in Longtooth, but Natasha, as her landlady, knew all her comings and goings down to the minute. And even if that weren't the case, Longtooth was so small and the next decent-sized city —Fairbanks—so distant, that there was no reasonable excuse for any other obligations.

"Don't worry about a fancy dress or a gift. It's just food and music."

There was absolutely *no* reason for Grace not to attend. She understood that. But that didn't stop the sickening dread from churning her stomach and squeezing her throat. "Sure," She made herself say. "That sounds fun."

Natasha smiled, and her gaze traveled around the dining

room. She was probably picturing all the single men she could throw at Grace. "Good. It will be fun. Everyone will be glad to meet our new resident." She replaced the carafe on the coffee machine and disappeared into the kitchen.

Saturday was five days away. Every moment that her mind wasn't occupied, Grace knew she would spend dwelling on the upcoming social gauntlet. Her breakfast turned into sawdust in her mouth. She choked down another few bites, picked up her coat, and left.

TRUE TO HER EXPECTATIONS, Grace spent the following days working herself into an absurd lather over a simple party. She knew her fear was irrational and that the right thing to do was to attend the party. She didn't want to be a socially incompetent basketcase, but she couldn't seem to get out of her own head.

Her social anxiety wasn't normally so overwhelming—or at least, it hadn't been in the past. Before everything that landed her in Longtooth, she'd only hated loud, crowded places like bars and clubs. They made her feel antsy and irritated and like time slowed to an unbearable crawl. But after everything with Alex went to hell in a handbasket, she couldn't stand crowds. Couldn't stand to be in any place where she didn't know everyone present—where she couldn't keep an eye on them all.

And that's exactly what this party would be—a crowded, loud space filled with an unknowable number of strangers who'd surround her on all sides. She wouldn't know anybody, but they'd all know her. They'd all be watching her.

Friday night, she didn't sleep at all. She lay in her bed, shivering from both the perpetual cold inside of her and the nervous dread of the next day's party. A thousand different scenarios played through her mind—all the ways things could go wrong—and the night passed too quickly. She only realized it was dawn because she heard other doors opening and closing in the hall. The voices of her neighbors greeted each other with sleepy good mornings.

She got up, showered, dressed, and hauled herself downstairs. She was exhausted, but even if she went straight back to bed, she'd never fall asleep. Her eyelids were heavy and her brain was soup, but her body was filled with nervous energy. The party was less than ten hours away.

"Gracie," Natasha greeted her with worry in her voice. "Are you alright?"

Grace knew she looked terrible. The bathroom mirror had shown her what a night of no sleep had done to her already hollow-eyed, haggard face.

"I'm fine," Grace said calmly, trying to hide the unhinged weirdo who lived inside her skin.

"Are you sure?" Natasha's golden charm bracelet clattered as she reached across the counter and pressed the back of her hand to Grace's forehead. Grace surprised herself by relaxing against Natasha's touch. A gentle warmth radiated from her skin, seeping into Grace's.

Natasha let out a little gasp. "You're cold as ice!"

"I'm alright." She touched a hand to her cheek, even though she knew her icy fingers would feel nothing. "I always run a little cool."

Natasha gave her a skeptical look. "There is cool, and then there is frozen. You look half-dead, *myszka*. You should be in bed."

It suddenly occurred to Grace that if she played up her "illness" into the afternoon, it'd be the perfect excuse to avoid the party. She wouldn't even have to beg off. Natasha would order her to bed, and she could hole up in her room where it was quiet and secure.

Don't be such a fucking coward, her own mind hissed at her. "No, really, Natasha. I'll be fine. I just need coffee and something to eat."

Natasha frowned, but she poured a cup of coffee.

When Grace finished breakfast, she allowed Natasha to badger her into returning to bed. She did need to get some sleep if she was going to survive tonight's party. But just that thought alone was enough to ensure she didn't sleep at all. She huddled beneath the blankets and went right back to her brain's favorite activity—constructing elaborately catastrophic scenarios that could happen at the party and then torturing herself by playing them on repeat.

She stumbled back downstairs around supper time. The dining room was already being shifted for the party. *HAPPY NEW YEAR* decorations were being replaced with *HAPPY BIRTHDAY* ones. There were a few people at the diner counter. Grace took a seat between Wade Evers and Jessica Taaltsiyh.

"You feeling okay?" Jessica asked.

Grace flushed. If she were truly ill, their concern would be touching. But the fact was that she was a nervous wreck due to her own constitutional weakness. Every time somebody noticed how wretched she looked, it was just further confirmation of that weakness.

"I'm not feeling amazing," she admitted.

Natasha pushed through the kitchen doors, spotted Grace, and immediately made a beeline to her. "I think Harlan should take a look at you," she said.

Harlan Bennett was one of two physicians at the Longtooth clinic. He was an outsider from Georgia, and he was rooming at The Spruce. Grace didn't want Harlan confirming that there was no reason for her to be such a mess, so she brushed away Natasha's concern.

"No, really. It's probably just a little stomach bug," she lied. "I'll be fine."

"Where do you want the stereo, Tasha?" Caleb Kinoyit's voice sounded from behind Grace. Sudden tension stiffened her spine, but she didn't turn to look at him.

"On the back table," Natasha directed him. She turned her attention back to Grace. "If you have a stomach bug, you need to rest," she said, her tone brooking no argument.

"Stomach bug?"

Grace jumped at the sound of Caleb's voice again, directly behind her. He hadn't walked away like she'd assumed.

"Where'd she get a stomach bug? There's nothing going around right now, and she only eats at The Spruce."

Anger and anxiety warred with each other, churning Grace's stomach. She finally turned to face Caleb, putting her shoulders back and smoothing the weariness from her face. "Oh, wow, I didn't realize you were a pilot *and* a doctor."

He scowled at her, clutching a massive old boombox in his arms, and lifted his gaze to Natasha. "She looks fine," he said, and it was very decidedly not a compliment.

The impulse to argue with Caleb stood in diametric opposition to the need to hide her pitifulness. "Your opinion has been noted," Grace told him dismissively.

"Gracie," Natasha said gently. "If you're not feeling well—"

She wasn't, but that was entirely her own doing.

"—then maybe you should skip the party and get some sleep."

Grace's sympathetic nervous system heard *skip the party* and lit up like a Christmas tree. But no, she refused to be a slave to wonky brain chemistry. She was going to that damned party, and she was going to stand in that crowd of strangers, and she was *not* going to freak out.

"And you don't want to get anybody else sick," Natasha added.

Grace deflated on that one. Explaining that her condition was definitely not contagious was too mortifying. She shrugged. "Alright, if you think so." She got up from the counter. "Sorry to be a party pooper," she added lamely.

"There will be other parties," Natasha assured her. "I will send something up for you to eat. Go rest."

Not long after Grace had returned to her room, Natasha appeared with a tray bearing a bowl of soup and a sleeve of crackers. Her thoughtfulness made guilt twist in Grace's gut like a hot knife. She thanked Natasha profusely and took the tray. While Grace's hands were occupied, Natasha felt her forehead again.

"Still so cold," she said worriedly.

"I'll be fine," Grace promised.

While she ate her soup, Grace could hear the distant beat of music and the indistinct rumble of voices. The muffled noise of the party drifted up the stairwell, crept beneath her door, and circled around her. *Coward, coward, coward* the bass line whispered.

"*I know,*" she hissed back.

. . .

Long after the party had dispersed, Grace was still awake. The surrounding silence was deafening. An unfamiliar restlessness filled her. There was nowhere to go, nowhere she wanted to go. But she couldn't stay *here*, locked in this tiny room, staring out at the same stretch of road for hours on end. She pulled the wool blanket off her bed, wrapped it around her shoulders, and stepped into her slippers. Treading lightly, keeping close to the wall where the floor was less creaky, she made her way silently downstairs.

The dining room had been cleaned, but ghosts of the party remained. Tables weren't in their usual places. The rich, greasy smell of party food still lingered in the air. A pair of forgotten glasses sat on the diner counter. Grace crossed to where a small table was pushed up against the windows. She sank into the chair, drew her knees up to her chest, and gazed out into the night.

The sky was clear, the moon a thin sliver. Far to the right stood the garage for Spruce residents, a low, metal building. The rest of the view was uninterrupted Alaskan wilderness. A snow-blanketed forest climbed the sloping foothills, rising higher and higher, then giving way to the harsh beauty of the mountains. Their jagged peaks stood starkly against a star-flooded sky. After several years in Chicago, she'd almost forgotten how overwhelmingly beautiful the stars could be. A faint, green iridescence pulsed against the sky, fading and shifting almost imperceptibly. She squinted at it, tilting her head. Was it the northern lights?

Movement drew her eye down to the edge of the forest. From beneath snow-covered spruces, three wolves emerged. She drew in a shallow breath, stunned. They were massive, and yet they moved with such powerful grace. Two of the wolves were creamy white, while the third and largest wolf was silvery gray. Grace stared as they drew nearer and nearer to The Spruce, until they were only a few yards away from the window where she sat. Margaret had warned her the wolves came into town, but she hadn't expected to see any so closely.

Suddenly, the big gray wolf froze, lifting his head. The other two halted, looking back to him. He lifted his snout, scenting the air. He turned his head slowly until, finally, he was looking at the windows. Disturbingly perceptive amber-gold eyes seemed to stare straight at Grace. There was no way he could see her through the glare of moonlight against the glass, but she was pinned in place by the force of that gaze. After a long moment, the wolf finally looked away. Grace let out a slow exhale.

A second later, the gray wolf surged back into motion, followed by the other two, and they raced along the side of The Spruce, looping past the garage, and then cutting behind it, disappearing from view.

"Oh my god," Grace whispered. She'd never seen anything like it.

She sat for a long time, staring into the night, hoping the wolves would return. The Spruce was utterly and completely silent. The stars glittered overhead while the darkness of the dining room enveloped her like a cocoon. She felt like the only person in the world.

"What are you doing?"

Grace nearly jumped through the ceiling. Heart pounding, she twisted in her seat. A man's silhouette stood in the darkness at the other side of the dining room.

"Who's there?" She asked, drawing the blanket more tightly around her shoulders.

He stepped forward, and the faint glow from the

windows slid over him. Caleb Kinoyit. Wearing a parka and gray sweatpants, with his feet jammed into unlaced boots. Had he been outside? At two in the morning?

"I'm just stargazing," Grace told him.

He leaned against one of the thick wooden support beams, folding his arms as he regarded her. "You're over that stomach bug, I see."

She flushed, looking down at her hands. "How was the party?" She asked.

Caleb let out a soft huff of laughter. "You don't care."

Irritation had her shoulders rising. "I wouldn't have asked if I didn't care."

They were both quiet for a while. Grace tilted her head back and nearly jumped out of her skin again. Caleb had closed the distance between them, moving with perfect silence. He eased into the chair opposite her, folding his arms on the table and leaning forward. His face was mostly shadow, but she could see the outline of his profile, the dark gleam of his eyes. His parka was only partially zipped, revealing the hard lines of his collar bones, the shadow of dark hair on his chest. She tore her gaze away from him, looking back out the window. Why had he been outside, shirtless, at two in the morning? Before she could ask, Caleb spoke.

"For whatever reason," he said in a low voice, "Natasha and Margaret are both pretty attached to you."

Grace was silent, waiting for him to make his point.

"They're going to take it hard when you leave."

He said it like she already had plans to go. When she actually had no idea what she was going to do. She didn't really belong anywhere. She didn't belong in Longtooth, but she had nowhere else to be, either. Her hometown was essentially one giant cornfield, and the idea of returning to that featureless flatland filled her with an odd melancholy that felt like the dark side of nostalgia. She'd lived in Milwaukee for several years, and still knew people there, but none of those relationships were significant. Nothing about the city beckoned to her. Chicago had never particularly felt like home either and, since ending things with Alex, it had become her worst nightmare—an endless labyrinth filled with shadowed alcoves, glinting windows, watching eyes.

A place like Longtooth would be ideal, she realized. The town was quiet without being dead. People were close without being *everywhere*. And then there was the staggering beauty of the land—no flat farm fields, no dingy concrete. Just towering mountains, rugged forest, blankets of pristine snow, and brutally crisp air.

But it wasn't hers. She wasn't part of the Valley, she didn't have the history or the familial ties or the cultural connection that all the locals had. Caleb knew it. Grace knew it. Still, it stung. "Why do you assume I'm going to leave?"

Caleb's face was hard, but there was something bleak in his eyes when he said, "Because your kind always do."

Grace bristled, twisting back to face him. "My kind?"

"I'm just saying, don't let them get too attached. Don't let Natasha make you into the daughter she never had. Don't let Margaret—"

"It's none of your business who I do or don't get attached to." Grace pushed away from the table, got to her feet. "Good night."

Caleb got to his feet as well. "I'm not the bad guy for noticing you don't want to be here. You hide in your room as soon as you're done eating. You faked sick so you wouldn't have to spend a few hours getting to know people."

She went to her room every night because the effort of living was an exhausting, uphill battle. She faked sick because the idea of standing in a crowd of strangers made her want to peel her own skin off. It was nothing personal against the people of Longtooth. Grace knew if she'd met them on a one-on-one basis first, the party probably would've been fine.

"You don't know anything about me."

"I know enough."

She turned away from him, headed angrily for the stairs.

CHAPTER 5

After her witching hour run-in with Caleb, Grace didn't see him for several days. Not in the dining room, not in the hallway. One morning, on her way to school, she saw his plane take off, arcing over the Valley, then growing more and more distant. Occasionally, late at night, she heard the creak of his bedsprings as he got into bed. It was her only indication that he even still existed. She would've preferred to have no indications. He was a constant reminder that the weakness inside her wasn't just her own burden to bear—it affected other people, offended them, hurt them. She had to find a way to get over Alex, get over Chicago, so that she could behave like a normal human being. Seeing or hearing Caleb reminded her of her abnormality, her weakness, her failure.

So, when Lucia Alvarez sat next to Grace in the staff room at lunch and invited her to the Blue Moose—Longtooth's only tavern—she forced herself to accept.

"A bunch of us 'outsiders' need to get together for

drinks," Lucia said. "Harlan and Andrew already said they'd be there."

"Sounds great," Grace lied.

"But don't go to the Moose alone," Lucia warned, with the wary eyes of a woman who'd learned her lesson firsthand.

"Is it dangerous?" Grace'd had no intention of going to the tavern anyway, but it was good to know where the bad parts of town were. Even tiny towns had that one sketchy place that locals knew to avoid.

"Only that you might die of pity," Linnea Teague chimed in wryly. "Most of the locals are relation to each other, some way or another. And not many outsiders want to live up here. So the competition for your fresh, genetically distant lovin' is steep."

"I knew it!" Grace stabbed an accusatory finger at nobody in particular. "Natasha's been shoving me at any local who walks into The Spruce."

Lucia gave her a commiserating look. "I had to put my foot down with her. She's a little frosty with me now, but at least I can eat my breakfast without being evaluated as breeding stock."

Grace shrank a little. "I don't think I have the nerve for that."

Natasha had that well-meaning, broody-hen kind of maternal nature that Grace had always been a sucker for. Her own family wasn't neglectful, exactly, but they weren't quite as affectionate as other people's parents seemed to be. They'd always made sure she was fed and clothed, drove her to volleyball practice, and uncomplainingly paid for the cello she'd halfheartedly played throughout school. But they'd rarely showed up to her volleyball games or orchestra concerts. They could never remember her friends' names, never knew or asked if the boys she was hanging out with were friends or boyfriends. They never pushed her too hard to achieve, and they also never came down particularly hard on her when she messed up. Her mom was always occupied with her life's passion—breeding, training, and showing her champion Norwegian Elkhounds—while her dad was usually either fishing on the lake or in the garage, trying to fix his boat.

Natasha was the polar opposite—interested in Grace's life, concerned over her well-being, actively involving herself in Grace's future. And besides, Grace didn't think of her attempts to pair her off as turning her into "breeding stock." She saw Natasha more as a matchmaker who just wanted to see her kith and kin happily settled and loved. If her efforts made Grace uncomfortable, that had more to do with her own brokenness than anything else. Alex had ruined her for other men, and not in a good way. The thought of a relationship made her feel caged, sweaty. The faintest glimmer of interest from a man made her want to run for the hills.

"Are the men pushy?" Grace asked.

"They get friendly if you encourage them, but you don't have to worry too much. We're a tight community. Word gets around pretty fast, and everyone knows there'll be hell to pay when the aunties find out you've been up to no good," Tamsyn explained.

As far as Grace could tell, "auntie" seemed to be a Valley catch-all term for an elder woman. Since all the Valley locals seemed to be at least third cousins with each other, the odds were good that any older woman was an aunt to a good portion of them, anyway. But being an auntie wasn't about blood ties. It was about status. Even a woman with no children, no nieces or nephews, became an auntie once she passed a certain age, or carried a certain amount of authority. Grace could think of a few women off the top of her head who seemed to have "auntie" status, and she could easily picture any one of them giving absolute hell to somebody who'd crossed lines of acceptable behavior. It gave her a small measure of comfort.

"Alright," she said, feigning excitement. "Friday it is."

THE WEEK PASSED MUCH the same as the previous one had—if Grace didn't find some way to occupy her mind, then she obsessively fretted about the upcoming drinking plans. The Blue Moose might be even worse than a party at The Spruce. At least under Natasha's roof people were sure to mind their manners. The same couldn't be said of the Blue Moose. Anybody and everybody could walk into a bar.

By the time classes ended on Friday, Grace was a sweaty mess of pointless adrenaline. She drove back to The Spruce and took a shower in the time she had before they were supposed to meet at the bar. She changed into something more casual than what she wore to school, and then she sat on her bed and... waited.

When she was with Alex, and he never wanted to do anything or go anywhere, it had often been a relief. Grace knew she *should* go see friends, maintain relationships, even if only for her own sake. But doing so was frustrating and anxiety-inducing. Her extroverted friends always wanted to drag her to some loud, crowded place where there were tons of other people she didn't know and where she had to put on her exhausting fake-extrovert persona. While spending every night on her couch, staring at the television wasn't her preferred alternative, it seemed better—safer—than the endless whirl of bars and festivals and pop-ups and whatever other venues could cram a bunch of outgoing strangers together.

In fact, one of the many reasons Longtooth had appealed to her was for the distinct lack of nightlife.

So, as the clock struck down, she sat tensely on the edge of her bed, mind spinning through plausible excuses not to show.

Stomach bug? No, I already used that one.

Can't use a family emergency, they all know I have no family here.

Can't use a work emergency, half of them work with me.

Claim to be a recovering alcoholic? No. They'll all wonder why I agreed to meet at the tavern in the first place.

Time wound down and Grace had nothing believable. Angry at herself for being such a shivering little coward, she stood up and marched out of her room with maybe too much force.

"Ah!" Harlan just managed to jump out of her way before Grace mowed him down. Although, considering his size, it would've more likely been a case of Grace getting knocked on her ass. Harlan's build would've made rugby players weep with envy.

"Sorry!" She stumbled and righted herself against the wall.

Harlan stood with his hand on his heart for a second, eyes wide. "Jesus. Is the place on fire?"

"No. I was just…rushing."

After a beat, Harlan seemed to recover, straightening his coat with exaggerated dignity. "Couldn't wait to see me?"

"Absolutely," Grace agreed with a genuine smile. They'd had a few conversations here and there—before being politely broken apart by Natasha—and she'd come to the conclusion that Harlan was easy to like.

He returned her smile and the flash of his teeth against his neatly trimmed beard brought to her mind another man with a black beard and attractive smile. Unlike Harlan, that man seemed to hate her, so why he even crossed her mind was an annoying mystery.

"Well then, can I escort you to the Blue Moose, Miss Rossi?" He proffered a bent arm and she looped hers into it.

"Certainly you may, sir."

The hallway was too narrow for them to walk side-by-side, but Harlan insisted on "escorting" her, so Grace laughingly allowed herself to be hauled sideways along the hall and then down the even narrower stairway. When they emerged into the dining room, arms linked, stumbling and laughing, heads turned toward them. Natasha looked up from a conversation with Joanne Lance and frowned.

"Gracie. Harlan. What are you doing?"

"We're headed to the Moose, Mrs. Freeman," Harlan answered, straightening up, but still holding Grace's arm.

"Together?" Natasha's frown deepened.

"A bunch of us 'outsiders' are meeting for a few drinks," Grace explained quickly.

Natasha's gaze lingered on their linked arms as they made their way out of the dining room.

Outside The Spruce, they broke apart with a burst of laughter.

"You're in trouble!" Harlan teased her as they walked toward the tavern.

"So are you! You're supposed to be using your Southern charm on local women only. Didn't you read the fine print in your employment contract?"

"I can't help it if I'm irresistible. You'll have to be strong for the both of us, Grace, my love. No matter how difficult it is, you cannot fall in love with me."

"Oh, Harlan. It's too late." Flirting with Harlan was safe, harmless. There was no heat in the smiles he gave her, and despite his easygoing humor, he held himself at a certain remove. The few conversations she'd had with Harlan were always light, easy. He avoided personal topics, said little about himself.

"Here we are," Harlan announced.

Wedged between the Ankkonisdoy Guide Service office and a small engine repair shop, the Blue Moose was distinguished by a royal blue entry door. Harlan pulled it open.

"Ladies first," he said magnanimously.

Grace almost quailed, but she had enough pride to hide her anxiety. "Thank you," she said, swanning into the small entryway.

They had to pass through another bright blue door to enter the heat, noise, and crowd of the bar. Her heart kicked up a notch, and she found herself automatically searching all the faces for Alex. Logically, she knew he wouldn't be here. But instinctively, she had to reassure herself. She expected every half-shadowed face, every turned back, to be his. But almost every face was turned towards them when they entered, and Grace was quickly assured that Alex was not among them.

The Blue Moose was not quite like any bar she'd ever

been to. The actual bartop was built out of plywood and painted the same bright blue as the door. None of the barstools matched, and half of them looked handmade— repurposed rebar welded together for the legs and a mixture of plywood and upturned 5-gallon buckets used for the seats. Instead of a mirror behind the bar, there was a giant blue moose painted on the wall.

The tables scattered around the open space had also been salvaged. There was a giant cable spool with mismatched aluminum folding chairs gathered around it. There was an old wrought-iron coffee table whose glass top had been replaced with a sheet of plywood, flanked by two broken-down old sofas—one patterned with roses, the other a yellow and brown plaid. There was a battered vinyl card table whose legs had been reinforced with lengths of PVC pipe, surrounded by improvised seats made out of repurposed materials, including a large stump, two old car seats, and more five-gallon buckets.

Grace found Lucia, Andrew, and Eric sitting around an old wooden door that had been sawed down and balanced atop a fifty-gallon drum, also sawed down. It was surrounded by wooden kitchen chairs, none of which matched and all of them slightly damaged in some way—all the spindles missing from the backrest on one, a leg replaced by a piece of two-by-four on another, the arms snapped off on another. They weren't pretty, but they were all perfectly serviceable.

"Hey!" Lucia brightened as she caught sight of Harlan and Grace.

"Alright." Eric hopped up, gesturing for Grace to take his seat. "I've got the first round."

Grace fought the urge to glance at the clock above the

bar. If Eric was buying a round, common courtesy would dictate that the rest of them also buy rounds. Which meant five rounds at a minimum. How long was she going to have to be here? She had to make sure to get the next round so that she could slink off guilt-free when her anxiety finally drove her out of the bar earlier than everyone else.

"Grace! Lucia!" Jessica Taaltsiyh materialized out of the crowd with a smile and wave. She looked around the table, smiling at the men. "Hey, guys!"

Jess was as tall as Grace was, at five-ten, if not a little taller. But where Grace was thin to the point of being skeletal, Jess was as curvy as an Old Hollywood starlet. She had the same silky black hair and tawny skin as the rest of the locals, with a pleasantly heart-shaped face, and large hooded eyes with golden-brown irises. Grace had learned from a handful of conversations during breakfast at The Spruce that Jess had lived in Longtooth most of her life, but she'd spent four years in Fairbanks getting her bachelor's degree in accounting, then two years in Anchorage getting her masters and becoming a licensed CPA. In Longtooth, she didn't have any official title, but she seemed to work as the city's comptroller, overseeing the finances.

Her presence had a calming effect on Grace. Jess reminded her of Margaret in a lot of ways—ostensibly warm and friendly while managing to project an air of steadiness, watchfulness. The fact that a local had joined their little circle didn't hurt either—it stopped Grace's brain from categorizing the crowd in the bar as *us* and *them*.

Eric reappeared with the necks of several beer bottles clutched between his fingers. "Ah, Jess, I didn't see you. Can I get you a drink?"

"I'm set." She held up a bottle. "Thanks though."

"Alright everybody," Lucia cut in, motioning for quiet. "Grace is the newest of us outsiders, so—" she hefted her glass "—cheers to Grace! Welcome to Longtooth."

They all clinked bottles with Grace and a few people around them cheered. A whistle sounded from somewhere else in the bar, making Grace's ears turn red. "Thanks, guys."

"It's been a whole month," Jess said. "What do you think?" She was smiling at Grace in that same hopeful way that Margaret and Natasha often did. It kindled a little warm spot in Grace's chest, a beacon against the cold.

"I like Longtooth," she said honestly. "Everyone's been good to me, my students are great, and the mountains are almost too beautiful."

Jess threw an arm around Grace's shoulders and squeezed. "Yay," she said.

The conversation veered off into a discussion of the Teekkonlit Valley's natural beauty, and Grace let herself become a listener, nodding in agreement with everyone else's pronouncements.

"You have to get outside of town and into the mountains to really appreciate them," Jess told them. "Snowmachines are the best. On a night when the sky is clear, it's unbelievable."

"Aren't you worried about animals?" Grace asked. Even in the comparatively mild wilderness of Wisconsin, walking in the woods at night could be dangerous.

Jess opened her mouth to speak. For a moment she hesitated. Finally, she said, "The sound of the snowmachine scares them away." She nudged Grace with an elbow. "I'll take you out there one of these days."

"Yeah, absolutely. That would be cool." She missed having friends. Even if kindling friendships wasn't exactly

Grace's forte, she liked Jess. She was funny and smart and kind. For whatever reason, she seemed to like Grace too. And doing something like snowmobiling wouldn't aggravate Grace's anxieties. Away from enclosed crowds, away from male pursuers, with a specific task to focus on, she could have fun. Unlike the tavern, where—as much as she liked the present company—the surrounding crowd and noise left her fidgety and tense.

As everyone was getting to the bottom of their drinks, Grace stood up. "I've got next round," she declared, heading for the bar.

Every stool at the bar was filled by locals. She slipped between two sets of broad shoulders and leaned over the bar top to get the bartender's attention. The shoulders to her left suddenly swiveled to face her, and she found herself looking up at Caleb Kinoyit.

He scowled at her. "Thought you were too good for the Moose."

She scowled right back at him. "When did I ever say that?"

"Hey, Grace." Adam Toonikoh—the bartender and owner of the Blue Moose—stepped up to her. He nodded his head towards Caleb. "This charmer bothering you?"

"Usually. Can I get another round of whatever Eric ordered?" She gestured vaguely at their table.

"Sure thing. Five?"

Grace glanced back at the table again, checking Jess's drink. "Yeah. And add one of whatever Jess is having."

Adam moved down the bar to get bottles from the cooler. Without a specific conversation to focus on, the noise of the bar suddenly rose to the forefront. Grace glanced over her shoulder at the press of bodies behind her. She couldn't help searching every face. *He's not here. Stop being weird.* She forced herself to turn back to the bar, uncomfortable leaving the crowd at her back, but aware of how weird it would look to methodically scan the faces in the bar. She flicked a glance at the clock above the bar—not even an hour had passed since she'd arrived. Way too soon to duck out. She drummed her fingers on the bar top, ears acutely attuned to the ruckus behind her. Her body was tense, waiting for danger, but she affected a posture of casual unconcern. She glanced down the bar, wishing Adam would hurry up with those beers.

After a moment she realized Caleb was still looking at her. His expression was blank, but his gaze was intensely focused. His scrutiny prickled her skin. Feigning unconcern, she raised her eyebrows, meeting his gaze. "Can I *help* you?"

His brows drew together. "You don't like crowds," he said.

What was giving her away? Could he see the way her palms were leaving sweaty marks on her beer bottle? Did he notice how often she looked at the Pabst clock above the bar? Embarrassed at being caught out for her social incompetence, she forced a careless shrug. "They're not my favorite," she admitted.

His expression deepened into a frown. "Is that why you—"

"Holy hell!" A pair of big hands descended on Caleb's shoulders, cutting him off. "Caleb Kinoyit—*socializing?*"

Caleb twisted back, and his frown faded into an expression of exasperated amusement. "Isaac," he said dryly. "Does Margaret know you're in town?"

The other man emerged from behind Caleb, leaving one beefy arm slung around Caleb's shoulders. He was built like an ox, all stocky brawn. The two of them resembled each other, although Caleb was taller and leaner.

"She knows." He clapped Caleb reassuringly on the chest. "My exile's over." The newcomer's eyes lit up when they landed on Grace. "And *who* is this?"

"Easy, man," Caleb muttered, putting a staying hand on the man's chest. He shrugged away from Caleb and pushed forward, crowding into Grace's space. He towered over her until she had to tilt her head back to look him in the eye.

"Hello, sweetheart. Isaac Murray. Who would you be?"

Grace hated being the recipient of such blatant male interest. It felt like she was guarding her wallet from a pick-pocket, but wasn't allowed to yell *thief!* A frisson of discomfort tugged at her flight-or-fight response, but she quashed it with a well-practiced social smile. "I'm Grace," she told him. "I'm the new English teacher."

"Ahhh." Isaac rubbed thoughtfully at his bearded jaw. "So *you*'re the pretty little schoolteacher I've been hearing about." He threw a satisfied glance at Caleb, who stared back flatly.

"What have you heard about me?" She started to lift her beer for another drink, then thought better of it. She could just imagine the leer on Isaac's face if he saw a long bottle-neck pressed to her lips.

"All good things," Isaac assured her, leaning on the bar top in a way that caged Grace in. She pretended not to notice.

"You must not have heard them from Caleb, then." She leaned over, as if to look at Caleb, and used the movement to slip out of Isaac's pin.

"Uh-oh." Isaac turned a smirk on Caleb. "Sounds like you're on little Gracie's shit-list."

At her height, Grace hardly qualified as "little." And the only people in Longtooth who could get away with calling her "Gracie" were Margaret and Natasha.

"Nope," she corrected Isaac with a tight smile. "*I'm* on *his* list."

Before the conversation could go any further, Adam appeared like a heaven-sent miracle. He placed a tray laden with brown bottles on the bar in front of Grace. She handed him cash, deposited her nearly-empty bottle, and took the tray. She turned a brittle smile on Caleb and Isaac. "You guys have a nice night."

Caleb frowned at her. She turned away before either of them could say anything, and slipped through the crowd.

"Who's the beefcake at the bar?" Lucia asked when Grace reached the table, a slightly predatory gleam in her eyes.

"That's my new friend Isaac, and you're welcome to him," Grace told her.

Lucia smiled dryly, looking past her. "Your *friend* doesn't look like he's interested in substitutions."

"What do you—" She turned to see Isaac parting the crowd like a rolling boulder, his gaze pinned on Grace. "Ah shit," she muttered.

"Gracie, you disappeared before I could buy you a drink." He leaned onto the table, his solid bulk forming a wall between Grace and the others. "What are you having?"

"I'm calling it a night after this one," she said, lifting her drink. "But thanks anyway."

"When I just got here?" He reared back to address the rest of the table. "Tell her she can't go!"

The others didn't notice the DO NOT she was telegraphing with her eyes.

"Come on, Grace," Lucia objected. "Stay!"

"It's *Friday night*," Eric pointed out. "In Longtooth. What else could you possibly have going on?"

"The man makes a solid point," Jess said, lifting her fresh drink.

Grace turned pleading eyes on Harlan.

He smiled. "Aw, come on, Grace. Don't make us shut the party down early."

She sighed. "Alright. One more round."

"Two," Isaac pressed.

"*Two!*" the others roared.

Grace threw her hands up. "Fine!"

The table cheered. She tried to look amused, but that old panicky dread was creeping in. *You're fine*, she told herself, taking a breath. *You're safe. It's only for a few hours. You'll be fine.*

She managed to hold it together. Two more rounds helped dampen the panic and annoyance, to the point that she actually found herself laughing at Isaac's obnoxious passes, fending him off with increasingly blunt rejections.

"I see you looking at my beard, Gracie. Go on, give it a feel."

"I was only trying to figure out if you're part-bear." The fact was, she *was* looking at his beard. Isaac wasn't unattractive. It was his pushiness that put her off. But she liked the way his smile looked against the black scruff of his beard and the warm tan of his skin. It was how Caleb looked, on the rare occasion that he smiled. Except Caleb's face was leaner. His smiles were a little sharp, a little feral.

Isaac's grin stretched wider. He caught Grace's wrist and brought her hand to his cheek. His beard rasped against her palm. "Can't keep looking at me like that, Gracie. Gives a man ideas."

If she was looking like anything, it was because the image of Caleb smiling—even just in her imagination—sent an alarming spark of heat straight through her. She pulled her hand away from Isaac's grasp. He held on for a second—just long enough to show her that she couldn't get away if he didn't want her to. When he finally released her, she jerked back, all humor gone. The mild beer buzz vanished with a bolt of fear.

You're safe. You're fine. There are too many people around. Nothing will happen. But reminding herself of the crowd had the opposite effect—the panic rose again. Suddenly, she was aware of every noise, every voice. The sound of a dozen other conversations buzzed in her ears like a swarm of bees. The sound of laughter was a raucous jeer. The bodies all around her seemed to press in. Their heat surrounded her, a feverish contrast to the bitter cold beneath her skin. Sweat prickled over her chest and back.

She drew in a jagged breath. "I have to use the bathroom." She backed away from Isaac and slipped through the crowd, weaving her way towards the narrow hall at the back of the bar.

At the end of the hall, there was a single unisex bathroom. Grace locked herself inside and slumped against the door. The wood was mercifully cool, and the heaviness of the door muffled the sounds of the bar. She drew in long, steady breaths for a while, concentrating on the in and out of air until her hands stopped shaking. Feeling steadier, she pushed away from the door and went to the sink. Wetting paper towels, she reached under her sweater and swiped away the tacky feeling of dried sweat on her chest and back.

When she emerged from the bathroom, Isaac was waiting just outside the door, blocking her way. She glanced down the dim hall towards the light and noise of the bar. Everyone else was only ten feet away, but it felt like a mile.

"Oh, hey," she said, hiding her discomfort. "Bathroom's all yours." She went to move past Isaac, but he caught her arm and spun her back. It was a surprisingly graceful move that ended up with her back pressed against the wall and Isaac's big body looming over hers. He put his hands against the wall on either side of her shoulders, his massive arms caging her in place.

"We've been dancing around each other all night," Isaac murmured, leaning in close. "And my feet are getting tired."

"Yeah, sorry, but that's not what's happening here." Grace tried not to let her panic show.

"Then why are you trembling, Gracie?" He pulled one hand away from the wall—not the side she needed for escape—and ran his knuckles softly over her cheek. "Damn, you're freezing. I bet I can warm you up."

"Isaac, wait—"

His mouth came down on hers, silencing her. She turned her head and shoved at his shoulders, but he was an immovable wall. His lips moved down her jaw, her neck, leaving a clammy trail in their wake.

"Listen, Isaac—" Grace twisted away from him, but was still trapped between his arms. "Stop. I don't—"

His mouth landed on hers again, humid and suffocating. She slapped at his shoulder, once, twice. She made a fist, but before she could figure out where to punch him, his body was suddenly wrenched away from hers. She staggered, falling back against the wall, and looked up to see—

Caleb?

Caleb's face was a mask of pure rage. His dark eyes seemed to gleam with some inner fire, making them shine like amber. He threw Isaac back against the other wall, then turned to Grace. He caught her by the elbow, steadying her. His touch was as hot as an iron. She gasped and flinched away from it.

He immediately drew back, giving her space. "Are you okay?" he demanded, his voice a raw snarl.

Heart pounding, stomach sick, Grace nodded mutely.

Isaac suddenly lunged forward. Caleb twisted to meet him, slamming him back against the wall again. Grace shrank back from the fight, wedging herself against the far corner.

"*Argh!*" Isaac wrestled against Caleb's hold. "Get your own woman!" he growled.

Two more men appeared, rushing down the hall to help Caleb subdue Isaac. "Hey now," one of the other men scolded. "What'd you do this time, Isaac?"

"Grace?" Harlan stood at the other end of the hall, Lucia next to him. A crowd had gathered behind them. "Are you okay?"

Caleb and the others had successfully pinned Isaac. Grace slipped past them and sprinted out of the hallway. Lucia caught her by the arms. Her touch was a warm glow against the cold beneath Grace's skin. "Hey, Grace. It's okay," she soothed. "Let's get out of here." She glanced up at Harlan.

He was staring down the hall at Isaac, his handsome face turned harsh and cold.

"Harlan," Lucia prompted.

He looked back at them. After a second, he smoothed his expression. "Sure. Let's call it a night."

The crowd parted for them. Pitying looks were cast Grace's way, which only made everything worse. If she could've dropped through the floor and tunneled her way out of Longtooth, she would've done it.

ALONE IN HER ROOM, Grace sat on the edge of her bed in the dark and stared out at the street. She could see The Blue Moose up the road. Light spilled through the bar's front window, casting a pale rectangle on the street. Shadows and silhouettes moved within it, made by the people who'd seen her inglorious departure—they were probably still talking about it.

Just as cold as ever, she turned away from the sight, tried to put it out of her mind. But she couldn't.

She'd hoped coming to Alaska would give her a reprieve from the darkness that had plagued her in Chicago. She'd thought getting away from the claustrophobia and anonymity of the city would give her a chance to reset, to recover herself. But she was just as messed up here as she'd been there. She couldn't handle one pushy guy in a small-town bar without being completely overset.

She wanted to leave Longtooth. But she didn't know where else to go. Not back to Chicago. Not back to her little hometown. She didn't belong anywhere. She definitely didn't belong here. But what else was there?

Her mind raced in circles, replaying the events at the bar, replaying her last few months in Chicago. Twisted up by memories she didn't want, she crawled beneath the covers and faded into panicked dreams.

ALEX HAD ALWAYS BEEN HANDSOME. *Tall and muscular, with a jawline that could cut glass, thick hair like spun gold, and piercing blue eyes. She'd been lost at first sight. That handsome face stared at her now, forehead creased with concern.*

"Where are you, Grace?" he asked. His voice was faint, distant.

"Leave me alone," she begged.

They stood in darkness, just the two of them. No earth, no sky. Just endless black, and the penetrating gleam of Alex's lovely blue eyes. She was afraid to look into those eyes. She'd always been a sucker for their soulful depths.

"Please, Grace." He tried to step closer, but she stumbled back, keeping the distance between them.

"Go away, Alex." She backed up more.

"Grace, please. Just tell me—"

"No!" She staggered back another few steps. She didn't dare turn her back on him. But she stumbled further and further away, the distance between them growing.

"Grace!" his voice was fainter now.

Still, she scrambled backward.

"Grace!" She almost couldn't hear him.

She finally turned away from him, ready to run for all she was worth. But when she turned around, there he was. He reached for her—

Grace woke abruptly to the jarring tone of her morning alarm. She was slicked with sweat, heart pounding and breath whistling as if she'd run a marathon.

You're safe. He can't find you.

Sitting up, she silenced her alarm, then walked to the shower on trembling legs.

It took her a few minutes to work up the nerve to go down for breakfast. She knew how small towns worked. By now, all of Longtooth would be buzzing over what had happened at the Blue Moose last night. She was going to have to suffer more pitying looks, nosy questions. People like Harry Lance were bound to take Isaac's side.

The dining room fell quiet as soon as she appeared. The usual morning crowd was all there, plus the extras who came by for breakfast on Saturdays. Harlan and Lucia were at the counter, with no space to sit near them. Caleb Kinoyit was seated at a small table by the windows, his assessing gaze traveling dispassionately over Grace. She blushed hotly—a mixture of both embarrassment and anger. Squaring her shoulders, she made her way to the counter and took the open seat between Wade Evers and Jessica Taaltsiyh.

"Hey, Grace," Jessica said with a studied casualness.

"Morning," Wade said, also studiously mild.

"Good morning," she said to them both. Around them, conversation gradually resumed.

Natasha appeared in front of Grace. She made no effort to disguise the concern in her eyes. Mercifully, she didn't ask about last night. "Good morning, Gracie. Coffee?"

Grace nodded. "Yes please." Aware of the entire dining room's scrutiny, she was already sweating. "Can I get scrambled eggs, too?" She had no appetite, but she was determined not to let anybody see how off-kilter she was.

"Of course." Natasha poured the coffee and disappeared into the kitchen.

"We're supposed to get snow on Monday," Wade said, cutting into his fried moose steak.

"Yeah?" Grace picked up her coffee mug. She was already wired. She probably should've asked for decaf. But that would've been admitting her nerves to everyone, so she took a hearty slug.

"Just a few inches. Nothing terrible," Wade said.

Grace cupped her frozen hands around her mug. "I like when it snows," she said inanely. "It's cozy."

"*Cozy?*" Harry Lance's voice cut through the air, three seats down from her. "Wait until you see a *real* Alaskan snowstorm," he warned. "You won't think it's so cozy then!"

Any other day, Grace would've been struggling not to tell Harry to go fuck himself. Today, his abrasiveness was a soothing balm amidst the walking-on-eggshells pleasantness of everyone else. "What's so tough about Alaskan snowstorms?" she asked, needling him. "Are there Ice Giants?"

"You laugh now. You won't be laughing when there's ten feet of snow dumped on you overnight! And minus-forty air temps! And—" Harry ended his tirade on his own, something Grace wouldn't have guessed to be possible.

She realized that the entire dining room had suddenly gone silent. She twisted in her seat, looking around. A few feet away, Caleb rose from his seat, and for a moment, she thought he was the cause of the sudden silence. But then she saw the figure standing in the lobby entryway, and her stomach plunged.

Isaac. He walked into the dining room, coming straight for Grace. Out of the corner of her eye, she could still see Caleb, standing, watching. Behind her, the kitchen door swung open, and Natasha sidled out, arms crossed.

Grace sat frozen in her seat, rigid as a corpse, watching Isaac approach. He stopped in front of her. There was a mottled purple bruise around his left eye, still swollen, and a scabbed-over split in the middle of his bottom lip. His expression was devoid of the obnoxious cheerfulness from last night. Above the edge of his beard, his cheeks were flagged with color.

"Grace," he said, his expression somber. His deep voice carried through the absolute silence of the dining room. "I apologize for mistreating you last night. I was drunk—"

"Is that a fucking excuse?" Harry growled, surprising Grace.

The red in Isaac's face deepened. "I was completely out of line and it won't happen again. If there's anything I can do to make it up to you, let Natasha know, and it'll be done. Anything." His words were stiff, uncomfortable. He glanced at Natasha. Her face was hard as stone as she stared him down. Finally, she nodded.

"I'm sorry," Isaac said. "I'll leave you alone." He turned and left.

Grace watched him go, sweaty and tense all over again. All around her, conversation resumed. Caleb sank back down into his seat. The air was different somehow. The walking-on-eggshells feeling gone.

"That's what happens when the aunties get you," Jessica said, licking her fork.

Grace glanced sideways at the small table where Caleb sat with William Freeman. He suddenly looked up, straight at her. His expression was cool, his dark eyes completely unreadable. Neither of them could seem to look away, until finally, Natasha called her attention with a plate of eggs.

She talked distractedly with Jess while she replayed Isaac's apology in her mind. While she picked at her eggs, she saw Caleb head out to the garage. With no time to grab her coat, Grace dashed into the cold after him.

"Why are you following me?" Caleb demanded flatly, his

back to her. He reached his truck and disconnected the block heater.

"I never thanked you for last night. So, uh, thank you. And I know you had something to do with Isaac's apology. So thank you for that, too."

Caleb whipped around to face her, anger writ across his face. "Don't insult me by thanking me for basic decency," he snapped.

Taken aback, Grace found herself reacting with anger instead of her usual exhaustion. "Well fuck you, then. I was just—"

"I didn't do anything for *you*," he interrupted her. "I was stopping my cousin from making a huge fucking mistake. The aunties are the ones who took a strip off his hide. So why don't you go throw *them* a parade for having moral standards."

Grace stared at him, completely at a loss for how to respond to such unwarranted hostility. "I have no idea what your problem is," she said, backing away. "But I'll be sure not to *insult* you with my presence again." She turned and left him.

Back inside, she made her way up the stairs to her room, thinking about Isaac's shiner and split lip. Somehow, Grace doubted the aunties had done that to him. And he hadn't had those injuries when she'd left the bar last night. Caleb obviously didn't like her, but he'd still dished out a punishment in her defense. And she hadn't missed the way he'd stood and watched when Isaac gentered—he'd made *certain* she got that apology.

Outside her door, Grace paused, key in hand. That didn't mean he wasn't a prick. It just meant he was a prick with principles. There was no reason for her to be slightly turned on by the fact that he'd beaten an apology out of Isaac. Seriously. It was primitive and uncivilized. She was *not* going to think about how big and strong Caleb was.

Shit. Alright, so he was strong. But there was no need to wonder what all that strength looked like shirtless.

Goddamn it.

Or naked.

Fuck.

CHAPTER 6

Grace had been determined not to be a stereotypical, unprepared, lower-48 outsider when she arrived in Longtooth. She was a veteran of brutal winters and frigid cold. She knew how to drive on icy roads. She was fully aware of how dangerous wild animals could be—even if her experiences with skittish black bears and whitetail deer didn't quite compare to grizzlies and moose. She'd grown up in a rural town, and she understood the social undercurrents of small, tightly-knit communities, even if she hadn't really integrated into this one.

But despite all that, city life had softened her just a little. She'd gotten so accustomed to certain conveniences that she'd forgotten they were luxuries and not standards. Like when she'd been taken aback to find out there was no espresso machine, and she would therefore not be having her usual double-shot macchiato. Instead, she had three cups of black coffee with an omelet. The old GMC Jimmy she'd bought did not have remote start—or remote anything

—and so the first morning she had to drive to school without heat because she'd forgotten to go out early and warm it up.

More crucially, it hadn't occurred to her that she couldn't get twenty-seven used copies of *Watership Down* delivered affordably to the interior of Alaska a week before she needed them for her freshman class. The ubiquitousness of free same-day delivery had really skewed her sense of logistical realities. So far, she'd managed to keep her occasional blunders to herself. But she was looking at a minimum of three weeks before she'd have the next books for her freshman classes, which meant she was going to run into trouble getting books for her other classes, too.

Margaret Huditiltik's office was in the secondary school building, in the small administrative hub where the guidance counselor, Lynn Daaldinh, and the school secretary, Joanne Lance—Harry's wife—also had offices. Grace knocked on Margaret's open door and stepped inside.

Margaret looked up and her eyes lit up. Her approval continued to surprise Grace. At Grace's last school, the administrators had seen her as a self-righteous nuisance who couldn't follow simple guidelines.

"Gracie! Come in. What can I help you with?"

"Hey, Margaret. Just a quick question. Is there a way for me to get books shipped quickly from Anchorage to Longtooth?"

She frowned thoughtfully. "How many books?"

Grace tried not to cringe as she admitted, "Uh, probably around a hundred and eighty-three." The exact number of students at Teekkonlit Valley Secondary.

Margaret's frown turned into a fond smile. "The kids are enjoying your classes, Grace. You're doing a good job. Submit an expense request to Joanne on Monday, and I'll make sure it's approved. You can go with Caleb on his next flight down to Anchorage and get the books you need."

"*With* him?" Grace balked. She wasn't a huge fan of that tiny plane. And the pilot radiated palpable dislike whenever he had to be in her presence.

"Yes." Margaret steepled her fingers and regarded Grace over them, smiling faintly. "Is that a problem?"

"No. Of course not. That'll be great." It was a relief to know she wouldn't be paying for all those books out of pocket. It hadn't occurred to her to have the school pay for the books. Her last school would only provide books approved by the curriculum, so she'd gotten accustomed to buying her own copies of the books she wanted for her students. With Teekkonlit Valley being so small, she hadn't expected to be given any sort of budget for her unconventional reading list.

"Good. I think Caleb's running to Anchorage tomorrow." Tomorrow being Saturday. "I'll get in touch with him and then give you a call with the details."

"Perfect. Thanks, Margaret."

"Thank *you*, Grace."

GRACE HAD RETURNED to her classroom and switched her indoor shoes for snow boots when she remembered that she had a question for Margaret about the state testing coming up in the spring. She hesitated outside the door when she realized Margaret was on the phone with somebody else. Grace leaned against the wall outside the office, waiting for Margaret to finish.

"—exactly why we wanted her," Margaret said patiently

to whoever was on the other line. She listened quietly for a moment. "I *am* taking your concerns seriously," she responded, her patience beginning to sound a little thin. "But nobody else is picking up on what you're sensing. I think you're letting the past color your judgment." A brief silence. "Alright, listen to me, pup, because this is an order—you are escorting Grace Rossi to Anchorage tomorrow."

Outside the office, Grace stiffened. Margaret was talking to Caleb. About Grace. And, even without hearing his side of the conversation, it was obvious he wasn't happy. Any hope that his apparent dislike was all just in her head instantly evaporated.

"And you will treat her with respect. Consider her my ward."

What? Grace considered marching into Margaret's office to demand an explanation but decided she didn't want her to think she'd been eavesdropping. She backed away silently and made her way out to her truck. As she drove the short distance back to The Spruce, Margaret's conversation replayed in her head.

What "concerns" was Margaret taking seriously? What concerns could Caleb possibly have about Grace? Was he still mad because she wasn't a social butterfly? Was he mad about her students' reading lists? It was the only thing she'd done since arriving in Longtooth that could be considered even remotely controversial. Somehow, she doubted Caleb cared that her students were reading modern sci-fi and fantasy novels instead of Hawthorne and Faulkner. So, for whatever reason, he somehow considered her a danger. Which was absurd. If Natasha wasn't so persistent, Grace would spend all her free time holed up in her room, bothering nobody and doing nothing.

When she pulled into The Spruce's garage, her phone began to ring. It was Margaret.

"Hello?"

"Hi, Grace. Caleb said to meet him in The Spruce's dining room at six tomorrow morning. You can ride with him to the airstrip."

Oh boy! We'll get to spend even more time together! Grace swallowed her dismay. "Okay..." she said, still baffled by the conversation she'd overheard.

"Is that alright?"

"Um. Yeah. Yes."

"You okay, Gracie?"

"Fine. I'm good. Looking forward to picking up some books."

In the morning dark, Grace and Caleb drove in silence to the airstrip. Grace stood uselessly to the side while Caleb pulled the big canvas covers off the plane and began a minute inspection of every part. This plane was bigger than the one he'd flown her from Anchorage to Longtooth in. It was banana yellow, with a row of square windows down each side of the fuselage. It sat on the gravel runway, wheels protruding from massive aluminum pontoons. Caleb stood on one of the pontoons, examining something on the wing. Grace pulled her fleece dickey higher over her face and watched him work. It was minus-twenty, but there wasn't much wind, so it was almost tolerable. She concentrated on not shivering, so Caleb wouldn't be able to judge her for being a fragile outsider.

Bright halogen lights lit up the space beside the pole building. The forest pressed close around them, branches whispering softly against each other in the dark. She kept her gaze on the plane and tried not to imagine a grizzly stalking them from the cover of the trees.

When the plane was ready, Caleb gestured for Grace to get in. She climbed up onto the pontoon, and into the passenger seat, glancing out at the surrounding darkness as she reached to pull the door shut. At the edge of the forest, several pairs of eyes gleamed back at her. Her heart jumped, and she froze with the door partially ajar. As her eyes adjusted, she could dimly make out the bodies of several bears.

No, not bears, she realized. Wolves. Really, really big wolves.

She jerked the door shut and twisted in her seat, frantic for Caleb to get inside.

"Caleb!" she croaked.

He appeared at the pilot's side door and pulled it open. All of his face was covered except for his eyes, and he still managed to convey complete and utter disdain.

"*Wolves!*" Grace whispered, pointing out her window.

His expression blanked. Not fear. Not disbelief. Just a complete non-reaction. He hauled himself up into the pilot's seat with casual unconcern. When he finally pulled his door shut, Grace let out a little sigh of relief.

A few minutes later, they were accelerating down the runway. Grace closed her eyes as the forest raced closer and closer to the nose of the tiny plane. Her stomach dropped as the sound of wheels rumbling over gravel abruptly cut away. There was only the smooth swoop of each upward climb and the rush of air.

Once the plane leveled out, she opened her eyes. Caleb was wholly focused on the instrument panel, reading dials and making adjustments. His methodical, unruffled confidence went a long way in easing her fear of the small plane. She released her grip on the seat and made herself look out the window. The whole world was spread below them—a dark sea of treetops enclosed by jagged mountains. The river meandered through it all, a twisting, ice-white serpentine. The sight of it took her breath away. She leaned forward, enthralled. Out of the corner of her eye, she saw Caleb turn to look at her. He watched her for a second, then turned his attention forward again.

The flight to Anchorage was long and silent.

They landed at an airfield on the edge of the city. Caleb's deep voice came through Grace's headset, startling her, as he communicated with ground control. It was the first she'd heard him speak in over an hour. He hadn't said a single word to her during the flight—speaking only to communicate with other pilots and air traffic controllers on the radio. While his words were mostly perfunctory, he spoke to them with a comfortable ease that left Grace feeling slighted. He was nicer to complete strangers than he was to her.

When they were wheels-down, she sighed and eased her grip on the seat. Caleb taxied the plane through a field of other planes. There was an old F-150 in storage at the hangar where Caleb parked the plane.

"Where are we going?" Caleb asked. It took Grace a second to process that he'd spoken to her. His deep voice was carefully neutral, but dislike still gleamed in his eyes.

"Why don't you take care of your stuff, and I'll take care of mine, and we can meet back here," she suggested.

"There's only one truck."

"I can get a ride." She was already opening the rideshare app on her phone.

His big hand splayed over her phone screen, capturing her hands and making her jump. The heat of his skin was like a brand, and she jerked away from him, dropping her phone on the frozen ground. She hadn't realized he'd gotten so close. He moved too silently for someone of his size.

Caleb bent to pick up her phone and tossed it to her. "I'll drive. Get in and tell me where we're going."

Grace sensed that, should she try to resist, she'd have to get pretty dramatic about it before he'd yield. So she got into the truck and searched for Anchorage bookstores. While she searched, Caleb made a call on his phone. Grace was only peripherally aware of him giving directions to somebody, talking about cargo and weights. He chuckled at something the other person said, and she looked up in time to catch the flash of his smile.

"No, I'll have to catch you next time. I've got something I have to handle today." His gaze flashed to Grace and his smile dropped.

Suppressing the urge to flip him off, she looked back at her phone.

Caleb ended his call and tucked his phone into his jacket. "Where are we going?" he asked flatly.

"Here." Grace pulled out the old ashtray—clean—and set her phone on it with the navigation pulled up.

Caleb glanced at it and put the truck into gear. He was silent as they drove out of the airfield and into the city. Grace had only been in Longtooth for a few weeks, but the size of Anchorage, the traffic, the people—it was overwhelming. She found herself scanning the faces of strangers on the sidewalk, in cars as they passed. She searched the windows and doors of passing buildings.

Calm down, she told herself. *Everything's fine.*

The first store they went to was a large, independent bookstore. Caleb trailed behind her, a silent, looming shadow. He stood by, glowering silently while she searched the shelves and counted copies and hunted down salespeople to ask if they had more copies of certain titles in storage. She'd just returned to the spot where she'd left Caleb, having managed to accumulate a surprisingly sizable stack of *The Parable of the Sower*, when she realized he'd disappeared.

She stood on her tiptoes, peering across the store, but couldn't see his bearded, shaggy-haired head anywhere. She walked the length of the central aisle, looking down rows of shelves, and finally found him in the History section, leaning against the shelves and reading a book about Genghis Khan.

His hands were so big, he could span the entire book— both covers—in one hand. Grace watched as his rough fingers turned the page, his focus never wavering. The sight of such a big, rugged man, fully engrossed in a book of historical nonfiction sent a staggering bolt of attraction straight through her body. Flinching like a startled rabbit, she backpedaled before he saw her. Suddenly overheated, she unzipped her parka and tugged at the collar of her sweater. She returned to the fiction section and resumed book-hunting.

Grace had three stacks of books on the floor beside her when Caleb returned. She glanced up to see him towering over her, his expression impassive as he scanned the titles she'd gathered. His jacket was partially unzipped, and she could see the edge of a paper bag with the store's logo sticking out. He'd bought a book. Maybe even several.

She had a sudden image in her mind—*Caleb, back in Longtooth, laying in a bed that looked like hers, engrossed in a thick history book. His big body was relaxed, his shaggy hair mussed. He licked one rough fingertip and turned the next page.*

Her whole face heated, and she twisted away from him, pretending to be totally intent on assembling her stacks of books. Without a word, Caleb crouched and gathered them up.

"I can carry them," Grace objected, letting her hair swing over her burning cheeks.

Caleb didn't respond, but he didn't let her take them from him either. He brought them up to the counter and set them down for the cashier. Grace added a small armful of single copies of a few other titles.

"Can you put these on a separate receipt?" she asked the cashier.

Caleb frowned. "Isn't the school paying for the books?"

Grace laid her hand over the individual titles. "These aren't for the school. They're my own, to loan to students who are looking for something to read for fun."

Caleb's dark eyes narrowed as he regarded her. She raised her eyebrows in question. Her blush had mostly receded, but she could feel her cheeks warming again. After a moment's silent interrogation, he shuttered his expression and turned away from her, staring impatiently out the window at the parking lot.

Grace wanted to grab his jacket and bellow, *WHY DON'T YOU LIKE ME?* But she was depressed, not deranged, so she swallowed her aggravation and waited for the cashier to bag her books. After she'd paid, Caleb swooped in and grabbed the bags before her outstretched hand could close around the handles. Were he any other person, she'd thank him for the kindness. But his intense dislike charged the air between them like crackling static, and his insistence on carrying things for her felt condescending. She glowered at his back as they returned to the truck.

"That everything?" Caleb asked as Grace climbed into the passenger seat.

"No, I couldn't get enough copies. We have to go to another store and try to make up the difference. We might end up going to a third and fourth store if I can't get enough at the next one."

Caleb let out a long-suffering sigh and put the truck into gear. Ignoring his pissiness, she set the route on her phone and propped it in the empty ashtray so he could see the map.

The next store was a large chain. Grace was able to get nearly everything she needed, but she was still two copies short of *A Wizard of Earthsea*. They drove to a third bookstore, located inside a mall. As they walked through the parking lot towards the mall entrance, Caleb suddenly froze. He lifted his chin, dark eyes scanning the parking lot. A soft wind sifted over them, and he inhaled deeply.

"Caleb...?"

"Shh."

He closed his eyes, inhaling again. He opened them, staring intently at the shadowed alley between two fast-food restaurants. His gaze was sharp, laser-focused. Grace followed his line of sight, but she couldn't see anything other than some dumpsters.

"What are you—"

"Nothing." He turned away and continued towards the mall as if nothing had happened.

She trotted to catch up to him. "Seriously. What were you—?"

"Did you come to Alaska alone?" he asked suddenly.

Grace frowned. "You know I did. You're the one who flew me to Longtooth."

"But what about your flight to Anchorage? Did you come with anybody?"

"No." She'd been very specifically trying to get *away* from people by coming up here, but he didn't need to know that. "Nobody even drove me to the airport in Chicago. I took a cab. Why does it matter?"

They reached the door and he pulled it open for her. Grace hesitated, once again put off by what she'd consider a nice gesture from anybody else.

"Do you plan to stand out here all day?" Caleb demanded.

She scowled at him, but he wasn't even looking at her. His gaze was trained on that alley again, his brow furrowed.

Unnerved, she scuttled inside the vestibule. Caleb followed on her heels, reaching around her to pull the next door open as well. The material of their coats *shushed* as his chest brushed her shoulder and his arm curved around her. Even through all their winter layers, she felt his touch spread over her skin like warm honey. Gooseflesh crawled up her neck as a shiver chased down her spine. She hurried through the door, putting space between them.

At the bookstore, Grace found the last two copies she needed. She sighed her relief and paid for them. On the way back out to the truck, Caleb resumed that hyper-vigilant watchfulness, like a dog who's heard a stranger at the door. It made Grace uneasy. She nervously scanned the parking lot, instinctively stepping closer to Caleb.

Inside the truck, Caleb reached across her to lock her door. She pressed back against the seat, away from the brush of his arm. He put the truck into gear and pulled out immediately. Grace just managed to click her seatbelt as he pulled into traffic. He leaned forward, peering intently through the windshield. His gaze swept methodically over the street and surrounding buildings.

"Why are you being weird?"

Caleb didn't answer her. But as they wove through city streets, getting further from the mall, his posture relaxed and his watchfulness eased. He still wasn't exactly a picture of careless nonchalance, but electric tension was no longer snapping off of him.

They returned to the airfield and Grace frowned over at Caleb. "Didn't you have anything to do in Anchorage? Don't tell me you flew here just so I could buy books."

"I had some cargo to pick up. It was loaded while we were in town."

"Oh." She relaxed back against her seat. "Does that mean we're flying back now?"

"Did you need to do anything else?"

"No."

"Then, yeah. We're headed back." He bit off the words so tersely, as if even answering a simple question was such an imposition. He pulled the truck into the steel outbuilding and put it into park.

Driven by some impulse best left unexamined, Grace decided to antagonize him by continuing to speak. "So, what book did you buy?"

He scowled at her, unclipping his seatbelt. "What?"

"You bought a book. I saw the bag. What's the book?"

"There is no book."

She leaned across the bench seat and knocked on his chest, rapping her knuckles against the flat, hard rectangle stowed inside his parka. "Liar. Why won't you tell me? Is it embarrassing?" His jacket was unzipped far enough that she could snake her hand inside. "*How to Win Friends and Influence People?*" she suggested as her fingers closed around the top of the book.

Caleb's big hand closed around her wrist, stopping her from pulling it out. She wouldn't let go of the book. He wouldn't let go of her wrist. She was trapped with her fist pressed against the warm, firm plane of his chest. Heat seeped from his body to hers, traveling up her arm, flooding her lungs. She let out a shaky breath and looked up to find Caleb staring down at her. Their eyes met, and held. His grip tightened on her wrist, and there was a flare of heat in his eyes, a subtle golden gleam. Grace felt herself falling into those dark, unfathomable depths—first only in her mind, but then her body was leaning into his and then—

"What are you hoping to accomplish here?" Caleb asked, his gaze still searching hers.

"What?" she asked, still dazed.

"You came for the Alaskan adventure, right? Winter in the Arctic, job in some bumblefuck backwoods, flights on a puddle jumper. You need to fuck a local before you go back to your real life?"

Grace jerked her hand out of his grasp and shoved back to her side of the truck. Humiliation washed over her in cold, clammy waves. To her utter horror, she felt tears burning at the corners of her eyes. "I don't understand why you're such a prick to me," she said through a tight throat. "I've never done anything to you! I just want to do my job and be left alone. Is there something wrong with that?"

Caleb stared at her, his straight black brows pushed together in a frown. "Why'd you come to Longtooth? Tell me the truth."

"You don't want to hear it," she told him with grim certainty.

"Let's see if I can guess. You wanted to escape the mundane hustle and bustle of your old life. You wanted *an adventure*." He said the last in a mockingly saccharine voice. An unfriendly grin tugged at the corner of his mouth. "You wanted to live somewhere wild and untamed and rugged. You wanted—"

"I wanted to get as far as I could from my stalker ex-boyfriend!" Grace spat out angrily.

He clapped his mouth shut. The mean smile dropped off his face. "What?"

"I had a restraining order. He kept breaking it. The police couldn't do anything. I just wanted to get away. Far away. So, *no*, I didn't come here for the *magic of Alaska*. I came here because, of all the very distant places I applied to, the Teekkonlit Valley district was the first to offer me a job."

CHAPTER 7

Grace had thought that the worst thing about Alex was that he was boring. He didn't hit her, didn't call her names, didn't scream at her. He wasn't cruel.

And yet, being with him had exhausted her. It took her so long to leave him, not because she was afraid, but because it was so hard to muster the energy. There was no clean, decisive reason to give him. There was no final straw, no glaring fault. She was just tired—of him, of herself, of everything.

The longer they stayed together, the harder it was to disengage from him. Whenever she expressed discontent— *Alex, can't we do something besides sit at home watching crime documentaries? Alex, do we always have to eat the same takeout every night? Alex, why don't we ever hang out with friends anymore?*—he seemed genuinely shocked. Instead of answering her, he'd just parrot her words with a baffled look on his face. *Friends?* he'd ask, as if the concept had never occurred to him. *You want to see your friends?*

Grace remembered the faint line between his brows,

while he stared at her like a puzzle he couldn't solve. They never did get around to going out, trying a new restaurant, or seeing friends. Somehow, the conversation always moved on to something else, and they passed yet another night slumped on the couch, watching *Unsolved Murders*.

When she finally found the motivation to end things, Alex had just stared at her with that same puzzled frown, echoing her words like a senile macaw. *Over? We're over? You're...leaving me? Me?* He couldn't have been more incredulous if the couch had broken up with him.

It wasn't until after the breakup that he started to scare her.

After Grace had packed Alex's very few things and taken his key back, he kept turning up places where she was—her usual coffee shop, the grocery store, her favorite bookstore—and spoke to her as if they were still together. When she didn't play along, he acted as if *she* were the unreasonable one, reacting to her discomfort with bafflement.

The few friends who hadn't given up on Grace during the self-imposed isolation of her relationship were not shy about expressing their joy over the break-up. They insisted on dragging her out to bars and clubs—to "get over" him. But in every crowd, he was there, watching her. Clubs had never been her favorite thing to begin with, but after Alex, the idea of going out left her panicked and shaky. When she wasn't at school, she stayed home, alone and miserable, but repelled by the idea of doing anything else.

The final straw came when she'd walked into her apartment after a late night at school, and found him sitting placidly on the couch, waiting for her in the dark.

"What are you doing here?" she demanded, clutching at her racing heart.

He got up, looking both concerned and confused by her fear. "You invited me. Two years ago."

"And I uninvited you! Two months ago! Get out of my apartment!" She pulled out her phone and dialed 9-1-1.

"Grace. Don't do this. You need me."

"Just leave. Get out now." She shrunk away from his outstretched arms and he dropped them to his sides, that perpetually confused frown on his face.

"This isn't how it works. You can't leave me. You can't live without me, Grace. You're mine."

"9-1-1, what's the address of your emergency?"

Grace looked at him, begging him with her eyes as she recited her address to the emergency operator. Still looking utterly shocked, Alex stepped around her and finally left.

When the police arrived, he was long gone. They said there was nothing they could do. When she pushed, they half-heartedly suggested she could file a restraining order, so she did.

She hadn't seen Alex in person since then, but little clues to his continued presence kept appearing. Flowers left anonymously at her apartment. Her car brushed perfectly clean when every other vehicle in the school parking lot was covered in three inches of snow. A coaster from the bar where they'd met, tucked into her mailbox. A box of her favorite chocolates left on the hood of her car in a parking garage. Worst of all was the disappearance of her memento box. It had been filled with personal, sentimental objects she'd collected over the years. After Alex left, it was gone from her closet, and she never saw it again.

Grace did everything she was supposed to. She documented every incident and contacted the police. But with no concrete proof that the gifts were from him, they said there was nothing they could do. They couldn't track him down. He had no forwarding address. The job he'd told her he had didn't actually exist. The few friends of his that she'd met couldn't be tracked down, either.

That's when she'd decided to leave. The city felt claustrophobic—she wanted somewhere wide open, with few people. There were too many places and faces to hide behind in a big city. She'd hoped getting far away from Alex—and away from the monotony of her life—would help wake her back up, bring back the old Grace, who cared about things and wasn't just drifting through each day on autopilot. So she'd looked for jobs in Alaska and Hawaii and the Rockies and the Appalachians, and the Cascades. She'd even looked at a few international opportunities—teaching English in Japan, in Costa Rica, in Ukraine.

Margaret Huditiltik and the Teekkonlit Valley school district were the first to offer her a position, and that's what made the decision for her.

But now, here she was, all the way in Alaska, and nothing had changed. She was still hollow and frozen inside. She was still existing purely out of the habit of being alive. And Caleb, with his sneering mockery, had been a little bit right. She'd come to Alaska partly in search of change. Just like every other naive outsider.

CHAPTER 8

The flight back to Longtooth was a quiet one. Grace could practically *feel* Caleb ruminating over what she'd told him. She vacillated between humiliation and anger. How had she read him so wrong—to think he was going to kiss her when he actually loathed her? But what right did he have to assume the worst of her, when she'd done nothing to deserve it? By the time the Teekkonlit Valley came back into view, she wasn't humiliated or angry anymore. She was just tired.

The sun had risen and fallen during the time they'd spent in Anchorage, and they returned to Longtooth the same way they'd left it—in total darkness. When they landed on the rough little airstrip and Caleb killed the engine, Grace turned to face him.

"Please don't tell anybody what I told you. About my ex."

He considered her for a moment, not speaking.

"*Please.*" She didn't want everyone pitying her. She didn't want them to think of her as a doormat with terrible taste in men who ran away from trouble instead of facing it.

Finally, Caleb said, "I won't say anything." He regarded her for a moment longer, looking as though there were something more he wanted to say.

"What?" she prompted.

He opened his mouth. Closed it. Frowned.

"*What*, Caleb?"

Finally, he shook his head. "Nothing." He dug in his jacket pocket, fishing out his keys. "Go start the truck. I'll bring your books out."

They drove back to The Spruce in yet more silence. Without a word, Caleb helped her carry all the books to her truck and load them in the backseat. In the distance, they heard the haunting song of a wolf's howl. Caleb turned his head towards the sound, listening.

"They sound close," Grace said, shivering.

His gaze was distant, pinned somewhere above the tree line. "They're not."

They walked into The Spruce together. It was dinner time, but Grace wasn't hungry and she didn't want to socialize. She was physically and emotionally exhausted.

"Hey there, Gracie," Arthur greeted her as she walked into the dining room. "Caleb."

"Hi, Arthur." Grace bypassed the counter, heading for the stairs. "Can you let Natasha know I'm not going to have dinner tonight?"

"Everything okay?" It might have been her imagination, but Grace thought his gaze landed accusingly on Caleb.

"She's fine," Caleb said.

Arthur ignored him. "Should I have Tasha send something up for you?"

"I'm alright, thanks. I have some stuff in my fridge." She had nothing in her fridge. But she needed to get away from everybody and everything. She'd survive until morning on an empty stomach. She made her way upstairs, listening for the sound of Caleb's footsteps. To her great relief, he didn't follow her.

It was only five in the evening, but she changed into an old t-shirt, turned off all the lights, and fell asleep.

"GRACE..."

The voice called her out of the peace of sleep.

"Wake up." The voice was familiar, but she struggled to place it. "Get up, Grace."

The covers slid away as she sat up. Moonlight slanted through the window, limning the edges of everything in her room. And there, on the Juliet balcony, the silhouette of a man. A scream rose up in her throat, but couldn't escape.

"Hello, Grace. I've been looking for you."

She recognized the voice finally—Alex. He shifted closer and the moonlight slid over his pale, angular face. He looked so severely handsome, he could've been carved from ice. His eyes glinted like silver shards. A smile pulled at the corner of his mouth.

"Let me in, Grace. It's cold out here."

She tried to scream, tried to leap out of the bed, but her body didn't cooperate. Instead, she crawled towards the window. Alex's smile grew as she approached.

What are you doing? she screamed inside her head.

"There you go, honey. Open the window. Let me in."

Grace's throat ached from trying to force out a scream. She remained silent as her hands rose to the window sash.

Alex watched her, his expression fond, expectant. "Keep going. Let me in."

She gripped the window latch with a trembling hand. She fought against the impulse to open it, tried to recoil. She was locked in place, her entire body clenched, fingers aching from the leeching cold of the glass.

Alex sighed. "Come on, Grace. I worked so hard to find you. Just let me in."

Her hand clenched spasmodically on the latch. "*No,*" she whispered.

Alex's face smoothed to blank shock. It was the same way he'd looked whenever she'd suggested thy see friends or leave the apartment. "*What?*"

Grace drew in a haggard breath, filling her lungs to the brim. "*NO!*" she screamed for all she was worth. "Leave me alone!" She threw herself away from the window. Her body tangled into something heavy and large, and she screamed again as she fought against it, bucking and thrashing. She hurtled off the bed and landed on the floor with a thump.

Her own scream was still echoing in her ears when she woke up—for real this time—laying on the floor beside the bed, tangled in the heavy weight of the quilt. Her eyes flew to the window—empty. The snow on the balcony rail was pristine, undisturbed.

A dream. It had just been a bad dream.

Through the wall between Grace's room and Caleb's, she heard a crash. A split-second later, she heard his door bang against the wall, and then he was pounding on her door, making it rattle and shudder in the frame.

"Grace!"

She scrambled to her feet, pulling the door open before he busted it down. Caleb surged over the threshold, nothing more than a hulking silhouette in the darkness. He caught Grace by the shoulders and pinned her against the wall, angling his body over hers like a shield as he looked frantically around the room. The heat of his body rolled through Grace like an explosion.

"I'm fine!" she said quickly. "I just had a nightmare. I'm sorry for waking you up, I didn't—"

"Quiet." He scanned the room intently. His big body was still positioned over hers, and when she put a hand on his shoulder to push him away, she realized he was shirtless. She jerked her hand back at the same time he flinched away from her touch, as if they'd burned each other. Finally, there was space between them. Enough for Grace to see that he was barely dressed at all—only a pair of gray sweatpants, hanging low on his hips, not tied at the waist. He'd clearly dressed in a hurry. Probably no underwear.

Shut up, brain.

"Why aren't you wearing a shirt?" Grace demanded, trying to hide a spike of adrenaline behind a show of dismay.

The moonlight poured over his skin, leeching warm bronze into silver, and highlighting the swells and valleys of his broad, tautly muscled body. A thick white scar curved over his left shoulder and swooped across the broad plane of his chest. Black hair furred his chest, arrowing down his flat, hard stomach, disappearing beneath his low-slung waistband.

Grace forced her gaze back up to his face and found him staring down at her body. It was then that she realized that she was in similar dishabille—wearing only a baggy t-shirt and thin cotton panties. Caleb's dark eyes shone golden-amber in the moonlight, and a predatory smile tugged at the corner of his mouth. She could only stare back, struck dumb by a bolt of pure sexual attraction.

His golden gaze lifted from her bare legs to her face.

"Why aren't you wearing any pants?" he demanded, something playful and rough in his voice.

Embarrassment overcame attraction, bringing her back to her senses. "Shut up," she huffed, resisting the urge to tug her t-shirt lower.

The smile faded from his face, and he turned away from her, stepping deeper into her room. He closed his eyes, inhaling deeply—just as he had at the mall in Anchorage.

"What are you doing?" Grace picked up the quilt while his back was turned and slung it over her shoulders, allowing it to fall around her legs like the folds of a cloak.

"You screamed," Caleb explained.

"I was having a nightmare."

"You screamed at someone to leave you alone."

"Because I was having a nightmare."

He went still for a moment, regarding her thoughtfully. "Was it because of what you told me about your ex?"

Grace's first impulse was to lie. She hated being seen as weak. And Caleb was clearly not an emotional safe harbor. But she was still angry at him for everything—the wrong assumptions he'd made about her, the way he'd treated her because of those assumptions, and most of all, because he'd somehow gotten her to tell him about Alex when she hadn't wanted anybody to know about that whole mess.

So, instead, she lifted her chin and met his gaze. "Yes. I dreamt that Alex found me. Now, could you leave? I've had enough of uninvited men forcing their way into my space."

Even in the dark, she could see Caleb's warm skin blanch. He recoiled as if she'd hit him and turned immediately to leave. But as he passed by her bed, he suddenly halted, staring at the window with predatory alertness.

"Hey!" She objected as he got onto the bed. He was only

crawling across to reach for the window, but there was still something uncomfortably intimate about seeing him on her mattress, his legs tangled in her rumpled sheets. "I asked you to leave." She clutched the quilt tightly around her shoulders.

"Quiet," he said.

"Stop barking orders at me!"

Caleb ignored her, unlatching the window and lifting the sash. Bitter cold poured immediately into the room, chilling Grace into silence. She shivered and watched as Caleb stuck his head out the window and did that deep inhalation thing again, like a dog scenting the wind.

Grace stared at him, brow furrowed. "What in the actual hell are you doing, Caleb? This is really weird."

He pulled his head back in and locked the window. "Just checking the window lock. Sorry for bursting in." He got off the bed. "I'll leave you alone." He gave her a wide berth as he left the room, closing the door quietly behind him. Grace followed and locked it, standing with her hand on the latch long after she heard his own door close and lock.

The window was at her back, and she was terrified to face it. What had drawn Caleb there? He couldn't have possibly known that Alex had been there in her dream. So why had he gone to it?

Through the wall, she heard the groan of bedsprings as Caleb returned to his bed. Unwanted heat flushed through her, and she turned abruptly away from the door.

Beside her bed, the window and the Juliet balcony were empty.

Just a dream, she told herself.

CHAPTER 9

When Grace came down for breakfast on Monday, the only available stool was next to Caleb. She'd managed to avoid him all of Sunday, and she'd almost put Saturday's nightmare out of her mind. But the sight of his broad shoulders covered in faded blue flannel brought to mind the sight of those same shoulders clothed only in moonlight.

A shiver chased over her skin and she froze at the bottom of the stairs, nervous. Of all the valley's inhabitants, the one who liked her the least was the one who knew her greatest vulnerability. Sitting beside him, speaking to him, felt like exposing her jugular to a knife.

Refusing to be cowed, Grace blew out a harsh breath and forced herself across the dining room. Prepared for Caleb's stony silence, she dropped into the seat next to him with emphatic carelessness.

"Morning," Caleb said quietly.

She blinked and swiveled to stare at him. "What was that?"

"*Good,*" he enunciated crisply. "*Morning.*"

An itchy flush spread over her skin, a combination of anger and embarrassment. "No you don't," she told him in a low voice. "Don't suddenly start treating me like a decent human being. If I wasn't worth your time before, don't put yourself out just because you know about my crazy ex now."

"What's this?" Natasha appeared with a coffee pot, glancing worriedly between the two of them. "Caleb, be polite to Gracie."

"I am!"

"Well, you can go ahead and knock it right off," Grace snapped, grabbing her mug so viciously that piping hot coffee sloshed over her hand. She hissed and snatched her hand back.

"Are you—" At her look, Caleb fell silent, though his brows were raised so high they'd disappeared into his shaggy hair.

Grace scowled at him. "Don't be nice to me because you think I'm a victim."

"For fuck's sake," he groused, turning away from her.

After that, breakfast was a quiet affair.

AT SCHOOL, Grace went to the administrative office first thing to turn in the expense request for the books.

"Oh yeah," Joanne said, flipping through the receipts stapled to the form. "Margaret told me about this. It's all good. The cost will be reimbursed on your next paycheck."

"Thanks, Joanne."

"Is that you, Grace?" Margaret called from her office.

Grace leaned in. "Hey, Margaret."

Margaret was at her desk, reading glasses on, staring at

her computer screen. She gestured vaguely for Grace to have a seat, her attention mostly arrested on the screen. "How'd everything go in Anchorage?" she asked.

"Fine. I got the books."

Margaret glanced up, something knowing in her eyes. "And Caleb?"

Grace's jaw clenched. Forcing herself to relax, she said, "He was fine."

"Hmmm."

"Really. He carried books and held doors like an old fashioned gentleman."

"*Hmmm.*"

Giving up, Grace sighed. "He clearly hates me, but I don't care. Not everybody is going to like me in this life."

"Honey, Caleb doesn't hate you."

Grace gave her a skeptical look. "Come on, Margaret."

"I know of at least two reasons why Caleb's acting the way he is, and unfortunately I can't share either of them with you."

"Why not?"

"One is Caleb's business and the other is Valley business."

That stung, the implication that Grace wasn't privy to Valley business. "So you think of me as an outsider, too?"

Margaret's face fell. "Oh, no, Gracie. It's not like that. It's just—it's not something I can discuss."

"I get it," Grace said, ignoring the little hurt that still lingered. She started to rise, but Margaret gestured for her to stay.

"You look good, Grace," she said, pulling her reading glasses off so she could survey her. "You look healthier than when you first arrived."

In the month since she'd come to Longtooth, Grace had gained fifteen desperately needed pounds thanks to Natasha's hearty meals. Over the last couple of weeks, she'd been thinking that her reflection didn't look so haggard anymore, but she wasn't sure if that was just wishful thinking. Hearing it confirmed by Margaret let her believe it was true. The shadows beneath her eyes were fading. Her skin no longer looked so fragile and dull, wasn't laying so close to the bone. When she caught sight of her naked reflection after taking a shower, she no longer looked like a bleached-out scarecrow. Her hips and breasts had filled back out and her skin, though always pale, had a healthy olive tone again.

She could stand to gain another ten pounds, but either way, Grace was happy to see her body looking vital again. She was happy to *feel* vital again. She wasn't at a hundred percent, though. She was still having nightmares about Alex. Crowds of strangers still made her panicky—she lived in dread of the next party Natasha might invite her to, and a team of huskies couldn't drag her back into the Blue Moose. But life wasn't the exhausting slog it used to be. Socializing with the other regulars in The Spruce's dining room was something she was starting to look forward to. Even generally negative emotions, like the irritation she felt for Caleb Kinoyit, were a welcome change from the numbness she'd been living with for so long. The perpetual coldness was still inside her, but it seemed to be receding, at least a little.

After school, instead of holing up in her room until dinner, Grace decided to sit in the dining room and grade essays. She dropped her coat and bag in her room, and then trotted back down the stairs with a stack of essays and a red pen. As she rounded the corner into the dining room, she skidded to a sudden halt.

Caleb was sitting at a table by the windows, silhouetted by a gently falling snow. He was looking down, intent on the open book in his hands. When she stepped into the dining room, he looked up at her and her stomach dipped.

Oh god.

Oh god oh god oh god.

He wore *glasses* to read. A pair of scholarly, slightly dweeby, *horn-rimmed glasses.* Grace stood frozen in place, staring at him. Those nerdy glasses with that messy beard and his wind-burnt cheeks and his big hands and—*ugh.*

Caleb frowned, brows drawing together. He pulled his glasses off. "What do you want?" He spoke impatiently, but his voice was deep and rich, making her acutely conscious that he was a *man.* As if she hadn't noticed before. But really, how dare he? How dare he be so fucking hot and also be such a massive jerk? How dare he be the first man to break her out of the numb, sexless haze she'd been living in? He'd made it clear that any attraction on her end was some kind of personal affront, so *of course* her stupid, masochistic brain had to fixate on him.

But that was exactly it, wasn't it? Men who wanted her made her feel trapped, panicky. It was much better, much safer, to want somebody who didn't want her back. Because then she'd never have to worry about getting trapped in another suffocating, inescapable relationship. She'd never have to worry that he'd try to keep hold of her the way Alex had. Because Caleb didn't even want her in the first place.

Safe.

Grace relaxed a little. "Nothing," she told him, and it was more of an answer than he realized. *Nothing* was exactly what she wanted.

And that's exactly what Caleb gave her. He turned his

attention back to his book, sliding his glasses back on. Grace ignored the little pang of lust that tightened her stomach and took a seat at the counter. She turned her back on Caleb, so she wouldn't be distracted by the sexual potency of his mountain-man-scholar look and took the first essay off the stack. They were far from friends, but she felt safe having him at her back.

As Grace worked on essays, a few more people wandered into the dining room. The sound of clanking pans and running water came from the kitchen. Natasha appeared briefly to start a pot of coffee brewing, then disappeared back into the kitchen. Grace had gotten through four essays when Jessica Taaltsiyh wandered in.

"Hey." She dropped onto the stool next to Grace, bumping her shoulder against Grace's—a friendly gesture she'd seen other Teekkonlit locals do to each other. Grace welcomed the brief wash of warmth that pulsed through her. Just as quickly, it faded.

She set her essays aside and talked with Jess as more and more regulars filtered in for dinner. Elena Morris came in and took the seat on Grace's other side, nudging her shoulder against Grace's the same as Jess had done.

"Have you gotten out of town yet?" Elena asked. "Seen the mountains up close?"

Grace shook her head. "I want to. I keep meaning to."

"We'll take you," Jess decided. "Me and Elena. This weekend?"

"Can't," Elena said. "I'm going to be in Eagle Ridge this weekend for my nephew's First Moon."

"Already?" Jess asked. "How old is he?"

"Just turned fifteen."

"No! I was in high school when he was born!"

"What's a First Moon?" Grace asked.

"Uh..." Jess and Elena both looked at each other, at a loss.

Finally, Elena ventured, "It's sort of like a bar mitzvah."

Jess nodded. "Yeah. Like the whole, coming-of-age, you're-a-man-now thing."

"Or a woman," Elena added.

"Or you're-a-woman-now," Jess agreed. "It's an old Teekkonlit Valley tradition."

"Anyway—" Elena clapped her hands on the countertop, and Grace got the distinct sense she was purposely changing the subject. "I'm free the weekend after that."

"Same. Snowmachines?" Jess asked.

Elena nodded. "Dead Dog Pass?"

"Perfect."

Grace looked askance at them both. "You want to take me to a place called *Dead Dog Pass?*"

"Don't worry," Elena assured her with a pat on the arm. "The dog died a long time ago."

Time passed pleasantly in conversation with Elena and Jess. Wade Evers came in just as the kitchen officially opened for dinner.

"Gracie," he greeted her, tugging on her ponytail as he passed by.

Grace had noticed early on how touch-friendly the Teekkonlit locals were with each other. They were always sharing casual, platonic touches in passing and in greeting. As the weeks went by, some of the more familiar people had begun to extend those little touches to Grace. She appreciated them, enjoyed the glow of warmth they imparted. But she wasn't yet brave enough to venture her own touches. She enjoyed the contact way too much, in a completely non-sexual way, and for her to initiate it felt somehow greedy.

For the first time, after dinner, she felt the impulse to stay in the dining room and socialize, rather than going to her room to sleep. Even so, it felt weird to stay. She'd established a routine, and people would notice if she deviated. She stood up and looked around the dining room, uncertain. Everyone else seemed to be settling into a familiar routine—Jess and Elena had plopped onto the loveseat in front of the TV in the lounge. Harry and Joann were still sitting at the counter, chatting with Max. Nobody even looked Grace's way—they were used to her leaving. How awkward would it be to try and insert herself into their routines?

"You play cribbage, Gracie?"

She looked to her left and saw Wade sitting at a table with Connor and Lucia. "We need a fourth to play teams."

Wade had his own house in town, but he almost always ate breakfast and dinner at The Spruce. Grace couldn't remember when or where she'd learned it, but she knew that his wife had died two years ago, and that he'd apparently nearly followed her in his grief. His children and grandchildren were enough to keep him anchored to this side of the veil, but loneliness kept him at work or at The Spruce until he needed to sleep. When Grace had first arrived, she never would have guessed at the sorrow hiding behind his good-natured chatter. But now she could see it—a shadow in his eyes when he smiled, the faintest echo of something missing when he laughed.

"You'll have to refresh me on the rules," she said, settling in the seat next to him.

It was late when Wade decided to call it a night. Grace bid him goodnight and made her way upstairs. She dug into her coat pocket for her phone so she could plug it in, but her hand found only empty fabric. She reached into the other pocket. Then the chest pocket. Still no phone. She checked them all again before she accepted that she'd left it in her truck.

She needed her phone—it was her alarm clock. She huffed out an annoyed breath and pushed her feet back into her boots. She crept down the hallway as silently as possible. It was nearly eleven at night, and she didn't want to wake anybody who'd managed to get to sleep at a more reasonable hour. The dining room was empty and silent when she reached it, the lights dim. She passed through to the rear door that led to the garage.

She dashed quickly through the cold and into the unheated garage. Her phone was sitting on her passenger seat, and so cold that it refused to turn on. She tucked it into her coat to let her body heat bring it back to life. As she trudged up from the garage, she noticed movement at the far corner of the building. In the faint glow of the security light above the kitchen door, she saw—a wolf? She squinted, trying to make the image resolve into something else. But it did not. There was a big, iron-gray wolf pawing at the kitchen door like a pet dog who wanted to be let in. Grace froze in place, dumb as a rabbit, and stared.

To her horror, the kitchen door swung open. She tried to shout a warning, but her throat was as frozen as her legs. She watched in helpless horror as Natasha appeared in the doorway.

The wolf sank to its haunches in front of her, ears pricked, tail swishing. Grace's horror turned to astonishment as she watched Natasha throw her hands up in an annoyed gesture. She motioned the wolf into the kitchen.

The massive animal trotted inside, and the door swung shut behind them.

A dog, Grace told herself. It must've been a dog. A giant, wolf-like dog.

A few seconds later, the door swung open again. Natasha held it as the wolf-dog trotted back out, a large bone clutched in its maw. Natasha made a shooing gesture at the animal, and it raced off, disappearing into the woods.

She watched it run, and when she turned back to go inside, she caught sight of Grace. Natasha stood still for a moment, watching Grace watch her. Finally, she waved and closed the door.

Back inside The Spruce, Grace went straight to the dining room. Natasha emerged from the kitchen's swinging door just as Grace reached the counter.

"Gracie," she said pleasantly. "What are you doing up so late?"

"I forgot my phone in my truck," Grace answered impatiently. "Was that a *wolf*?"

Natasha shrugged. "I am not a zoologist."

"It looked like a wolf. It looked like you were giving raw meat *to a wolf*." Grace remembered Margaret's warning when she'd first arrived—wolves came into town fairly often. Well, maybe that was because a crazy woman was *feeding them*!

"Maybe it was a large dog." Natasha shrugged.

Grace stared at Natasha, completely flummoxed. It was dangerous to feed wild animals. And illegal. And dangerous!

Natasha regarded her blandly. "It's getting late, Gracie. Aren't you tired?"

Taking the hint, Grace stepped back from the counter, giving Natasha one last wary look. She climbed the steps to her room, still not totally sure of what she'd seen. When she reached the top landing, Caleb was coming down the hall towards her, wearing sweatpants and an unzipped parka with nothing underneath. His feet were shoved into unlaced boots.

"Where are you going at this time of night?" Grace asked, trying not to stare at his bare chest.

"Sorry Miss Rossi, do I need a hall pass to leave my room?" Caleb was bearing down on her, hogging the entire hallway. Grace was forced to press against the wall as he passed. Even so, his shoulder brushed against hers and the back of his hand knocked her hip. She glared at his back as he bounded down the stairs.

Did he take up the entire hallway on purpose? Did he do it to everyone else? What happened when he and Harlan passed in the hall? Grace doubted Harlan wilted against the wall like a shrinking violet. Annoyed, she resolved to take up her fair share of space the next time they passed each other. If Caleb didn't want to make room, then it was hardly Grace's fault if he caught her elbow in his kidney.

CHAPTER 10

The next morning at breakfast, Connor Ankkonisdoy dropped onto the seat next to Grace.

"Hey, Grace. How'd your first month in Alaska go?"

"Not too bad. Especially now that the days are getting longer." In mid-February, the sun was up for nearly eight hours. It was a huge improvement over the measly three hours of daylight they were getting when she'd first arrived.

"Just wait," Arthur told her. "By summer you'll be wishing for a little more darkness."

"So, you're getting settled in?" Connor pressed.

Grace nodded and sipped at her coffee. "Yeah, I think so. I've got my reading lists taken care of, lesson plans mostly set—"

"So I guess that means you've got some free time now."

Ah, shit. That familiar old panic started to squeeze her.

Connor leaned in. "If you wanted to see the northern lights maybe we could—" He suddenly cut himself off, wrinkling his nose. "You been seeing Caleb Kinoyit?"

Grace frowned. "Not intentionally. Why?"

"You smell like him." Connor flinched as soon as the words left his mouth.

"I *smell* like him?" she repeated incredulously.

"Sorry, it's, uh, an expression around here," Connor said, looking panicked. "It means, uh…"

"It means there's a rumor you're together," Arthur cut in. "And that's the polite way of putting it," he added.

So there was a rumor they were sleeping together? How? Did everyone assume their mutual antagonism was just a symptom of their raging sexual tension? That was a bit of a stretch, considering their hostility mostly manifested itself through complete avoidance of each other.

"I can assure you that's not going on," Grace said dryly. "Caleb would sooner cut off his—" she caught herself before the word "dick" popped out of her mouth "—*hand* than touch me with it."

Arthur chuckled, but Grace got the sense it wasn't inspired by her wit. It was the slightly gleeful chuckle of a man who knows something you don't.

"What?" She glared at him, with no real heat behind it.

"Aw, sweetheart." He got up, taking his coffee with him, giving her shoulder a squeeze. "Don't think too hard on it."

Easier said than done. As she drove to school, Grace replayed the conversation over and over in her head. What about Caleb's behavior towards her would indicate that he was in any way interested? Yes, she was reluctantly attracted to him. But only to his face, and his body, and his smile, and how he looked when he was reading, and how competent and in-control he was as a pilot. But that was it. His personality needed more work than big muscles and intense eye contact and unexpected literary interests could make up for.

But if that was the case, why did she want to believe in Arthur's knowing smile?

As she parked at the school, she pushed Caleb out of her mind and focused on the day's plans. First things first, a writing workshop for her freshman where they hammered out the basic format for writing an essay. She got to her desk half an hour before students would start arriving. She pulled out the sheet on which she'd printed twenty ridiculous essay prompts and then opened the top drawer to grab her scissors. She needed to cut the prompts apart so she could put them in a bowl and have the students draw them at random.

But when she reached into the drawer, her fingers brushed against an unfamiliar shape. She pulled the drawer out further and peered into the back. Sitting just above her scissors was an old leather dog collar. She stared at it for a long time, unblinking. As if in a daze, she finally managed to reach out and pick it up. The tags tinkled against each other, and in the light, she could read them—one was an old rabies tag, but the other said *FREYA*.

Grace dropped the collar. It hit her desk with a jangle.

The last time she'd seen this collar, it'd been in the little wooden chest where she kept all her other sentimental things. The chest had been filled with the usual kinds of mementos—her favorite childhood stuffed animal (a fat yellow bunny named Sunny), an arrowhead she'd found in a farm field when she was nine, an old green glass coke bottle she'd somehow managed to reel in on one of the very few occasions when her dad had taken her fishing with him, a loose stone she'd stolen from a medieval castle wall during her semester in France, the friendship bracelet she'd worn throughout middle school that matched the ones her three best friends had also worn, the tassels from her high school and college graduations, her late grandmother's wedding ring, and... the collar from her dog, Freya, who'd passed away when she was sixteen.

The chest had disappeared right after she broke up with Alex. He'd known it had existed. Had even asked to see inside it. Grace had no proof he'd stolen it, but it was the only rational explanation. Nobody else had been in her apartment between the time she'd last seen it and the time it went missing—not even her landlord or repair people.

Grace stared at the collar. *There's got to be a rational explanation.* Probably...probably the last time she opened the chest, she took the collar out? And then accidentally put it in the cabinet where she kept her school supplies? And then somehow packed it away in Chicago without noticing, and then also unpacked it in Longtooth without noticing?

Could that happen? It had to. The only other explanation was that Alex was in Longtooth. But the only way to get into Longtooth in winter was by plane. And Caleb knew all the comings and goings of all the flights in and out of Longtooth. Even if he and Grace weren't exactly best pals, it would've somehow gotten back to her that another outsider had arrived in Longtooth.

That made sense.

"Grace."

She jumped about a foot in the air and spun around, clutching her chest.

"Oh, honey, sorry." Margaret stood in the doorway, looking concerned. "Is everything okay? You're white as a sheet."

"I'm fine. I just...nothing. I'm fine." She picked up the collar and dropped it back in the drawer.

"Are you sure?"

"Yep." She shut the drawer and put it out of her mind. "Something I can help you with?"

"Just some happy gossip for you. The book your Seven-and-Eights are reading? Oscar Nobody?"

Grace laughed. "*Octavian Nothing.*"

"That's the one. Well, a few of the kids in your class have been talking with their cousins over in Eagle Ridge and apparently it's become a big hit over there." Margaret's smile turned saturnine. "Tom Tremaine is annoyed with you."

Grace had never met Tom Tremaine, but she knew he was the English teacher in Eagle Ridge—the Teekkonlit Valley's second-largest town, less than half the size of Longtooth. "Why would he be annoyed with me?" Grace asked, even though she could guess. It was the same reason the other English teachers were always annoyed with her in Chicago.

"Because his kids are on the verge of staging a mutiny. They want to know why they have to read 'boring books' when the Longtooth kids get to read 'cool books.'"

Grace couldn't help cackling. Odds were good that Tremaine's students were reading "classics." She appreciated those books and enjoyed many of them, but she was also well aware that those kinds of books turned a lot of kids off of reading entirely. "Tell Tom he can borrow my reading list any time."

Margaret grinned at her. "I don't think I want to ruffle Tom's fur any harder." She turned to leave, but at the door, she paused and looked back. "Good job, Gracie."

The cold receded a little more, and Grace smiled.

. . .

SEVERAL HOURS LATER, Grace was in her seventh-eighth grade split class, listening to her students debate about the meaning behind different character names. She looked up from her copy of *Octavian Nothing: The Pox Party*. "Alright, who can tell me—Caitlin? Are you okay?"

The girl in question was gripping the sides of her desktop, her face slick with sweat. An unnatural tremor ran over her body like ripples in a pond. A shadow seemed to rise beneath her skin—the skeleton of something inhuman, with wicked fangs and pointed claws and gleaming golden eyes.

Grace blinked, and the shadow was gone. Caitlin was just a normal thirteen-year-old girl—albeit, one who was desperately ill. She shuddered and let out a pained groan.

Grace had only taken half a step towards her when the rest of the class sprang into action. The four kids nearest Caitlin hauled her to her feet and rushed her into the hall. The rest of the students gang-rushed Grace, forcing her into the corner behind her desk.

"*What* are you doing?" she demanded, trying to weave her way through them, and finding herself constantly thwarted.

"Don't worry, Ms. Rossi. They're taking her to Mrs. Teague—she's Caitlin's aunt," Gwen Yidineeltot said as she caught Grace around the waist and hauled her back. She was only a lanky thirteen-year-old, half a foot shorter than Grace, but she was wickedly strong. It took considerable effort to break out of her hold.

"All of you!" Grace snapped. "Out of my way!" She managed to force her way free of their blockade and burst into the hallway. Linnea Teague's classroom was next to hers. The door was closed, and when Grace tried to open it, it was locked and a poster of the color wheel had been pressed over the window.

Grace pounded on the door. "Linnea! Is Caitlin in there?" she called.

"Yes," Linnea called back. "I'll handle it. You can go back to your room."

An eerie, inhuman howl punctuated the end of her sentence.

"What on earth is happening?" Grace shouted.

There was a beat of silence, and then the sound of a struggle—something scrabbling heavily, desks squealing across the floor, and teenagers exclaiming incoherently.

"It's a health condition that runs in our family," Linnea called back, sounding strained. "I'll take care of it. If you want to be helpful, get Margaret and send her to my room!" Her tone was brusque, bordering on angry. Even though Grace wanted to kick the door off the hinges, she backed off. She turned back to her classroom and found her entire class standing in the hall, watching her. There was a wariness in their expressions. They knew exactly what was going on. But nobody wanted Grace to know.

Was it contagious? Historically, when isolated population groups made contact with outsiders, diseases ran rampant. But this wasn't the Columbian Exchange. The people of the Teekkonlit Valley had access to the wider world via plane and, once the ice receded, by road as well. Grace's initial thought had been that Caitlin was having a seizure, but with the way the class had been so intent on keeping her away, the wary way they watched her now, had her second-guessing that. So what was wrong with Caitlin—and why was it a secret?

"Alright," Grace said, trying to project confidence and

failing. "Everyone back in the classroom. Pick up where we left off with our discussion about character names. Michael, you're the discussion leader until I get back."

As soon as they were all inside, Grace pulled the door shut and sprinted down the hall to the administrative offices. Teekkonlit Secondary was small, and it took her all of ten seconds to get there. Joanne looked up when she burst in, half-rising from behind her desk.

"Grace, what's—"

"Is Margaret in her office?"

"Yes, but she's—"

Grace threw Margaret's door open. She was on the phone, glasses on, frowning at something on her computer screen. "Yes, that's—Grace?"

"Something happened with Caitlin Evers. She's—I don't know. Linnea told me to get you."

"I have to go," Margaret said into the phone. She dropped it in the cradle and was on her feet in the same instant. "What happened?" she asked, already making her way out of the administrative offices.

"I really don't know." Grace had to jog to keep pace with Margaret's urgent pace. "Caitlin looked really ill—like she was going to vomit? Or was it a seizure? I just don't know. The rest of the class brought her to Linnea, and that's the last I saw."

"Good," Margaret said, a small measure of urgency fading from her posture. "Linnea knows how to handle this."

"She said it's a health condition that runs in their family."

"Yes. It's nothing to worry about. Happens from time to time. Caitlin will probably need a little time off of school, but she'll be perfectly fine."

They rounded the corner to the short hall where Grace's and Linnea's classrooms were. Linnea's door was still shut, the poster still pressed over the window. Grace wanted to ask Margaret what the health condition was—why her students had reacted the way they did. But it wasn't her business, and it was illegal for her to ask.

"Go ahead and get back to your class," Margaret told her, giving her a squeeze on the arm. "For the sake of Caitlin's privacy, leave your door shut until the end of this class period. We don't need the rest of the student body gawking at her while we get her out of the building."

The cloak-and-dagger mystery of it all had Grace completely unbalanced. It couldn't be diabetes, or a food allergy, or asthma. Teachers were always made aware of those conditions, given instructions for an emergency. What could possibly be so serious that everybody else seemed prepared to respond—but that Grace wasn't allowed to know about? She recalled the unnatural way Caitlin's body had rippled with tremors and the shadow that had seemed to pulse beneath her skin. That last bit had been Grace's imagination or a trick of the light, but she could still picture it so clearly.

"Grace?" Margaret squeezed her arm again. "She'll be fine, I promise. Go back to your class."

There was nothing else she could really do. "Okay. Well. Let me know if I can help."

Grace stepped back into her classroom and the buzzing conversation died immediately. They definitely hadn't been discussing *Octavian Nothing*.

She returned to the spot where she usually leaned on her desk while teaching. "Alright. Where'd we leave off?"

She was distracted for the rest of class. Her students were

suspiciously well-behaved. Not that they were ever bad, but their participation was so universally enthusiastic—never letting the discussion lull, never letting a question go unanswered—that it was like teaching an entirely different class. *They're probably all keyed up from the excitement with Caitlin,* Grace told herself. *This is not a conspiracy to keep you distracted while Caitlin and her mystery-ailment are secreted away.*

When the bell rang, Grace walked to the door behind her students. Linnea's classroom door was open again, her own students filing out. Grace thought about walking over to ask her if everything was okay, then decided against it. It was clear nobody wanted her to know anything. She tried to tell herself that the uneasy suspicion she felt was unwarranted. Their family had some kind of genetic disorder, and they didn't want to make it public knowledge. Fine. Grace could understand that.

As the day progressed, it preyed less and less on her mind. By her final class, she hadn't stopped worrying about Caitlin, but she'd come to accept reality. Caitlin's health condition was private. In this case, "private" meant that all the locals knew about it, and how to respond to it. But Grace didn't, and couldn't, because she was an outsider. To the Teekkonlit Valley, no matter how hard she worked at her job, no matter how much she cared about her students, no matter how friendly she was to her neighbors or how much of an effort she made, Grace would always be an outsider. It wasn't a new feeling. But Longtooth had started to feel a little different from everywhere else she'd lived, and it was the first place where she felt her outsider status as an insult. She wasn't allowed to care for them the way they cared for each other.

The realization of where she stood in Longtooth hung

over her head for the rest of the day. The cold inside of her seemed to deepen, becoming sharper and more brittle. Her whole body ached. Her fingers and toes were ice. She put another sweater on top of the one she was already wearing, but she couldn't stop shivering. She wanted to go back to The Spruce and sit in front of the big stone fireplace in the dining room, but she also wanted to lock herself in her room where her unfixable loneliness wouldn't be exacerbated by the empty friendliness of everyone else in the dining room.

WHEN SHE FINALLY GOT BACK TO The Spruce, Grace parked in her assigned spot in the garage and, for a moment, just sat there. She couldn't bring herself to trudge into the dining room and face the gulf between herself and the locals. They were friendly to her, and they were content to let her live here, but it was becoming more and more clear that she wasn't truly one of them, and never would be.

It's Valley business. Margaret's words continued to ring in Grace's head. Margaret had tried to walk it back, but it was too late. She'd said what she meant. Grace wasn't privy to Valley business, because she didn't belong in the Valley.

Grace's throat tightened. It was just like Chicago. She had a job, and a home, and people she could even consider friends, but she was a second thought to all of them. Nobody considered her a priority. Her staying or going wouldn't really affect anybody's lives in the long run.

Hollowness seemed to cave in her chest. She hated this feeling. She hated feeling sorry for herself.

She heaved a heavy sigh. She'd thought it would clear her head, push away the bad feelings, but the sigh just brought them up to the surface. She couldn't remember *not* feeling lonely. She couldn't remember the last time she'd felt welcome and loved and wanted. Was it when her grandma was still alive? That long ago? Hot tears pricked at her eyes.

Until now, Grace hadn't really admitted to herself that she'd chosen to move to a small place like Longtooth partly because she'd been hoping to find a way out of the loneliness. Maybe a smaller community, more tightly knit, would be the answer. But witnessing that tight bond only made her loneliness more stark in comparison. One tear streaked down her cheek, then another, and then she was just hunched over her steering wheel, dragging in shuddering breaths and squeezing her eyes against the hot flood.

Sudden pounding slammed against her window. She jerked upright.

Oh, for fuck's sake. It was Caleb. He peered into her window, frowning as if he'd just caught her doing something criminal.

"What are you doing in here?" he demanded, his voice slightly muffled by the closed window.

Grace pressed her hand to her face. "Please just go away."

"Did somebody do something to you?"

"No."

"Grace," he said skeptically.

"I said I'm fine," she growled. "Nobody did anything to me."

"Then why are you—"

"Because I'm a fucking mess! Alright?"

Caleb didn't say anything for a moment, just regarded her with that steady, expressionless gaze. Finally, he stepped back from her truck. "Don't let the cold get you."

He left.

Grace leaned against her seat, head tipped back, blinking over and over until her tears dried up. She stayed in the truck for a while afterwards, letting the cold soothe the redness from her eyes and nose.

When Grace went inside, dinner was already in full swing. Natasha greeted her brightly and Grace forced a smile for her. She ate quickly, quietly, then went upstairs.

She knew that isolating herself away from everybody else was self-defeating. But if she tried to hang around and forge a meaningful connection with people who saw her only as a visitor in their lives, she'd end up crying again. So she shut herself in her room, pulled out an old comfort read, and crawled into bed.

CHAPTER 11

Things were a little stilted at school the next day. Caitlin was conspicuously absent, and everybody was very carefully not talking about her.

At the end of the day, as Grace watched her last class pack their things and file out of the classroom, she resolved to stay late at school. She wouldn't have to face all the regulars at The Spruce and pretend she didn't see the invisible wall between them and her. She had protein bars in her desk, so she wouldn't starve, and she'd be able to get a bunch of grading done.

Before she could slump into her chair and get to work, she realized one of her students had hung back. Daniel Gray, a quiet, stern-faced kid who never spoke up in class.

"Hey, Daniel. What's up?"

"Um, do you have any more books like *Unwind?*" he asked, referring to the book they'd just finished last week.

The dark cloud that had been hovering over Grace suddenly evaporated. She straightened, trying to keep herself from leaping out of her chair in excitement. Excessive cheer might chase him off. She managed to restrain herself to a smile.

"There are sequels to *Unwind,* actually," she told him. "I don't have any copies, but you might be able to get them through an interlibrary loan system." The school's library was housed in a room no bigger than Grace's classroom, erratically organized, and entirely unstaffed. Checking out books operated on an honor system, in which the only form of accountability was a self-policed logbook. Grace wasn't sure if the library was connected to a wider system, or if an interlibrary loan was even possible.

Daniel's expression shuttered. "That won't work."

"It might. I'll have to look into it and get back to you. In the meantime, I think you might like—" she turned to her bookshelves, considering the spines "—*The Hunger Games.*"

"I already saw the movies."

"Hmm... how about *The Maze Runner?*"

"Saw that movie, too. Never mind, I gotta go. My uncle's waiting for—"

"No, wait!" Taking a gamble, Grace pulled *The Lightning Thief* off the shelf. It also had a movie adaptation, but what popular YA book didn't these days? "What about this one?"

Daniel looked down at the cover. Grace could tell whatever prompted him to ask for another book had already waned.

"Come on," she wheedled. "If you don't like it, you don't like it. No big deal. But I think you will like it. It's pretty good. The main character has to prevent a war between the gods. There's mystery! And mortal peril!" She held the book in front of her face and made it dance enticingly. "*You know you want to read me, Daniel,*" she intoned in a ghostly voice. "*Take me,*" she crooned. "*Flip my pages...*"

Daniel looked more mortified than enthused, but he snatched the book out of her hands, which Grace counted as a win. From the hallway, she heard a derisive snort. She looked up to see Caleb Kinoyit leaning against her doorway. His expression was pensive as he watched the two of them. How long had he been standing there?

"Ready?" Caleb asked. For a second Grace was confused, and then she realized he was talking to Daniel. Caleb must be the uncle Daniel had mentioned. Once again, she was reminded of how tightly the Valley residents were connected to each other.

"Yeah." Daniel slid *The Lightning Thief* into his backpack and turned to leave.

"Hey." Caleb kicked at Daniel's heel as he walked out the door. Daniel stumbled and scowled at him. Caleb's expression was just as unhappy. "What do you say?" he demanded, tilting his head towards Grace.

Daniel flushed. "Thank you, Ms. Rossi."

"You're welcome, Daniel. Keep it as long as you want."

Caleb regarded Grace over the top of his nephew's head, his expression contemplative. He seemed like he wanted to say something. Grace watched him, trying to keep the warm flush on her chest from creeping up to her face.

Daniel elbowed Caleb. "You just gonna stare at my English teacher, or can we go?"

A low sound rumbled in Caleb's throat. Daniel looked immediately chagrined and skittered out the door. Caleb pushed off the door frame, giving Grace a nod before following his nephew down the hall. She stared after the two of them. Had Caleb just... *growled* at his nephew?

· · ·

GRACE STAYED at school until eight in the evening. When she came in the back door of The Spruce, the dining room was empty except for Natasha, sitting at the diner counter refilling salt shakers.

"Gracie," she looked up, dismayed. "Did you eat?"

"Yeah." Grace plopped down on the stool next to her. "Natasha, do you think of yourself as an outsider?" Not only was she not from the Valley, or even Alaska, but she wasn't originally from the U.S. Was she privy to the secrets that were being kept from Grace? Did she know about the health condition that ran in Linnea Teague's and Caitlin Evers' family?

Natasha considered Grace for a moment, her lips pursed. Finally, she resumed filling salt shakers. "When I first arrived in Longtooth, everyone called me 'Arthur's Polish girl' instead of my name. My English was not as good back then, and some people thought that was funny. I did not know a lot of the little things that everybody who grows up here knows, and *everybody* thought that was very funny. Arthur's mother and father ran The Spruce back then. I helped in the kitchen, and I am a very good cook, but Arthur's mother was never happy with anything I made."

Remembered annoyance flickered over her features.

"But Arthur was always on my side. The locals started to treat me as one of theirs. It happened faster with some people than others, but now I am one of them. Even his mother eventually acknowledged that people like my food." She looked up from the salt shakers and smiled at Grace. "I was not born in the Valley, but I am from here, now. It is my home." She set the last salt shaker aside and pushed the spout down on the salt canister. "Why do you ask? Has somebody insulted you?"

Not intentionally. "No. I just..." Grace shrugged. "I'm not sure I belong here. I think everybody sees me as a visitor." A visitor they liked well enough, but not somebody worth trusting and confiding in. Not somebody who'd invested her own trust and effort into the community.

Natasha squeezed Grace's forearm. "You have to do what I did."

"Marry a local?"

Natasha snorted. "No—well. That wouldn't hurt. But if you want to be treated a certain way, you must demand it."

Grace frowned. Demanding to be *wanted* kind of negated it. Wanting had to be voluntary if it was worth anything. "Hm."

"You don't believe me," Natasha said airily, "But you will see. I'm right about this."

"I'll take it under consideration." Grace picked up her bag and got to her feet. The day had been long and emotionally exhausting. It wasn't even nine o'clock, but she was ready for bed.

She reached the top of the stairs just as Caleb was leaving his room. After a split-second of hesitation, she continued towards him. He looked right past her as he strode down the hall, taking up too much space, as usual. She remembered her resolution to stop shrinking herself for him. Natasha's advice bolstered her. If Mr. Broad-As-A-Barn couldn't be bothered to make room, then neither could Grace. She shoved her shoulder against his as they passed.

"Oh, excuse me," she drawled carelessly as she reached her door. "I didn't see you there."

As Grace dug in her bag for her key, Caleb remained rooted to the spot where she'd bumped against him. She glanced over. He had his back to her, big shoulders hunched as he clenched and unclenched white-knuckled fists. Suddenly, he turned. His eyes gleamed in the dim light. Awareness prickled over Grace's skin like static.

He took one step towards her.

Another.

"What are you—"

He grabbed her suddenly, pulling her against him. Burying his face in the crook of her neck, he inhaled deeply.

Instead of screaming and struggling like a sane woman would, Grace clung to him, tilting her head back to give him better access to her neck. His nose and his lips pressed against her throat and the touch seared her. His heat sank beneath her skin and boiled her blood. Warmth like she hadn't felt in years radiated through her. The perpetual ice beneath her skin suddenly cracked and thawed.

His exhalation was hot and humid. His beard tickled her, sending gooseflesh racing over her skin. He clutched a fistful of her hair and brought it to his face, inhaling deeply again. A satisfied sigh rumbled in his chest like thunder. With her arms wrapped around his neck, her body pressed to his, Grace shivered.

God, how long had it been since she'd been touched like this? Since she'd *wanted* to be touched like this? Too long.

But why him? Why this man who seemingly hated her when there were any number of strapping Alaskan mountain men ready and willing to show her a good time? Instead, she was getting all revved up for the one who'd made it clear that she was, at best, an unwelcome annoyance.

Her sense returned, and she let go of him, pushing at his shoulders. He released her immediately, staggering back like a drunk. Her breathing was just as ragged as his as they stared at each other across the narrow hall.

"What the hell?" Grace demanded, her voice embarrassingly unsteady.

Caleb said nothing. His eyes, which had always looked nearly-black before, had lightened to warm brandy. Silence stretched tautly between them.

Caleb was the first to move. He turned his back on her. "Go inside," he said hoarsely.

Another dismissive command. Anger burned again, an incendiary to her already-heated blood. "Fuck you."

Caleb spun around. The golden gleam in his eyes looked too bright, wild. "Are you offering?" he snarled.

"Maybe!" Grace blurted angrily.

He moved like lightning. Suddenly, she found herself pinned to the wall with his big body looming over her. His hands slid from her hips up her ribs. Heat blossomed in the wake of his touch and she arched helplessly against him, needing more. Caleb's gaze met hers. His eyes paled to glittering gold.

Grace gasped. "Your eyes—"

He released her, shoving abruptly away. Without a word, he left, thundering down the stairs and out of sight. In the wake of his absence, the ice crept back into her veins, chilling her once again. She touched her hand to her cheek. Ice cold, as usual. But for a brief moment, when Caleb had been touching her, she'd been filled with heat. She wanted it back.

GRACE DIDN'T SEE Caleb for several days after that. Not at breakfast or dinner. Not in passing in the garage or the hallway. She tried to ask where he was without asking about him directly.

"So," she hedged while Natasha poured coffee. "Smaller crowd for breakfast today, huh?"

Natasha glanced around the dining room. "Ah, yes." A knowing smile curled her lips. "Caleb is not here."

Grace's ears burned. Luckily, her hair was covering them.

Natasha's smile deepened. "He flew out to Anchorage for a supply run. The weather down there has kept him grounded. I've heard he should be able to return today."

"Oh." Grace shrugged. "Well, whatever."

She couldn't stop thinking about the heat of Caleb's touch. The memory kept sliding into her mind at inconvenient times—in the middle of staff meetings, or while she was grading assignments, or during dinner, leaving her staring off into space with her fork halfway to her mouth.

She managed not to get distracted when she was teaching, but in the spare moments between classes and after school, her mind went straight back to him. At the end of the day, as her last class filed out after the final bell, her brain jumped immediately to him.

It took her a moment to realize that not all of her students had left. Daniel Gray hovered near her desk.

"Oh—Daniel. Sorry, I was just... thinking about something. What's up?"

He handed a book over—*The Lightning Thief*. "It was good," he said. "Thanks." A boy of few words, he immediately turned to leave.

"There's a sequel," Grace called after him.

He turned back. His expression, as usual, was flat and guarded.

Grace swiveled in her chair to pull the next book off the shelf. "It's part of a whole series. Interested?"

He walked back to her desk. "Sure."

She carefully smoothed away her smile before turning back to face him. "Keep it as long as you want."

"Thanks, Ms. Rossi."

He left. Grace gathered her things and floated out of the building on a happy glow. When she got back to The Spruce, the glow abruptly extinguished. Caleb was back. His truck was back in his space in the garage. A strange nervousness overtook her as she walked inside the building. The dining room was empty, and she let out a breath. She was halfway up the third flight of stairs when she heard the tread of heavy footsteps approaching. Her heart began to pound in her chest.

Could be Harlan, she told herself. *Or Eric.*

But it wasn't. She reached the landing at the same time Caleb did. He stopped so abruptly at the sight of her, you'd have thought she was covered in anthrax. Perversely, his reaction calmed her. With Caleb in retreat, Grace had control of the field.

"Hello," she said, a little breathless.

His expression didn't change, but something about him seemed to sharpen as he observed her. "Hi," he said impatiently. He gestured at the stairs behind her. "You going to get out of my way?"

"No." She took a step towards him and reached for his hand. She only wanted the briefest of skin-to-skin contact, to see if his heat would warm her again.

Caleb caught her wrist before she could catch his hand. But it was enough. His big, calloused fingers closed around the delicate bones of her wrist. Heat bloomed beneath her skin, making her gasp. She looked up at him, dazed.

"Caleb," she breathed. "You're *so* warm."

His eyes gleamed and suddenly he was no longer retreating, no longer holding Grace at arm's length. He closed in on her, backing her across the landing until she was pushed against the wall, caged by his body. His expression was murderous as he looked down on her. But when he reached out, instead of strangling her, he gently cupped her jaw. Grace sighed as the incendiary heat of his touch sank into her. His thumb stroked across her cheekbone, her bottom lip.

When he spoke, his voice was a gravelly rasp. "Why do you keep playing with me?"

"I have no idea what you're talking about," she murmured. She laid her hand over his, pressing his palm against her cheek, savoring the fresh bloom of heat beneath her skin. Nothing melted the ice inside of her the way Caleb's touch did. Not Natasha's maternal fussing. Not Margaret's collegial friendship. Not Jess and Elena's light-hearted affection. Just Caleb and this unwanted, inexplicable attraction to him.

He slid his hand down the column of her throat. Her eyes slid shut as she tilted her head back for him. He stroked his thumb over her pulse. "If I hadn't been the one coming down the stairs, then who'd be touching you right now? Adam? Connor? Harlan?"

Grace's eyes flashed open and she pushed away from him. Shame and humiliation flooded her, a different heat from Caleb's touch—sickening and clammy. How could she have fooled herself again? After Anchorage, hadn't he made his opinion of her perfectly clear? He may want her physically, but for whatever reason, he'd long ago decided she was untrustworthy and dishonest.

She turned her back on him and walked away without speaking. Mortified tears burned at the corners of her eyes.

"Grace, wait—" he called, sounding contrite. She heard the pound of his booted footsteps coming after her.

She swallowed past the tightness in her throat. "Wait for what? More insults?"

Caleb kept pace with her angry march. "I'm sorry, Grace. Stop for a second and let me—"

"Just stop talking to me." She was a sucker for a sincere apology, and she refused to be suckered again. She needed to stay mad forever because she clearly couldn't trust her own good sense to keep her away from him. "And stop following me. Go away."

He halted immediately, allowing Grace to storm past him. Dammit if his immediate acquiescence didn't make her a little less mad at him. *Boundary-respecting asshole!* she fumed ineffectively. She needed something better than that. *He keeps making you think he's going to kiss you, and every time it ends in insults.*

Yeah. That's the stuff. She ripped her door open and slammed it shut behind her.

CHAPTER 12

Saturday night, after dinner, Jess and Elena met Grace out the back door of The Spruce with three snowmobiles.

"You know how to operate one of these?" Jess asked.

Grace scoffed. "Please. My entire childhood, there was always a bare minimum of two snowmobiles in our garage."

"*Snowmobiles?*" Elena smirked. "You're in Alaska now. They're called snowmachines."

"Oh, excuse me, *snowmachines*," Grace said, pretending at annoyance.

"Oh my god, it's like she was born here." Jess grinned as she tossed Grace a helmet. "We're going up into the mountains."

Despite her bravado, it was one of the toughest rides Grace had ever been on. Jess and Elena knew the terrain like the backs of their hands, and they raced over it at top speed. It was all Grace could do to keep them in sight. As soon as they reached the mountains, the trail turned into a nearly constant incline. Grace's forearms and shoulders ached from the effort of steering, her thighs burned from clenching the seat. Under her winter gear, her entire body was sticky with sweat. When she saw Jess and Elena slow to a halt, she nearly wept in gratitude.

They'd stopped on a broad ridge high above the valley, hundreds of feet above the tree line. There was nothing to obstruct their view, except for the surrounding mountain peaks. In the distance, Longtooth was a faint twinkle of light. Overhead, the sky was a tapestry unlike anything Grace had ever seen before.

She sat astride her snowmobile, arms folded over the handlebars, and stared in absolute wonder at the impossible beauty of the Arctic night. The sky wasn't black at all—it was studded with an infinite array of diamond-bright stars, twinkling white, yellow, blue, purple, pink. They clustered in whorls and blooms, with the Milky Way forming a beautiful wake through it all. That bright ribbon of starlight ran down to the horizon, like a celestial road, and in that moment, Grace truly believed if she just kept going, she could reach the end and walk upon it. Her hands curled inside her mittens, wishing she could swipe her fingers through it. What would magic feel like? The wind and the earth were perfectly still, perfectly silent, as if the whole world was holding its breath in awe. She felt her face mask sticking to her cheeks, hot and damp, and realized she was crying.

Jess turned towards her, flipping up the visor on her helmet. "Well?"

Grace swallowed past the tightness in her throat. "Beautiful," she said inadequately, her voice hoarse.

She didn't belong anywhere in particular—not in her decaying hometown, not in Milwaukee's industrial hustle, and not in Chicago's overwhelming everything. But maybe she could choose to belong here, in this otherworld, where the sky was made of diamond dust and magic. Where the killing cold was somehow melting the ice inside of her. Where people like Margaret, Natasha, Jess, and Elena thought she was wonderful just for the simple act of being herself.

"I wish I could live here," Grace said faintly, not intending to be heard. But Jess and Elena both cocked their heads towards her.

"You do live here," Elena said.

Grace shook her head, not sure how to articulate the uncertain yearning she felt. "I mean... I don't really have anything tying me here. All the locals have such deep bonds, and I'm an outsider. You're all family, and I'm not."

Jess regarded her for a quiet moment, thinking. "Family isn't just born," she said. "Family can be chosen." A sneaky smile tugged at the corner of her mouth. "But if you want to make it official, I can think of several local boys who'd be more than happy to bring you into the fold."

Grace grinned beneath the cover of her helmet. "Yeah, well, for every interested guy, there's another who can't get rid of me soon enough."

Elena scoffed. "Don't let Harry get to you. He's not happy unless he's got something to complain about."

"It's not just Harry."

"What? Who else?"

"Caleb wants me gone."

Jess and Elena both laughed.

"Are you serious?" Elena asked.

"He's made it pretty clear."

Jess shook her head. "Caleb's been sniffing around you since the day you landed."

Grace flipped her visor up just so she could give Jess the incredulous look that statement deserved. "Are you drunk most of the time, Jess?"

Jess laughed.

"I know he's your cousin and you guys get along just fine, but he really doesn't like me."

"I think you make him nervous," Elena said. She turned to Jess. "Remember Brenna? He doesn't want a repeat of that."

Grace frowned. "A repeat of what?"

Jess and Elena shared a speaking glance. Finally, Jess shrugged. "Alright, normally I'd keep this to myself. But apparently he's being a dick, so I guess he deserves it."

Grace raised her eyebrows, waiting.

"About five years ago, this nurse from the lower-48, Brenna McIntyre, took a job in Longtooth at the clinic. She and Caleb started hooking up. Caleb thought it was serious, but Brenna didn't. She was only planning to stay for a year or two. Just a fun adventure before she settled down into 'real life' back in Kansas or wherever."

Grace raised her eyebrows, unimpressed. "I mean, that's too bad, but it's not exactly the sob story I was expecting."

Jess sighed. "It's hard to explain without spelling out every little detail, but basically, Brenna let Caleb think she was interested in something long term in order to keep him on the hook. For a solid year. But then when he started talking mating—"

Elena coughed harshly.

"—marriage," Jess said, "she immediately broke it off with him."

"Okay, that's shitty," Grace conceded.

"And she immediately started fucking this outsider, Dan

—who you've never met. He left Longtooth a few months after she did."

Grace sighed. "Alright, fine. That's really shitty."

Elena grimaced, adding, "And Dan's room was on the other side of Caleb's, so he got a constant earful of their—"

"Alright, I get it. I can understand why he doesn't want to get into a relationship with an outsider. But the thing is, I'm not trying to get into a relationship with him! He has no reason to—"

As she spoke, Grace saw faint movement along the top of the ridge. She turned just in time to see a silhouetted figure slide into the shadow of a large spruce.

"Did you see that?" She pointed at the spot where the shadow had been.

Jess and Elena lifted their heads. "I don't see anything," Jess said.

A slight breeze brushed past them. Jess and Elena both closed their eyes and inhaled through their noses.

"What's with the sniffing thing you weirdos do?" Grace demanded. "Caleb did that in—"

"Start your sled," Jess said urgently, turning her ignition. The alarm in her voice had Grace obeying immediately. "Go! Back the way we came. Now!" She flipped her visor down and pinned the throttle, arcing around Grace in a spray of snow.

Adrenaline spiked through Grace, and she pinned the throttle down. Jess and Elena flanked her all the way back to Longtooth. When they reached The Spruce, Jess hustled her inside.

"Don't worry about the sleds," she said. "We'll take care of them in the morning."

"Why did we have to race back?" Grace asked.

Elena and Jess exchanged a dark glance.

"There was a bear," Jess said at the same time as Elena said, "I saw a moose."

They looked at each other again.

"Uh, it could've been a bear," Elena said. "I didn't get a close look."

"Moose or grizzly—" Jess shrugged "—you don't want to mess with either one." She herded Grace towards the stairs. "Go ahead and get some sleep. I have to go talk to Margaret."

"At midnight?" Grace asked.

"She's my aunt, she won't mind. See you tomorrow."

Jess and Elena hustled out of The Spruce, leaving Grace alone at the bottom of the stairs.

"Well. Goodnight," she said to the empty room. Some of the brightness she'd been feeling dimmed away. There was something they weren't telling her. Something they didn't trust her to know. After the fun she'd had with them, it was a sharp reminder of where she really stood.

She was an outsider.

THAT NIGHT, Grace dreamt of Alex again.

His handsome face was creased with sorrow. His usually perfect blonde hair was messy and rumpled. His eyes were dark with grief. "Grace," he pleaded. "My Grace. Come back to me."

Cold splintered through Grace like a million needles. She folded over, breathless from the pain.

"You have to come to me, Grace. There's only one way this can end happily for everybody."

She hauled in a frozen breath. It shredded her lungs, and she choked on it.

"Stop fighting this, Grace. Stop fighting us. Come back to me. Now. Come back—"

"No." The word emerged as the faintest rasp. But it stunned Alex into silence. "Leave me alone." Her voice became a little stronger, a little clearer. "Go away!"

He stared at her in shock. "You can't mean that," he said faintly. And then he was gone.

WHEN GRACE MADE it down to the dining room, breakfast was nearly over. Her arms, shoulders, and back ached so badly from last night's snowmobiling, it'd been almost impossible to pull her sweater over her head.

"Well, look who decided to wake up," Jess said as Grace slid onto the stool next to her.

"I slept like shit last night." She winced and stretched her arms. "It's been a few years since I went on such a long snowmobile ride. I feel like I've been hit by a truck."

Jess frowned. "Aw, Grace, I didn't think of that. We should've started you with a shorter ride."

"No way. I'd crawl back on my hands and knees just to see that view again. The last few years, all I've done is work, eat, and sleep. I forgot how good it feels just to do something for fun. It made me realize how much I miss my old hobbies."

"Why'd you stop?"

Grace hesitated. She was still unpleasantly aware of the distance between her, an outsider, and the locals. Even Jess, who'd been one of the most friendly to her, was not really comfortable with her. It had been made abundantly clear last night when she and Elena wouldn't tell Grace what was going on. But even in ordinary conversations, it was there.

They were all friendly and kind and earnest, but even so, there was a guardedness that they tried to cover behind easy smiles and nimble changes in conversation. A lot of people might not even see it. But Grace was an expert at fooling people with those same tactics.

"Too busy living it up in the big city?" Jess prompted when Grace's silence had gone on too long.

Her guess was so far off the mark, it spurred Grace into answering honestly. "Got sucked into a bad relationship. Lost interest in the rest of my life." She shrugged. "Anyways, when I packed to move to Longtooth, I didn't pack any of my hobby stuff because I thought I'd stopped caring about it. Now I'm realizing that I just... forgot." Forgot how to enjoy things. Forgot how to feel anything.

"What hobbies?" Jess asked. "You might be able to get some of the stuff around town."

"I used to knit." Grace plucked at her sweater, an Icelandic sweater with the traditional decorative yoke. "I actually knitted this. And most of the other sweaters I own."

"You did this? Wow." Jess fingered the colorwork on the sleeve. "Getting knitting stuff should be easy. Give Caleb some cash next time he makes a run to Fairbanks or Anchorage, and tell him you want yarn and knitting needles."

The thought of asking Caleb for anything made her stomach curdle. "I'm not going to do that," she said flatly.

Jess's expression flickered—Grace could see her decide not to argue. "Fine. What else did you do for fun?"

"I liked baking. Just to relax. But that's not really an option here."

"Why not?"

Grace gestured at the kitchen door. "This is a commercial

kitchen. Even if Natasha were willing to let me play around back there, there's probably some health code against it."

Jess snorted. "This is Longtooth. There are no health inspectors. And there isn't a soul in the entire Valley who'd complain about how Natasha handles her kitchen." The door suddenly flapped open, and Jess turned. "Hey—Natasha! Can Grace use the kitchen to bake for fun?"

Natasha set a mug in front of her and filled it. "Grace, you didn't tell me you like to bake!" Her eyes lit up. "Of course you can use the kitchen. Today?"

"Oh, I—well, thank you—but I don't actually have anything planned. I didn't even buy any ingredients."

Natasha scoffed. "I have ingredients. Do you know how to make a babka?"

"I've eaten babka, but I've never made it before."

Natasha smiled. "I will teach you to make my grandmother's babka. It is how I stole Arthur."

"You *stole* him?" Jess echoed.

Natasha looked smug. "Oh, yes. He came to Poland to meet a girl whose family knew his family. Both families expected they would marry. But I found him, and I decided he was mine. Poor Anastazja never had a chance."

"Natasha!" Jess sounded scandalized, but she was grinning broadly. "I never knew you were such a minx!"

Just then, Arthur came into the dining room carrying a bucket full of tools.

"Arthur!" Jess called. "Is it true—did Natasha steal you from another woman?"

Arthur smiled good-naturedly. His gaze settled on Natasha, something steady and reverent reflecting in his eyes. "She didn't have to steal anything. I was all hers the first moment I saw her."

Natasha's wicked little smile softened. "Arthur," she said quietly.

He winked at her. "If you ladies will excuse me, there's a burst pipe that needs my attention."

Grace watched the entire exchange with a strange little ache in her chest. It grew and grew until something inside her seemed to crack. She had to look away.

"So," Natasha said, a little breathy, her cheeks slightly pink. "We will make babka. After breakfast."

Grace nodded, still trying to get past the strange emotional charge that Arthur and Natasha's love for each other had imparted. "Okay. Thanks, Natasha."

"There you go," Jess said, nudging her. "That's one hobby restored. Now we just have to get you some knitting supplies."

There was no way Grace was asking Caleb to go out of his way to get anything for her. She'd order them online, pay the extra charges, and wait the ten thousand years it took for deliveries to reach the interior of Alaska. Caleb was going to be the delivery boy either way, but in this case, he'd just be bringing a load of packages to the post office, and Grace could pick up her stuff from Wade.

When she finished her breakfast, she turned to go upstairs and found Caleb sitting at the table behind her with Harlan and Connor. His gaze flicked up to meet hers, his expression unreadable. Grace looked away, passing their table without a word. She climbed the stairs, wondering how long he'd been sitting there.

Back in her room, she changed into a shirt she didn't mind getting flour and cinnamon all over. Then she spent the afternoon making babka with Natasha.

They sat at the workbench, drinking coffee while the

dough went through its first rise. Grace asked Natasha about growing up in Poland and listened to stories about her brothers and sisters, her parents, her family's farm.

"I sort of grew up on a farm, too," Grace said. Her maternal grandparents had owned a dairy farm, and she'd grown up just down the road from them. She'd started working on the farm very young, doing the fun stuff like bottle-feeding calves. By high school, she was milking before and after school, planting alfalfa hay in the spring, baling the hay in the fall, and doing all the other messy, backbreaking tasks necessary to keep a small farm afloat. Even after moving away, she'd still worked on the farm when she came home to visit. But grandpa passed away five years ago, and Grace's mom and uncle sold the farm.

"Ah, this must be why I like you so much," Natasha told her. "Farmers are a special kind. Hardworking."

They commiserated over the endless, exhausting, glamourless work of farming. Natasha told Grace more about her first few years in Longtooth, and the ways she'd struggled to adapt.

"It does not happen overnight," she said, and Grace knew she was referring to their conversation from a few nights ago.

Grace shrugged, but she couldn't think of anything to say. Natasha's situation had been so different from hers. She'd come here as a *wife*, tied to the Valley by love and by law. Grace was just here because of a job—a job that she could do anywhere, and that could be done by anyone with the certifications. That transient feeling wasn't helped by the fact that she lived in a hotel. She reminded herself that plenty of locals lived at The Spruce—Caleb, Jess, Elena, Connor, and Max. But their situations were different from hers, too. They lived in The Spruce because they were single and worked in town. But they had family all over the valley —parents and grandparents and siblings whose houses they could visit, eat at, stay at, any time. All Grace had was her little room.

If she could find what Natasha had found, maybe she'd feel more welcome here. More wanted. Immediately, Caleb appeared in her mind's eye. She shoved him away. She didn't need that humiliating reminder. Her chest still felt cracked. Nobody had ever looked at her the way Arthur and Natasha looked at each other—and she didn't think anybody was ever likely to. Even the guys in Longtooth who'd made no bones about their interest in her—Adam, Connor, Isaac— only looked at her the way a golden retriever looks at a hamburger.

"There is going to be another party this Saturday," Natasha said suddenly. "You might have heard—for Linnea and Roland Teague's twentieth wedding anniversary."

Grace remembered Linnea mentioning something about it at school a couple weeks ago. Linnea hadn't asked her to come, so she'd assumed, with a mixture of hurt and relief, that she wasn't invited. She realized now, that simply mentioning the existence of a celebration might be construed as an invitation in Longtooth.

"Roland's a Teague and Linnea's an Ankkonisdoy, so between the two of them, they're related to almost every-body. It will be a big party. You can meet the rest of the Valley."

Grace swallowed the anxious little whine trying climb out of her throat. If she wanted to stop being treated like a temporary visitor, she was going to have to suck it up and start socializing. If only she could meet the rest of the Valley in small groups, rather than in a huge crowd. But that wasn't feasible. So a crowded party it was.

"That sounds great," she lied cheerfully. "This Saturday?"

"Yes. There will be music and dancing and drinks and I'm making a cake. A very big cake." Natasha got up to fetch the ceramic bowl with the rising dough from its warm spot next to the oven. She pulled the towel back to check on it. "Ah, here we are." She brought the bowl over to Grace. "See—twice as big. Now we punch it back down, and we shape it. Go on."

Grace did as directed. Surprisingly, the anxiety about the upcoming party had faded away to nothing after that initial spike. She worked the dough, enjoying the satiny feel of it, relaxed and unconcerned. A little while later, they had a piping hot cinnamon babka cooling on a wire rack.

"Whenever you want to bake, just let me know," Natasha told Grace as she cut thick slices for them and spread them with butter. "You can use the kitchen any time."

When they'd finished eating, Natasha wrapped the remainder of the babka up and made Grace take it to her room. "You are not so unhappily skinny as when you first arrived," Natasha told her, pinching the back of her arm. "But you could still carry a little more weight, I think."

Grace smoothed her hands over her hips. She was getting happier and happier with her shape, but she didn't disagree with Natasha. "Don't worry," Grace said. "A few more weeks of your cooking and I'll have to switch to elastic waistbands."

CHAPTER 13

On Monday, there were no classes, but the teachers had in-service training. Grace had to drive over to Eagle Ridge for the meetings, where she got to meet her accidental nemesis, Tom Tremaine. He was an outsider, like her, but he'd been living in the Valley for more than a decade now, and had married a local. He was friendly, but that didn't stop him from grilling Grace a little bit about her reading lists.

"How do you expect the kids to develop an appreciation for more challenging literature?"

Grace shrugged. "I don't."

Tom opened and closed his mouth, wordlessly appalled.

"Kids who enjoy challenging lit will pursue it on their own. Didn't you, when you were young?"

"Well, yes, but at the guidance of my teachers."

She picked an apple cinnamon muffin from the breakfast spread that had been put out for the teachers. "My upperclassmen do independent reading, and I steer the more analytical readers towards stuff that will challenge them.

But I care a lot more that they enjoy reading. They're going to develop better critical thinking skills from reading 'fun' books than they are from 'literary' stuff that they just skimmed, or looked up the cliff notes for. And even if they don't, then at least they had fun reading."

"So you prioritize 'fun' over learning."

"I think learning only happens if students are engaged with the texts. So, yes." Grace took a big bite of the muffin. It was possibly the best muffin she'd ever had in her life and she almost groaned out loud.

Tom's expression flickered. Warmth Grace hadn't realized was missing suddenly came into his eyes. She realized that this was the first real smile he'd given her since they'd been introduced. "I'm not sure I agree with you entirely," he said, taking a muffin for himself. "But I can see you care about your kids."

Ah, yes. That was the line she used to get at her old school all the time—if she cared about her students she'd be teaching "serious" books, clearly she just didn't want to do her job, et cetera. Tom had apparently been in the same camp until now.

"I do care," Grace said fiercely.

"Margaret told me," he said ruefully. "I should know by now not to argue with her."

Eagle Ridge's principal, Sheryl Toonikoh, called everyone to order shortly after that. They were all gathered in the school's gym/cafeteria/auditorium. The school housed all classes from K-12, so even though there were half as many students as in Longtooth, the building was about the same size as the one Grace taught in. Refilling her coffee and taking a seat at one of the folding lunch tables, she steeled herself against the tranquilizing effect that these trainings always had.

"Good morning, everybody," Sheryl said brightly. Outside the gym windows, the steel gray sky continued to darken as the wind picked up. "Looks like tonight's storm might be moving in a little faster than we expected. We might have to let some of you head out early."

Grace was the only teacher from Longtooth. Lucia had been meant to come with her, but she'd called early this morning to let Grace know she was too sick to come. Aside from Grace, the only other non-Eagle Ridge teachers were the four who'd made the trek down from Daghukkoda, a small village several hours north of Longtooth.

"Well. Let's get started. We've got a speaker today. This is Dr. Jensen. I'll let her introduce herself."

The in-service training was completely unremarkable. It was meant to be a four-hour session, and then they'd be released back to their classrooms for whatever work they wanted to get done. But, two hours in, the wind had begun to rattle the windows and the sky had turned nighttime dark.

"Alright, we're going to let our Longtooth and Daghukkoda teachers head out," Sheryl announced. "The snow's not supposed to hit for a few hours, but we'd rather you got home safely instead of driving through it."

THE DRIVE HOME WAS ROUGH. Grace's arms were getting sore from steering against the wind, which pushed at her truck like the hand of an angry god. Even without actual snowfall, the wind pushed a constant stream of powder off the snowbanks that swirled across the road and made it impossible to see where the shoulder was.

Things got worse when, halfway between Eagle Ridge and Longtooth, the Jimmy sputtered, coughed, and then died. Grace coasted to the side of the road and put it in park.

"This is *not* a good time for you to act up," she muttered at the truck as she tried turning the ignition again. The engine made a mighty effort to turn over, but just couldn't get going. She looked at the dash—no check engine light. A second later, she realized the fuel gauge was on E.

No. Impossible. She *never* let her tank get below half full in the winter, and she'd been especially vigilant about it since moving to Alaska. She had to stare at the fuel gauge for a few more seconds before it really sank in that she'd let her tank run down to empty in the middle of winter in Alaska on the day of a fucking blizzard.

She sagged back against her seat with a tortured groan. She was going to have to call The Spruce and ask Natasha to send someone to get her. Not only had she made an unbelievably brainless fuck-up, but everyone in town was going to know about it. Someone was going to have to drive all the way out here because of her.

With a heavy sigh, Grace reached into her pocket for her phone. It wasn't in the chest pocket where she usually kept it. She slid her hand into her other pockets—also empty. She checked all her pockets again. She grabbed her bag and dug through every divider and pocket. It was pointless, but she was still in denial, so she searched her glove compartment and cupholders. She checked under her seat. Then under the passenger seat. Then under the back seats. She clambered all over her truck, searching every nook and crevice that a phone could fit into. When she'd finished that, she checked her pockets again.

No phone.

Had she left it in Eagle Ridge? Or was it sitting on her nightstand back at The Spruce? It didn't really matter. Either way, she was stuck on the side of a rarely trafficked road with no gas and no phone. As if to emphasize her circumstances, the wind gusted so hard that the truck rocked on its tires.

Grace clutched the steering wheel and stared blankly out the windshield at the dark, empty road. The wind rocked the truck again and she closed her eyes and screamed as hard and long as she could.

It helped a little.

With a shaky sigh, she unclenched her hands from the steering wheel and clambered once more into the back of the truck. She had a roadside emergency kit back there, along with a few of her own additions. She pulled out the sleeping bag, the heat-reflective mylar blanket, and a pack of twenty hand warmers. On second thought, she grabbed the road flares and granola bars as well.

She waited until the truck had cooled to close to the outside air temp before she peeled off her scarf and ventured outside to tie it to her antenna. She'd knitted it herself from a gorgeous—and expensive—merino wool. It was silly, considering the situation, but she really had to talk herself into sacrificing it. It was a bright, vivid red, and it would flutter dramatically in the gusting wind. She didn't think anybody passing by would be likely to miss her just yet, but once the snow started falling and her truck was buried, the scarf might be the only thing that distinguished her from the snowbanks on the side of the road.

She tied it to the antenna and then went back inside her freezing truck. She activated two hand warmers and tucked one into each boot. She took her parka off and wrapped herself in the mylar blanket, then put the parka back on over it. Keeping her boots on, she wriggled into the sleeping bag. She activated two more hand warmers and stuffed them into her mittens.

And then she just waited. How long would it be before somebody in Longtooth noticed that she was missing? They all knew she was supposed to be out of town today. What if they assumed she'd decided to wait out the blizzard in Eagle Ridge instead of driving home? Could she last that long?

She clenched her hands around the warmers. She was strangely optimistic. Except for her face, she was almost too warm. The hand warmers claimed to last for 10 hours, but she knew from past experience she could get four hours of reasonable heat out of them. And she still had sixteen unopened ones. She told herself she was going to be fine and settled in for a long wait.

She periodically turned the ignition so she could check the clock, then turned it back off. She'd left Eagle ridge around noon. By two in the afternoon, nobody had found her yet, but the snow had begun to fall. It came down in big clumps, driven sideways by the wind. It had become truly dark by then, so she turned the headlights on. They'd eventually drain the battery, but she was choosing to believe that somebody would find her before then.

She debated about whether she should turn on the radio, then decided not to use the battery any more than she needed. After a few minutes, she started to dig for her phone so that she could read something while she waited for rescue, before she realized what she was doing and laughed hollowly.

There was really nothing else to do. She pulled the sleeping bag over her face and went to sleep.

CHAPTER 14

Grace was woken abruptly by a heavy thump against the driver's window. She jerked upright, confused about where she was and why she couldn't move any of her limbs. After a moment of panicked thrashing, she remembered. Going perfectly still, she peered at the darkness surrounding her. Her hand warmers had gone stone cold. Her face felt like an icy mask.

The thump sounded on the driver's window again. She twisted towards it, breathing shallowly, heart hammering. What if it was an animal? If she rolled the window down or opened the door, a grizzly could rip her head off like a champagne cork.

"Hello?" she shouted.

"Grace?" somebody shouted back.

"Yes! It's me!"

"Open the door!" he shouted, with an accusatory impatience that identified him immediately.

Caleb. Of course.

Grace worked her arms free of the mylar blanket, then

back into her parka sleeves, then struggled to find the zipper on her mummy sleeping bag with her cold-numbed hands.

"Would you open the fucking door!" Caleb shouted.

"I'm *trying!*" she snarled. Finally, she found the zipper and jerked it down, freeing her arms. She pushed the door open to the howling wind, dropping a curtain of snow on her head.

Big hands clamped onto her shoulders. After the absolute darkness of her snow-blanketed truck, Caleb's face was surprisingly easy to see. He wore a snowmobile helmet with the visor pushed up. He squinted against the wind, staring down at Grace with an expression of pure rage.

"What the hell are you doing out here?" he demanded furiously.

"Seemed like a nice night to go camping," she said caustically. "What do you think I was doing? My truck broke down."

"And you didn't think to *call* anybody?" He looked ready to wring her neck.

"I lost my phone!" Instead of being relieved at being rescued, she was so angry and embarrassed at her stupidity, she was on the verge of tears.

Caleb's grip eased on her shoulders. He shook his head and leaned past her to look at the dashboard. The gauges were all lit up, but the truck was so heavily blanketed by snow that they couldn't see the headlights at all. Caleb turned the key and pulled it out of the ignition.

"Come on," he said. He nodded at the sleeping bag and mylar blanket still wrapped around her. "Bring your kit."

"I'm not that cold. Once I get in a warm vehicle, I won't need—"

"I don't have a warm vehicle."

"What? How'd you find me?"

"Snowmachine. The roads are impassable right now." He reached out and unzipped her sleeping bag all the way. "Come on. Roll that up. You're going to need it."

That sounded ominous. "Why?"

"We're not going to make it back to Longtooth in this. There's a dry cabin not far from here. We'll hole up there until the blizzard passes."

Stiff from the cold, Grace stumbled as she stepped down from the truck. Caleb caught her by the arm. He grabbed her gear with his other hand and guided her to his waiting snowmobile without a word. He lifted the seat and stuffed her things into the compartment underneath. He stuck a spare helmet on her and strapped it beneath her chin when her fingers were too stiff to work the nylon through the buckle.

"Are you going to fall off?" he asked impatiently as she clumsily boarded behind him.

"Hopefully not."

"Seriously, Grace. *Don't* fall off."

"Oh, well, now that you told me not to, I definitely won't."

He growled, but faced forward and started the sled.

In the darkness and the swirling snow, Grace couldn't see what was coming at all. They dipped up over the snowbank and then plunged steeply down the embankment on the edge of the road. Trees appeared suddenly in the snowmobile's headlight, startling her. And then they were in the woods, weaving between trees, lurching over uneven ground. Even within the cover the forest, wind and snow drove at them. Grace closed her eyes, buried her face in Caleb's back, and held on tightly. Her thighs were clamped against his, and she could feel the flex of his muscular torso as he shifted with the movements of the snowmobile. It was uncomfortably intimate, but the discomfort was not as great as the fear of falling off.

The snowmobile came to a stop. In the glow of the headlight stood a rustic little cabin. A blanket of snow at least six inches deep covered the roof. Caleb grabbed the gear from the seat compartment and then led Grace inside.

She dug the flashlight out of her roadside emergency kit and flicked it on. The interior was about as sparse as a cabin could be. The uninsulated walls were just wooden planks nailed to the exterior timbers. Plywood platforms were mounted on both sidewalls, one above the other, forming rustic bunk beds. There were no bedrolls or mattresses of any kind. A narrow walking space ran between the bunks, leading to the back wall where a small wood stove sat next to an empty wood bin.

Caleb let out a sigh. "Of course it was too much to expect firewood." He looked over at her. "We'll have to bundle."

"Bundle?"

"We're going to share your sleeping bag."

"Are you serious?"

"It's for warmth."

"I've heard that one before."

He scowled. "Fine. Freeze to death."

It's not that she didn't trust Caleb. He might be an asshole, but he was an asshole with principles. The problem was, Grace didn't trust herself. She still hadn't forgotten how the heat of his touch rolled through her like an explosion. She couldn't forget the way he'd grabbed her in the hallway and pressed his face into her neck, and just *inhaled*—like he wanted to breathe her in and savor her. Like he *needed* to.

But she also couldn't forget the cutting things he said every time she'd initiated something. He didn't like her. Didn't trust her. Grace was unbearably attracted to him, and it hurt that he was so repulsed by her very existence. To share a sleeping bag with him, to have their bodies pressed together, knowing he loathed every minute of it, might be more than she could bear.

But what could she do? Caleb was right. Her only other option was to freeze to death.

"Alright…" she said uncertainly, not able to look him in the eye. "How are we going to do this?"

Caleb took off his jacket and spread it across one of the lower bunks. "Lay your jacket out. It's not much, but it'll pad the platform a little bit."

She did as he said, then stood shivering as she watched him roll out the sleeping bag.

"Take your boots off, but keep the liners on." He did the same, and then he unzipped the sleeping bag. "Alright then. Get in."

She hesitated for a second.

"Grace, it's fucking cold."

Like Joan of Arc going to the stake, she crawled onto the bunk and into the sleeping bag. Caleb turned the flashlight off, plunging the cabin into total darkness. The wind seemed to grow louder in the darkness, howling and raging as the cabin's walls groaned under its assault.

The plywood bunk creaked as Caleb sat down on the edge. The sleeping bag rustled as he found the opening. The plywood creaked again as he moved closer. He slid his legs in beside hers and then shimmied his big body in next to her. He was clearly trying to position himself with the least amount of intimate touching, which only made things worse. She'd rather have him accidentally touch her boobs than have to deal with the humiliation of him trying *so hard* not to.

Eventually, he seemed to conclude that no amount of maneuvering would prevent them from being glued together. With an impatient sound, he wrapped an arm around Grace's waist and pulled her back tightly against his chest. The intimacy of it paralyzed her.

"Zipper the bag," Caleb prompted.

His no-nonsense tone jarred Grace back into motion, and she pulled the zipper up, sealing them in together. Caleb's touch seared her as it always did, blooming a decadent warmth beneath her skin that sank all the way into her bones. She wanted to relax, to curl into his luxurious heat, but she couldn't bring herself to do it. Instead, she lay as stiff as a pole, with her arms crossed over her chest and breathing as shallowly as possible so that her body wouldn't move at all against Caleb's.

"So what'd you do to the truck?" Caleb asked. His mouth was so close to her ear, she felt the heat of his breath.

"I was driving it. The way they're meant to be used." Grace couldn't bring herself to tell him she'd run out of gas. He'd find out eventually, but she intended to never have a conversation with him about it.

"Anthony Daaldinh rebuilt that engine," Caleb said. "He's the best there is. If something went wrong, it's because of operator error. Do you even know how to drive stick?"

Grace may have blacked out for a split-second, out of pure murderous rage. "No, I've just been making my best guess all this time," she snapped. Her first car had been a manual, and she'd driven that beast for ten years. She'd started driving tractors, skid-steers, and combines at a dangerously young age on her grandparents' farm. And up until Grandpa died and the farm was sold, she'd still been driving them every time she went back for a visit. Growing up, her dad had always had ancient snowmobiles and Frankensteined dirt bikes to tool around on. She could drive anything on wheels or a track. She was pretty sure she could figure out how to drive a tank if the need ever arose.

"Does your 'best guess' include fueling it up every once in a while?"

Fuck. He knew.

Her face flooded with heat. "I can't believe this happened. I *never* let my vehicles get below half full in the winter," she said stiffly.

"I don't think 'never' is the right word here, Ms. English teacher." The laughter in his voice made her blood pressure spike. The worst part was that he was totally right. There was nothing she could say to defend herself. Any insults he lobbed her way would be impossible to fight without making herself a liar. She couldn't leave him thinking she was both stupid *and* unrepentantly so.

"It's the dumbest thing I've done since I was eighteen," she admitted, swallowing her pride. "It was insanely stupid, and I'm sorry that you got dragged into my mistake."

Caleb didn't say anything for a long minute. He shifted slightly, "What'd you do when you were eighteen?"

"What?"

"You said this is the stupidest thing you've done since you were eighteen. I want to know what you did that was stupider than this."

Grace's face burned even hotter. "Not telling."

He made an impatient sound. "I had to fight my way

through this mess to make sure you weren't freezing to death, and you can't even give me a simple story?"

Her face burned even hotter. She huffed out a breath. "I will tell you if you swear never to repeat it to another soul." He'd promised not to tell anybody about Alex, and he'd held true to that.

"Scout's honor."

She opened her mouth, then hesitated, brow furrowing. "Were you actually a scout?"

Grace couldn't see his face, but she would swear she could hear his smile. "No. But I promise not to tell, anyway."

"Very reassuring."

"Quit stalling. What'd you do when you were a genius eighteen-year-old?"

Grace couldn't quite bring herself to speak.

"If you tell me, I'll tell you how I got the scar on my shoulder." She knew exactly which scar he was talking about. A jagged line of silvery-white skin that ran across the top of his left shoulder and slashed across his chest. The only time she'd seen it, he'd been shirtless in her room. "I promise you it's not a flattering story."

Grace wasn't hesitating because of embarrassment. She was hesitating because Caleb knew more of her personal vulnerabilities than anybody in Longtooth, and she wasn't sure she wanted him to know any more. Especially since he seemed to want nothing more than her speedy departure from Longtooth. But his offer to share something of himself was hard to resist. Knowing something embarrassing about him might balance the scales between them a bit.

"Alright. Fine. So I grew up in a really small town—even smaller than Longtooth. But I went to college in Minneapolis. I'd never lived anywhere but my podunk little farm town, and I was kind of naive about people. I was driving back to campus from my part-time job when I saw a guy waving frantically at the passing cars. I couldn't believe nobody was stopping for him. So I pulled over and rolled my window down to ask him if he needed help. My car doors weren't locked. He pulled the passenger door open and got into my car."

Caleb tensed.

"He told me he needed a ride to his house. And instead of screaming and telling him to get out of my car... I drove him. I let this stranger sit in my car and direct me to a place I didn't know in a city I wasn't very familiar with. I could have been driving to my own murder scene. But I just... I just did what he told me to."

"*Grace*," Caleb said, aghast.

"I know. I look back on it, and I still can't believe... I don't know what I was thinking. I *wasn't* thinking, actually. I was only eighteen, and I'd never experienced anything like that, and I was just so scared when he got into my car that I went into autopilot." She let out a breath. A decade later, and she was still rattled by it. "He had me stop at this one house and said to wait for him, he'd be right back out. But as soon as he went inside, I drove away."

Silence followed. The wind roared and the cabin walls groaned. Caleb's arm tightened around her waist. He probably didn't mean anything by it, but it comforted her all the same.

"Anyways," she said hastily, "Now it's your turn. How'd you get that scar?"

He was quiet for a second. There was a thoughtfulness to his silence that made Grace uneasy. She wondered if he was trying to find the words to properly berate her for being so stupid. As if she hadn't berated herself enough for it in the intervening years.

But he didn't. "When I was a kid, we used to go sledding off of rooftops in town."

The tension lifted from Grace's shoulders.

"Well, we didn't actually use sleds. We'd just body surf down the roof, and then drop into the snowdrifts below."

"Sounds safe."

"Extremely," he agreed. "We were always getting in trouble for it. The adults kept warning us—we were going to break our necks, break our legs, there might be something buried in a drift that could hurt us, and so on. Turns out, they were right. I went diving off of Wade Evers' roof when I was seventeen without knowing that the night before the last snowstorm, he'd put some fifty-gallon barrels along the side of his house."

Grace drew in a sharp breath.

"Steel drums, too. Not just plastic."

She winced.

"I went down the roof on my belly, headfirst. Wade has the steepest roof in town, and it's aluminum. You can really get some good speed on it." He chuckled. "I hit the barrel so hard and so fast that I didn't even know what happened to me. Knocked me clean out. Next thing I knew, my friends were standing over me screaming my name, while someone else was sprinting off screaming for my ma. I couldn't breathe, I couldn't move. I thought I was dying. Someone got me on a sled—I don't even remember who—and took me to the clinic, but I was too busted up for Anna to fix. I needed surgery, and fast. I had to be flown to Fairbanks. I had a broken collarbone, three broken ribs, and a collapsed lung."

"You could've killed yourself!"

"Told you it wasn't flattering." But there was a smile in his voice when he said it, and it made Grace think of all the sledding accidents from her own childhood.

"When I was fourteen, I went sledding with a bunch of friends, and I ended up crashing into the guy I had a crush on while he was walking back up the hill. I broke his foot." She flushed as soon as the words were out of her mouth. Why had she even told him that?

But Caleb laughed. She felt his body shaking against hers and another surge of heat bloomed beneath her skin.

"That's nothing," he said. "When *I* was fourteen I was trying to impress the new girl who'd moved to Longtooth. I decided the best way to do this was by doing handstand pushups in the middle of math class. I lost my balance and smashed my face so hard against the floor that I broke my nose."

Grace felt bad for laughing, but she couldn't help it. "And she instantly fell in love with you?"

"Yes. If by 'fell in love' you mean 'was so scared of blood that when she saw my messed-up face she puked in the classroom trashcan.'"

"Yes, that's exactly what I meant." Grace was laughing again and Caleb was laughing with her, his arm tight around her. His breath coasted over her neck and ear. Somewhere during the conversation, their bodies had relaxed against each other like lovers spooning in bed. They both became aware of it at the same time. They shifted awkwardly away from each other—as much as they could, anyway, until Grace's ass was no longer cradled against Caleb's groin, his forearm no longer snugged up right below her breasts.

"We should sleep," Caleb said.

"Okay, goodnight!" Grace said too brightly.

The sound of the wind seemed to swell back into a roar, filling the awkward silence between them. Grace lay stiffly, listening to the cabin walls creak and pop. She was too conscious of Caleb's big body pressed against hers. She didn't think she was ever going to fall asleep.

And then, at some point, she did.

CHAPTER 15

Grace woke to total silence. No wind. It took her a second to understand why she was being halfway crushed by a warm weight against her back.

"Caleb."

"Mm." He buried his face against her neck, gusting out a warm breath.

A not-unpleasant shiver rippled through her. She shifted away from him. "Caleb. I think—"

His arm tightened around her, pulling their bodies flush together. Grace gasped as she felt the hot, hard press of his erection.

"Uh, Caleb. Wake up."

His lips parted and his teeth pressed against the tender skin where her shoulder met her neck. A low growl rumbled in his throat as he sank his teeth into her skin.

"Caleb!" She swung her elbow into his gut.

"*Oof!*" Caleb jerked back. He seemed to wake up in an instant, jerking away from her so hard he rolled off the bunk. Unfortunately, they were still zipped into the same sleeping bag. She was dragged along with him, and they landed hard, cracking their heads together.

They both hissed in pain. The broad strength of Caleb's body surged against hers as they fought to find the zipper.

"Goddamn it," Caleb snarled. "Quit squirming against me!"

"Quit getting in my way!" she shot back, slapping his big hand away from where it was blocking her reach. She finally caught the zipper tab and gave it a yank. Freed, she clambered back onto the bunk, away from the urgent press of Caleb's morning glory.

Caleb remained on the floor, tangled in the sleeping bag, rubbing at his temple. Grace pulled her parka on and zipped it up to her chin.

When they had the sleeping bag rolled up and her roadside emergency kit put back together, they pulled the cabin door open, only to find themselves facing a five-foot-tall snowdrift barring the doorway. They both grabbed handfuls of snow and bit into it, quenching a nearly painful thirst and subduing growling stomachs.

When they were ready, they had to dig their way out of the cabin. The snow was heavy and densely packed, leaving them both panting by the time they made it free. On the bright side, since they had no choice but to pee outside, all the deep drifts gave a lot of privacy. Grace nearly screamed as she cleaned herself up with a handful of snow, and then joined Caleb where he was digging out the snowmobile.

The snowmobile started up without a problem, and Grace was once again wrapped around Caleb like a koala on a tree. They plowed through the dense snow, cresting and dipping, bobbing and weaving their way through the forest. The sky was clear and blue. The wind was gone. The ground and the trees were covered in a pristine blanket of snow. Everything about it was beautiful.

THEY EMERGED from the woods near Grace's truck. She only knew where the road was because of her truck. And she only knew where her truck was because of the bright red scarf she'd tied to the antenna. The truck was covered in several feet of snow and buried in a drift up to the hood.

"You tied the scarf there?" Caleb asked. His tone was strange. So carefully polite. It was like talking to a stranger.

Grace found herself responding with the same contrived civility. "Yeah. I was hoping it would help somebody find me."

"I couldn't see it last night. But it was a good call. Anthony will be able to find your truck when he can get out here to tow it."

"Glad it was a worthy sacrifice. I knitted that thing myself."

Caleb looked over at it again, contemplating it for a second.

They dug away the snow around the driver's door until they could finally swing it open. Grace was kneeling on the driver's seat, reaching for her work bag when Caleb suddenly grabbed her hips and tossed her into the passenger seat.

"Hey!"

He jumped in behind her and pulled the door shut. "We've got a visitor," he said, panting a little.

The only window clear of snow was the driver's side window. Grace leaned towards Caleb, peering out at the snow-covered trees on the other side of the road. Suddenly, a massive moose passed into view. It had crossed in front of the nose of the truck, making its way across the road. It was the biggest animal she'd ever seen in person, and it was close enough that she could look it in the eye.

"Oh my god," she whispered. "Aren't they insanely dangerous?"

"Yes."

"Are we safe in the truck?"

"Probably. But don't make any sudden movements, just in case."

"Is that one female?"

"No, that's a bull. Moose shed their antlers in the winter."

"Then how do you know it's a bull?"

Caleb hesitated. "I... got a look at the family jewels."

Grace grinned and pressed her hand over her mouth. Caleb glanced at her, and a small smile tugged at the corner of his mouth. They sat in silence, watching the Moose as it meandered across the road and then disappeared into the woods.

"We'll sit for a couple minutes—let him put a little more distance between us."

While they waited, Grace picked up her bag and started double-checking it again for her phone. She'd already searched every possible nook and cranny. She knew it wasn't in there. But she couldn't help trying again.

Instead of her phone, she found something even more surprising. A string bracelet, elaborately braided from pink, blue, and purple thread. In the middle, lettered beads had been worked into the braid, spelling out *HAGS*. Grace stared at it for a long time. Long enough that Caleb noticed she'd gone as still as a statue.

"What's wrong?"

"This... this was stolen. It's been missing since—" Since she broke up with Alex and her box of mementos had disappeared with him.

"What is it?"

"It's a friendship bracelet." She turned it over, examining the age-grimed threads. "I made it in middle school with my best friends."

"Hags? You had good self-esteem, I see."

"It's our initials. Hannah, Alyssa, me, and Summer." Grace hadn't seen Hannah or Summer since high school, and she hadn't seen Alyssa since college. They'd all gone to different parts of the country, began new lives, and lost touch.

Caleb glanced from the bracelet to her rigid expression. "Are you alright?"

"I thought Alex stole this. I haven't seen it since the last time I saw him. I don't know how it got into my work bag. It makes no sense." She was starting to doubt her sanity. She looked over at Caleb. "Have you brought anybody into Longtooth recently?"

"No outsiders since you."

And the only way in was by plane. There was no way for him to be here. She thought of Freya's collar, tucked in her desk drawer. Maybe Alex hadn't stolen the mementos. Maybe he'd just scattered them around her apartment, and she'd somehow packed them up without noticing?

But why would he do that? None of it made any sense.

"There's no way he's here," Caleb said, as if reading her thoughts. "Nobody gets in and out of Longtooth without me or Margaret knowing."

Grace nodded stiffly and tucked the bracelet back into

her bag. "I know. It's just... weird. I keep getting these reminders of him." They were supposed to be *her* memories. They were from times in her life when Alex didn't even exist for her. And yet, somehow, he'd sullied them.

"Let's get back to Longtooth," Caleb said, cracking the driver's door open cautiously.

THE RIDE BACK WAS LONG. By the time they pulled up to The Spruce's garage, Grace's whole body ached from the effort of holding onto Caleb and shifting her balance with the snowmobile.

When she walked into the dining room, she was greeted by mostly good-natured jibes.

"She's alive!" Wade put his hand to his heart, faking astonishment.

"Hey, Grace, didn't Anthony tell you when he sold you the truck that you're supposed to put gas in it?" Adam teased.

"She's from Chicago. She's used to electric cars," Connor said. "Hey Grace, you know that's a block-heater you're plugging into, not a charger, right?"

She laughed dutifully at their banter and thanked her lucky stars that Harry Lance wasn't there. She could just imagine what he'd have to say about it.

Mercifully, she ended up getting a two-day reprieve from Harry, but on Thursday, he was sitting in the dining room when she came down for breakfast. The only open seat at the counter was two down from him. Grace took a steadying breath and sat down. Almost instantly, his grizzled silver head leaned over the counter, dark eyes narrowing on her.

"Told you not to take Alaska for granted, didn't I?" he

said. "Winter up here isn't a joke. Didn't I say that? You run out of gas in Chicago, and it's no problem. You run out of gas up here, you can die."

"Well, it depends *where* in Chicago you run out of gas," she said, curling her hands into fists so that she didn't flip him both birds.

"Won't make that mistake again, will you?"

Natasha appeared with a coffee pot and a mug. "Gracie," she said pleasantly. "Anthony called a few minutes ago and said you should swing by the shop before school if you can. There's something wrong with your gas tank."

The dining room fell silent. Harry's smug face went blank.

With every ounce of self-control she possessed, Grace leaned over casually to look at Lucia. "Think we could leave a few minutes early?" she asked.

"No problem."

Clenching her jaw against the vindicated grin that wanted to spread across her face, Grace leaned back in and picked up her coffee mug.

ANTHONY'S SHOP was small and warm. When Grace and Lucia got there, he had a truck up on the hoist, draining some kind of fluid into a pan. Max Freeman was there, leaning against a tool chest and chatting with Anthony. He greeted them with a subdued nod.

"Hey, Grace." Anthony wiped his hands on a rag as he came around the vehicle. "The good news is it's a quick fix— just have to wait for the replacement part to come in. There was a leak in your fuel line. It's definitely why you broke down." He pulled his phone out of his pocket. "I took some pictures of the damage."

She looked at the pictures. "How did this happen? Did I run something over?"

Anthony scratched at his collar, looking a little uncomfortable. "To be honest, I think somebody did this to your truck on purpose."

"*What?*" Lucia gasped. "Why?"

"You could have done it by running something over. But this cut—" he zoomed in on the picture "—is too precise. It was done with a knife."

"Who would do this?" Lucia demanded, clutching Grace's arm.

"That's my question," Anthony replied. "I told Max about it."

Max was the closest thing Longtooth had to any sort of criminal investigator. There were no police in the Teekkonlit Valley, but Max was authorized in some sort of official capacity by the state. When the Valley needed law enforcement, Max was the liaison. But the Valley rarely wanted the state's interference. The locals handled things in their own way, and Max was the one who facilitated it.

"Grace," Max said, calm, but serious. "Can you think of anyone who might have done this?"

Her mind went blank at the implication. Somebody in the Valley hated her enough to get her nearly killed in a blizzard.

"No—I mean... I don't know what I could have done—"

"You didn't do anything wrong," Max assured her quickly. "Sometimes people are just assholes. Can you think of any particular assholes who've been nursing a grudge against you? Someone who might think you did them wrong?"

"Oh my god," Lucia said suddenly. "Isaac Murray. After he attacked you at the Moose—"

Grace stiffened, heart hammering.

Max nodded. "I thought about Isaac, but I don't think he could have done it. The aunties sent him to work the fishery up in Daghukkoda after what he did. He hasn't left the village since he arrived, according to Sue Taalona."

"Sue would know," Anthony said thoughtfully. "Nothing gets past her."

Grace shoved her hands into her pockets so nobody would see them shake. "I just... I don't know who would have done this."

"Don't be afraid," Max said gently. "The whole Valley is looking out for you."

"Except for whoever sabotaged my truck."

Max's expression turned stormy. "I'll figure it out, Grace. We won't let you be hurt, okay?"

She nodded. "Yeah. Of course. Thanks, Max." She stepped back, pulling on Lucia's arm. "We should probably get to school."

"If you think of anything that might help, give me a call right away," Max said.

"I can't—I lost my phone. That's why I couldn't call for help on Monday. I'm waiting for a new one to get shipped in."

"Your phone went missing right before your truck broke down?" Max asked sharply. "When exactly did you last see it?"

Cold leached into Grace's bones as she realized why he was

asking—whoever cut her fuel line might have stolen her phone to prevent her from calling for help. "I—I'm not sure. I thought I had it in the morning when I left for Eagle Ridge, but I'm so used to always having it with me, I might just be imagining that I did."

Max was quiet, contemplative. "Alright," he finally said. "If you think of anything you saw out of the ordinary, anybody who's been acting strange, anything at all, have my mom get ahold of me."

Grace was silent in Lucia's passenger seat as they drove to school.

"It's going to be alright, Grace," she said gently.

CHAPTER 16

Despite the looming threat of whoever had cut her fuel line, the next few days passed peacefully. A bunch of people apologized for jabbing at her about running out of gas. Harry didn't exactly apologize, but he did go on a tirade about Not Being Able To Trust Anybody These Days, which Grace considered about as good as she was going to get from him. On Tuesday, Wade handed over a package—her new phone. On Wednesday, Anthony called to let her know her truck was ready.

Grace was never wholly satisfied with life. That unhappy otherness still stained every friendship, but she was trying not to let it take up too much space in her mind. She spent her days in class, her nights in The Spruce's dining room, grading assignments, preparing lesson plans, or reading for her own pleasure. Jess and Elena joined her most nights. On Tuesday and Wednesday, Caleb wasn't at breakfast or dinner. Not that Grace was looking for him. Elena told her weather had kept him grounded in Anaktuvuk Pass. Not that Grace was asking about him.

Thursday afternoon, his truck was back in The Spruce's garage. When Grace got to her door after school, she found a shopping bag hanging from the knob, stuffed full. She stared at it for a second. When that yielded no answers, she pulled one of the loops free and looked into it.

Knitting supplies filled the bag. There was a gorgeous set of steel needles in a black canvas case. There were nine different sizes, with interchangeable tips to turn regular needles into double-pointed or circular needles. There was a container of stitch markers. And then there were four skeins of a pure merino yarn in a gorgeous cobalt blue. Somebody had gotten her knitting supplies, and not just basic supplies, but *really* nice stuff. Whoever had gotten it either knew about knitting or had asked someone who did. Grace brushed one of the skeins against her cheek, thinking.

It hadn't escaped her that the knitting supplies had shown up after Caleb returned from a supply run. But who was really behind this? The only person she'd talked extensively to about knitting was Jess. Had she asked him to do it? Grace tucked the lovely cobalt yarn back into the bag and brought the whole thing into her room. It had to have been Jess.

At dinner, Grace sat beside Jess at one of the small tables by the windows, and quietly thanked her. "You have to let me pay you back. Those needles had to be insanely expensive and the yarn would've cost at least fifty dollars in the lower-forty-eight. God knows what it'd go for in Alaska."

Jess scrunched her face, clearly baffled. "No offense, Grace, but there's no way I'd spend fifty dollars on yarn. It wasn't from me."

Grace's stomach plunged. The was only one other likely culprit. "Shit."

Jess's expression transformed into one of glee. "It was Caleb! I told you he wants you!"

Grace shushed her, looking around the dining room. No Caleb.

After dinner, she went straight up to her room, gathered the knitting supplies back into the bag, and hung the bag on Caleb's doorknob.

Friday morning, the bag was back on Grace's doorknob. Clenching her jaw, she pulled it off and hung it back on Caleb's door.

Friday afternoon, she got back from school and found it on her door again. Swearing under her breath, and smiling despite herself, she hung it back on his doorknob. After a second, she darted into her room and snagged a roll of tape. Wrapping the tape around several times, she secured the bag to his doorknob.

When she came back up from dinner, she found the bag gone, but all of its contents were taped to the front of her door.

"Son of a bitch!" she choked out on a laugh.

As she pulled knitting needles and yarn skeins off her door, a door further down the hall opened up. Lucia poked her head out. "Grace? What are you doing?"

"Getting revenge. You have some time to help me?"

Lucia came into the hall. "I've always got time for revenge."

They sat on the floor in front of Caleb's room, pulling knitting needles out of their case and sliding them beneath his door. They opened the package of stitch markers and pushed them under the door, one by one. They unraveled each skein of yarn, coiled them into flat loops, and slid them in after the needles and stitch markers.

"So what's this all about?" Lucia asked as they worked the last skein of yarn beneath his door.

"I think he's trying to make up for being an asshole, and I'm not having it."

Lucia raised a single eyebrow. "By giving you knitting needles?"

"Hey, I like knitting," Grace said defensively.

Lucia shrugged. "When a hot guy buys me gifts, I usually just say 'Thanks, handsome. Why don't you come inside and let me demonstrate my gratitude?'"

"It's not like that. We actively dislike each other."

Lucia grinned. "Even better."

Grace got to her feet, then extended her hand and pulled Lucia up. "Thanks for the help. I'd still be unraveling those skeins if it were just me."

"No problem. This is the most fun I've had all week."

Grace realized very suddenly that she was having fun too. A lot of fun. And not just with Lucia. The ongoing battle with Caleb made her smile every time she thought about it. She couldn't wait for his retaliation. "Uh, yeah," she said unsteadily. "Longtooth can be pretty quiet."

"Especially when you're an outsider," Lucia said.

Which reminded her— "Hey, I'm sure you heard about Caitlin's episode. Do you have any idea what that was about?"

Lucia shook her head. "No, but all my students clearly know what's up. They're all being so shifty and weird about it. I know I can't pry into a student's health history, but it's freaking me out. She's in my Pre-Algebra class. What if she has an episode and I can't get help in time, or I do the wrong thing, or..." Lucia broke off with a frustrated sigh.

"I wonder if Eric knows anything."

"He might. I caught Elena Morris creeping out of his room three weeks ago."

"What!"

Lucia grinned. "I promised her I wouldn't gossip. Anyway, she's a local. She might have told Eric something about it."

"Way to keep that promise. Remind me never to—"

Heavy footsteps sounded on the stairs. Lucia and Grace stared at each other with wide eyes. In a panic, they shoved away from each other and sprinted to their own rooms. Grace eased her door shut just as the footsteps reached the top landing. They continued down the hall, passing her door. And then they stopped.

It's him! She pressed her ear to their shared wall, practically vibrating with anticipation.

She heard the rattle of his key in the lock, the creak of his door opening. And then... silence. A long stretch of silence, finally broken by a masculine chuckle. Grace pressed her hands over her mouth to silence her answering laughter. Caleb's footsteps continued into his room, and the door swung shut.

Heart racing, she spun away from her door and leapt onto her bed like a little kid. The bedsprings squealed as she bounced. She froze, wide-eyed. No sound from Caleb's room. She eased back against her headboard, grinning. "Your turn, Kinoyit," she whispered.

THE NEXT MORNING, Grace showered and dressed. The sun hadn't yet risen, and the hallway was dark when she opened her door. She stepped out—and was immediately tangled in an enormous net. She shrieked as she stumbled back into her room. It was all over her, clinging like a thousand little tentacles. She flicked the light on and realized she was tangled in beautiful cobalt yarn. Worked into the complicated net were all the knitting needles and stitch markers.

That Caleb had managed to weave a giant spider's web over her door without waking her was admittedly an accomplishment. Grace was a notoriously light sleeper. With a growl, she shut her door and began the work of carefully extracting herself from the yarn without damaging it. She spent several minutes carefully separating the skeins and winding them into tidy loops. She set them on her dresser along with the needles and the stitch markers. She needed time to think on her response—she had to top a giant spider's web.

When she made it down to the dining room, Caleb wasn't there. She scanned a second time, wondering if she'd missed him.

"Looking for someone?" Lucia asked with a grin.

"You know I am."

She cackled. "I saw the net. Impressive."

Jess came in behind them. "Hey, Grace. Hey, Lucia." She glanced at Grace. "What's in your hair?" She plucked it out and handed it over. A stitch marker.

Grace curled her fist around it with a growl. "Where is Caleb?"

Arthur Freeman looked over his shoulder from where he was seated at the counter. "Caleb flew out to Fairbanks."

An idea immediately popped into Grace's head. "Any idea how long he'll be gone?"

Arthur shrugged. "He said he'd be back for Linnea and Roland's party, but I wouldn't expect to see him before five."

"Perfect."

Arthur's brow furrowed. "Perfect for what?"

"Nothing to worry yourself about, Arthur. Jess, Lucia? Got time for a ride to the airstrip?"

"Yes!" Lucia said, bouncing with excitement.

"For what?" Jess asked, sounding as wary as Arthur.

"Vengeance," Grace told her with a feral grin.

She blinked. "Well. Alright."

OUT AT THE AIRSTRIP, they found Caleb's truck parked in front of the hangar. Like everybody else in Longtooth, he left his vehicle unlocked, which was convenient for Grace's purposes. Pulling both doors open, they started in the middle of the old bench seat, tying the first skein off to the rearview mirror. They wound it all over the cab, looping it through headrests, door handles, sun visors, the gear shift, the steering wheel, the gas pedals, the glove compartment, the heater vents, the seat belts. They hooked the stitch markers into the carpeting on the floors and used them as anchors for the yarn. When one skein ran out, they tied it onto the next and continued working. By the time all four skeins were used, the interior of Caleb's truck was an impassible labyrinth of crisscrossing blue yarn.

When they were done, they piled back into Grace's truck, giggling like children. Back at The Spruce, Grace was so impatient for Caleb's return, she forgot to be nervous about the upcoming crowd of strangers.

CHAPTER 17

The party was less than an hour from starting, and there was still no sign of Caleb. Grace went up to her room to get cleaned up. She put on one of her favorite sweaters—a form-fitting, snow-white sweater with the most intricate cabling she'd ever done, a repeating pattern of interlocking Celtic knots. She pulled on tight-fitting black jeans that she hadn't worn since she'd arrived in Longtooth, and slid her feet into a pair of delicate suede flats. She smoothed jojoba oil into the ends of her hair and brushed it until it shone. She took the time to put on a touch of makeup. It was more effort than she'd put into her appearance in months, and it felt good. She smiled at herself in the mirror.

When it was time for the party to begin, Grace made her way downstairs, fighting the nervous dread that always accompanied these sorts of events. The sound of voices drifted up to her, carrying over low music. The front entry doors creaked open, and more voices joined the throng. She took a deep breath and continued down the steps. But when she reached the threshold of the dining room, she froze. The Teekkonlit Valley had turned out en masse. The entire dining room was packed with bodies.

Grace shrank back, nervously scanning faces. Each time she recognized somebody, it was a relief. But there were just as many faces she didn't recognize. She spotted Jess on the far side of the room and tried to work up the nerve to wade through the crowd to her.

"Grace?" Caleb's voice rumbled behind her. She turned to face him, not even surprised by the wave of relief that washed over her. Somebody she knew. But when she actually saw him, that relief turned to dry-mouthed astonishment. He looked... different. Heat prickled beneath her skin as she took him in.

He was still Caleb, but, *sharper*. He still had the thick, black beard, but it had been trimmed, tidying the edges and pruning back the mustache to reveal surprisingly full, firm lips. His shaggy hair had gotten a much needed cut. It was still long, but now, instead of looking like carelessness, it was intentional. He wore a clean flannel shirt with no rips or frayed edges. The changes were subtle, but they made enough of a difference that Grace's attraction to him went from inconvenient to unbearable.

Her ears were burning with a flush that threatened to spread to her face. She forgot all about the yarn in his truck and her plans to antagonize him. "Caleb. Hi," she managed to choke out.

He brushed a strand of hair from her cheek. The calloused pad of his thumb left a bloom of fire in its wake. "You look nice," he said. A grin pulled those gorgeous lips back, revealing a flash of teeth. Grace's brain whited out for a second. "I'd never guess you spent the afternoon turning an innocent man's truck into a Gordian knot."

This was the part where she was supposed to banter wittily. But her brain had vacated the premises. "Well—I—uh...fair turnabout is—no. I mean, uh... that's what you get!" In a complete panic, she spun away from him.

And crashed into Max Freeman.

"Whoa, Grace." Max peeled her off, steadying her. "Buy a guy a drink first." Minus the Magnum P.I. mustache, Max was the spitting image of Arthur. He even had the same easygoing competence that made Arthur so likable. Looking at Max told Grace exactly what Arthur looked like twenty-five years ago. And why Natasha had decided to steal him.

But, as attractive and likable as Max was, there was no spark between the two of them. So Grace could smile at him and bring her brain back online. "Well, I've heard drinks are free tonight, so put it on my tab."

She could still feel Caleb's eyes on her, feel the space his body took up in the room. She moved away from them both, fighting her way through the crowd and over to Jess.

"Why do you look like you just ran a marathon?"

"I hate crowds and Caleb got a haircut," Grace wheezed.

"I didn't know you hate crowds."

"Yep." She went back to nervously scanning faces. When she accidentally made eye-contact with Caleb, she nearly leapt out of her skin.

"Well, that's understandable. But what's this about Caleb's haircut?"

"Shut up. I never said anything about Caleb."

"I'm pretty sure you did."

The man in question was currently making his way

across the room, gaze pinned on Grace. "Oh, no. Jess. Shit. I have to, uh—"

Jess followed her stricken gaze. Her expression transformed into mischievous delight. "You have to come with me." She grabbed Grace's arm and pulled her along the back wall, towards the table where drinks and snacks had been set up. "Don't bother with food." She twisted the cap off the top of a bottle labeled simply RED WINE and poured a generous glass. "This will help with the crowd thing. Might make things worse with the Caleb thing—depending on how you want that to go."

"I don't—"

She shoved the glass in Grace's hand and clinked her own against it. "Drink up!"

Grace took a healthy slug, and then another.

"There we go!" Jess topped her glass off, then dragged her back through the crowd. "I'll introduce you to some people. Then it won't be so bad."

And it wasn't. Jess stayed by her side. Grace met the parents of many of her students. She met the cousins and siblings of people she already knew. She got into a long conversation with Harry Lance's sister Lorraine about the difficulty of knitting cables with light-colored yarn. She ended up in a good-natured argument with Connor Ankkonisdoy's Uncle Geoff about the merits of Jack Kerouac. She astonished the hell out of Arthur's sister Ruth when she mentioned in passing that Natasha taught her to make babka—apparently Natasha guarded that recipe like a dragon with its gold. She promised Brigitte Yidineeltot—the mother of two of her students, aunt to several others, and cousin to her coworker Roger—that she could borrow a copy of *The Cloud Roads*.

Jess greeted a tall, dark-eyed woman with a hug. "Aunt Meredith, this is Grace Rossi. Grace, this is my aunt, Meredith Kinoyit." She grinned and added, "Caleb's mom."

"You know my Caleb?" Meredith asked with a warm smile, shaking Grace's hand.

"We're neighbors." Grace pointed upstairs. "Do you live in Longtooth?"

Meredith shook her head. "I'm closer to Eagle Ridge."

It surprised Grace how many people had come all the way from Eagle Ridge, and the even more distant villages of Kiyeedza and Daghukkoda. The roads connecting the Valley's towns and villages were unpaved, and often impassable in the winter. Even in good conditions, the winding drive from Eagle Ridge to Longtooth would take nearly three hours. But Arctic winters were long and dark, and Grace supposed a three-hour drive was worth getting out of the house and having a little fun.

"Are you the new English teacher?" Meredith asked.

Grace nodded. "How did you know?"

Meredith shrugged. "The Valley's small, and news travels fast." Her tone was casual, but her eyes were intent. She searched Grace's face for a moment, her own face unreadable. "Well, welcome to the Valley, Grace."

"Thank you. It was nice meeting you."

Jess pressed her on through the crowd. By the time Grace made it to the guests of honor—Roland and Linnea—she'd met just about everyone in the room, and made her way through two very full glasses of wine. She gave Roland and Linnea her heartfelt congratulations.

She and Jess drifted back to the periphery of the room.

"I don't *hate* crowds," Jess shouted, "but I'm not in love

with these giant parties. There's no room to move and having a conversation is impossible over all the noise."

"What?" Grace shouted.

Jess grinned and elbowed her.

The volume of the music rose, and bodies suddenly pressed in on Grace as the crowd backed away from the center of the room, leaving Roland and Linnea standing alone in a large circle. The previous song faded into silence, and then the opening of strains of *Unchained Melody* floated through the room. Linnea turned to Roland with a huge smile. He reached out for her hand, pulling her to his chest with a twirl.

Cheers and whistles traveled through the crowd. Roland and Linnea danced together in slow circles, so focused on each other that the rest of the world may as well have not existed. Grace watched them and felt that strange little crack in her chest fracture just a little wider. *I want that*, she thought wistfully.

As the song went on, other couples joined them, until the center of the room was filled with slowly revolving dancers. Grace saw Harry and Joanne, Arthur and Natasha, and dozens of others happily swaying in each others' arms. When *Unchained Melody* ended, half the couples drifted off the dance floor. *Jim Dandy* came on, and the remaining dancers broke from the dreamy romance of slow-dancing into the kind of barroom swing she'd only ever seen people from her grandparents' generation do. It was fast and enthusiastic and hectic. A distant memory played in her mind—Grandma and Grandpa tearing it up at a backyard party, both laughing helplessly after Grandpa accidentally twirled Grandma right into Aunt Debbie's rhododendrons.

"That's the smile of a woman who wants to dance." Max Freeman stood beside Grace, hand extended.

"I don't know how to dance like this," she shouted over the music, taking his hand anyway, following him to the edge of the dance floor.

"Just follow my lead." With a tug, he reeled her close to him. He caught her other hand, and away they went. Grace wasn't entirely sure *how* to follow, but Max managed to pull her into turns and spins, and she tried to match her footwork to his. She nearly kicked her shoes off three times. When the song ended, she was breathless and sweaty, but feeling light as a balloon. *Jim Dandy* bled into *Ain't Goin' Down*, and Harlan tapped Max on the shoulder, cutting in. Harlan guided her in an energetic two-step, wincing dramatically when she stepped on his feet.

"Your parents were really optimistic when they named you, huh?" he shouted over the music.

Grace swatted at him in mock offense, but her big smile ruined the effect. Harlan kept her for the next song, *Black Velvet*, laughing in delight when she managed to fall into step without being forcibly guided.

"Not too bad, *Grace*," Harlan told her as the last few chords played out.

The Way You Look Tonight came on, and Wade Evers appeared, stealing her for a slow dance.

Tamsyn Taaltsiyh claimed Wade from her after that, and Grace gratefully escaped the dance floor, desperate for a drink of water. Jess was standing at the drinks table, talking to Meredith Kinoyit, who watched the dancing with dark, unreadable eyes.

"Well, aren't you Miss Popular?" Jess turned to Grace

when she reached them. "Stealing all our men with your fancy footwork and your exotic midwestern charm."

"You figured me out," Grace told her, putting her empty water glass down and picking her wine back up. "First I'll seduce them with my inability to dance, and then I'll—*ack!*" A big body crashed into hers, sending her to the ground. She landed hard on her hands and knees. Her wine splattered across the floor like blood.

"*Caleb!*" Meredith shouted, sounding appalled.

"Grace! I'm so sorry!" Connor appeared at her side in an instant, hauling her to her feet. "Are you alright?"

"I'm fine," she said quickly, pushing her hair out of her face, straightening her sweater. She could feel dozens of eyes on her. Everyone was calling out to see if she was okay. She felt her face turning beet red. Her skin prickled with nervous sweat.

"Are you sure you're okay?" Connor pressed, stooping to peer into her averted face. Unconvinced murmurs surrounded her.

"Are you sure, honey?"

"You seem a little flushed."

"Why don't you—"

Natasha emerged through the crowd, an arm extended to Grace. "She'll be fine once you clodpoles learn to look where you're going. Come on, Gracie. You need a new drink." She looped her arm through Grace's and drew her away from Connor. Grace had to sidestep another male body and realized it was Caleb glowering down at her. His hair was mussed, but he still looked just as shockingly handsome as he had when he first walked in.

"Are you hurt?" he asked—but not in a nice tone. It was a

skeptical, slightly mocking question. As if Grace were making a scene for no reason. Like she enjoyed the attention. Anger flared hot and sharp. What she really wanted was for there to be *no scene at all*. She was embarrassed by the attention she was getting, and mortified by her helpless attraction to him, and here he was, being a giant tool bag about it all.

"I'm fine," she told him icily.

"Good," he said and turned away.

"Man, your social skills are stellar," she called after his retreating back. She couldn't help herself. The words just burst out of her. Hoots and chuckles followed her jibe, bright eyes bouncing between her and Caleb, drinks lifted to hide curling smiles.

He swiveled back to Grace with a sneer. "Swept *you* off your feet, didn't I?" His glance flicked to the spot where she'd been knocked down.

"I believe that was Connor," she corrected him archly.

Connor looked up, shoulders hunched sheepishly. "Uh, actually I tripped Caleb. He's the one who knocked you down."

Grace's gaze flew back to Caleb, who arched his eyebrows smugly.

Asshole.

"Oh no!" Natasha plucked at Grace's sweater. The formerly snow-white wool was splattered with red wine.

Grace stared down at it, keeping the despair out of her expression. "Well, that's ruined."

"No." Natasha pulled her behind the diner counter and through the kitchen's swinging door. "We can fix this."

The floor abruptly transitioned to hard gray tile as they wove between stainless steel kitchen racks crowded with massive cans and jugs of food. They swung past the walk-in cooler and freezer, and rounded a narrow stainless steel work table to reach the sink mounted on the back wall.

From a rack above the sink, Natasha plucked a big box of baking soda, a jug of white vinegar, and a bottle of blue dish soap.

"Sweater off," she commanded.

Grace shrugged out of it and handed it over. With only a thin camisole underneath, she was freezing. She wrapped her arms around herself and watched Natasha work. After dabbing a paste of soap and baking soda into all the stains, Natasha laid the sweater in the sink and poured vinegar over the whole mess. They watched it foam.

"I hope it works. I knitted that sweater myself." Grace's frustration boiled over. "Just what were they thinking, horsing around in a crowded room like that?"

Natasha looked smug. "Connor was going to ask you to dance. Caleb told him not to. It turned into a scuffle."

He was fighting over me? No. That couldn't be it. If Caleb wanted to dance with Grace, he could've cut in at any time. He just didn't want anybody else to dance with her. Was he protecting his friends from her?

Natasha bent down and began rinsing the stains. To Grace's surprise, the wine seemed to be coming out. After a moment, Natasha grimaced and straightened, fanning at her face.

"Are you okay?" Grace asked.

Natasha let out a snort. "Hot flashes," she grumbled. "I need air." She went to the back door and pushed it open. Cold air blasted in, raising goosebumps all over Grace's body. She huddled in on herself and shivered while Natasha stood on the threshold and sighed.

"Don't get old, Gracie. It's nothing but trouble."

"It can't be all bad," she said. "You get to watch your children grow up. See how their lives unfold. Guide the next generation."

Natasha looked back at her with a fond smile. "The Valley was lucky to get you." Beyond Natasha, shadows shifted at the edge of the forest. "You're a sweetheart, and I hope—"

One of the shadows detached from the others, racing forward with dizzying speed.

"Natasha!" Grace gasped, lunging for her at the same time the shadow descended on her. It ripped Natasha away from the doorway. With only a faint gasp of surprise, she was gone. The door slammed shut.

Grace bolted forward, wrenching the door open, scanning the darkness frantically. *There*—halfway to the tree line, two figures struggled against each other. The smaller of the two was being dragged inexorably towards the dark of the forest.

"Natasha!" Grace grabbed the nearest weapon—a meat cleaver from the magnetic knife strip—and sprinted after them, screaming her name from the very bottom of her lungs. "Natasha, hang on!"

The snow came up to Grace's thighs, forcing her to make awkward, lunging leaps. Another shadow flashed into sight on her left, coming from behind her. Grace gasped and stumbled—a wolf! It raced towards Natasha. Fear stabbed at her heart.

Two more wolves appeared after the first, closely chased by a fourth. They closed in on Natasha with unbeatable speed.

"Help!" Grace screamed, hoping someone in The Spruce

would hear her—realizing far, far too late that she should have called for help in the first place. But panic had overtaken her, and she'd leapt out the door without thinking.

The shadow that had taken Natasha straightened suddenly, and Grace realized it wasn't a wolf like she'd first thought—it was a man. A tall, powerfully built man who'd emerged from the forest without a coat, and who moved with inhuman speed.

At the sight of four wolves bearing down on him, the man dropped his hold on Natasha. The dark of the night seemed to condense around him, distorting his shape until Grace wasn't certain anymore that it was a man. With that same alarming speed, the shadow leapt to Grace. She slid to a halt, falling backwards into the snow. Time seemed to slow as she watched the shadow close in on her, reaching for her with hands made of midnight.

Out of nowhere, another wolf appeared, leaping in front of Grace and intercepting the shadow creature. They crashed together and landed hard, kicking up snow as they rolled. Both figures broke apart, and then the wolf lunged. Moonlight flashed over his silvery pelt, his bared fangs, and Grace realized she recognized him—it was the same big silver wolf she'd seen that night through the dining room windows. Vicious snarls rent the air as he lunged at the shadow again and again, sinking his fangs in and tearing away strips of fabric and flesh.

Grace scrambled to her feet, the cleaver still clutched in her hand. The shadow twisted and feinted, surged and fell back, landing a blow against the wolf that sent the animal sprawling. Blood sprayed the snow, vivid and steaming. The shadow straightened—suddenly in the shape of a man again. The moonlight flashed over his face as he turned to look at Grace.

Her heart stopped. A scream boiled in her throat, but she couldn't make a sound.

Alex.

Three more wolves raced in from behind Grace, leaping at him. Snarls and howls surrounded her. Just as quickly as he'd appeared, the shadow man with Alex's face condensed back into shapeless darkness. It fled from the wolves, racing over the snow with impossible speed. The wolves gave chase, also impossibly fast. The shadow disappeared into the darkness of the forest, and the wolves plunged after it.

Grace was alone again. The sound of her own breathing abraded her ears. She turned to where she'd last seen Natasha—there, still surrounded by wolves. She began running.

"Grace!" She heard a voice behind her. "Grace, stop!"

She glanced back. Jess was running to her, closing the distance between them with ease. Adam and Elena sprinted past her, racing towards Natasha and the wolves.

"Here!" Grace called to them, waving the cleaver frantically. "For the wolves!"

"The wolves won't hurt them." Jess reached her side. She grabbed Grace's weapon arm and carefully wrestled her to a stop. They were similarly sized, but Jess was far stronger than Grace. "Come on, Grace, it's going to be alright. I need you to come back inside with me."

"But—" Grace tugged against Jess's hold, twisting to look back. Arthur Freeman had Natasha scooped into his arms. Where had he come from? And... "Why is Arthur naked?" Grace asked faintly, letting Jess take the cleaver from her.

"Shh, come on," Jess soothed. "It's minus twenty and you're out here in a camisole and ballet shoes."

"I lost my shoes," Grace told her dumbly, allowing herself to be led back to the kitchen door. "They came off in the snow."

"Well, I hope they weren't expensive. You're probably not going to find them until spring." Jess got her back to the kitchen door. She tried to turn for another look at Natasha, but Jess hustled her inside. A crowd had gathered in the kitchen, watching the mayhem.

"Out of the way," Jess ordered. She led Grace through the parted crowd. "Someone get blankets. And someone fill hot water bottles." Grace was vaguely aware of bodies hustling to obey. Jess brought her into the dining room and pushed her to sit on the stone hearth in front of the fireplace.

A moment later, Arthur emerged with Natasha still cradled in his arms. Someone had draped a blanket over his shoulders.

"Put me down, kochanie," Natasha said weakly. "I can walk."

Arthur ignored her, his face a grim mask. He sank down next to Grace at the hearth, cradling Natasha in his lap and staring down at her with heart-rending grief on his face.

"Arthur," Natasha said softly, freeing one hand to cup his jaw. He shuddered, eyes closing as he leaned into her touch.

Grace felt like a voyeur, witnessing the raw emotionality between them. At the same time, the crack in her chest opened even wider. She rubbed at her sternum and looked away from them.

Jess reappeared with a heap of towels. She draped a few over Natasha. Arthur fussed with them, rearranging them with grave particularity. Jess knelt in front of Grace and began wrapping her bare feet with towels. Grace hissed as she realized they'd been warmed somehow. What was probably pleasantly warm to Jess felt like molten lava to Grace's frozen feet.

Connor came from the back hall, his arms loaded with blankets. He draped one around Grace's shoulders, threw another across her lap.

"She's not shivering," he said to Jess, concerned.

"They should change out of those wet clothes immediately," somebody said.

"Good luck prying Tasha out of Arthur's grip," somebody else said dryly. Nobody laughed.

"Grace, what did you see?" Jess asked.

Alex's face flashed into her mind, stark and handsome and terrifyingly familiar. *No*, she told herself. *Impossible*. It was a trick of the light—a trick of her terrified mind. It couldn't have been him. It couldn't have even been human, whatever it was.

"No questions," Arthur growled. "Not until Margaret gets back."

Grace looked up then, scanning the crowd. Margaret, Caleb, Harry, Elena, and Adam were gone. Were they outside? She had only seen Elena and Adam out there, and they hadn't been wearing coats.

"Ow," Grace hissed as sensation began to return to her feet in the form of a sharp, needling feeling beneath her skin. A small tremor ran down her spine. It seemed to spread slowly outward until her whole body was trembling.

Jess took note of the change, nodding with satisfaction. She lifted one of Grace's feet and examined it closely. "Doesn't look too bad," she said. "I think you're going to have a little frostbite, but you'll keep your toes." She stood up and helped Grace to her feet. "You need to change into some dry clothes." She eyed the thin camisole. "*Warm*, dry clothes. Come on."

Jess led her to the stairs. Her feet tingled painfully beneath her weight.

"Arthur," Grace heard Connor say coaxingly. "You know she doesn't run as hot as we do. You need to let go of her so she can get into dry clothes."

Arthur growled—literally *growled*—but when Grace glanced back, he was carrying Natasha down the back hall that led to their living quarters.

Back in her own room, Grace was shivering so hard, her teeth were clacking together like castanets. Jess helped her sort her clumsy, useless limbs into the appropriate places so that she could pull off her wet jeans, and step into long underwear and thick fleece pajama bottoms. She slid Grace's arms into the sleeves of a thermal shirt and pulled on a heavy sweatshirt over that.

As Grace struggled to pull on some thick wool socks, a sequence of images flashed through her mind. *Four wolves racing towards Natasha. Only three humans present—Adam, Elena, and Jess. Then, out of nowhere, Arthur at Natasha's side.*

Where had the wolves even come from? Behind her had been The Spruce's back wall, stretching nearly the entire length of the block. The only thing that made sense was that the wolves had come *from* The Spruce. And where had Arthur come from? There'd been four wolves to begin with. How many had been there after Arthur appeared?

She stared at the scene in her memory. An absurd suspicion took hold of her.

No. No way.

She'd been freezing half to death, jacked on adrenaline,

and terrified out of her mind. Her memory of events was not exactly reliable.

"Grace?" Jess crouched beside her, looking concerned. She'd frozen with one sock halfway on. "Are you okay?"

Grace looked into Jess's face, looking for any sign that she was hiding something from her—hiding something really, *really* bizarre.

Not possible.

Grace shook her head. "I'm fine."

She finished pulling her socks on, and Jess herded her to the bed. While Jess was heaping blankets on top of her, a knock sounded at the door.

Linnea Teague came in, bearing a tray loaded with supplies—hot broth in a mug, a hot water bottle, a thermometer, and a bottle of painkillers. "Harlan's with Natasha right now, but he said he'll check in on Grace in a little bit," Linnea said, setting the tray on the bedside table. "We need to keep her warm and give her aspirin." She lifted the hot water bottle and slid it beneath the blankets. "Don't put your feet directly on the hot water bottle. Harlan said it could make the tissue damage worse."

Grace nodded complacently, still shivering.

Linnea and Jess looked down on her, like two concerned farmers with a horse they didn't want to shoot.

"It's good she's shivering," Linnea murmured.

"Mm-hmm," Jess agreed.

"Get her to drink the broth while it's still hot," Linnea said. "I'm going to go see if Margaret's back yet."

Jess sat with Grace, holding the mug of broth so that she wouldn't dump it all over herself, and all but pouring it down the back of her throat.

Grace's shivering had begun to ease when there was

another knock at the door. Jess got up and let Margaret inside. Margaret was hastily dressed, in completely different clothing than she'd been wearing at the party. She had on sweatpants that were way too big for her, a pair of unlaced boots, and an oversized t-shirt that said *"What happens in Vegas..."*

"How is she?" Margaret asked Jess. They both looked at Grace.

"Fully cognizant," Grace said impatiently. She was tired of everyone speaking over her head.

"Gracie." Margaret came and sat on the edge of the bed, looking down at her with such warmth that Grace instantly forgot her irritation. "How are you?"

"Fine," she said. "Ready to sleep." It had to be well past midnight by now.

Margaret smoothed the edge of the top comforter, tucking it snugly against her. "Of course you are. But before you go to sleep, I need to know exactly what you saw. What happened."

Alex's face flashed into her mind again, and she flinched.

"Grace?" Margaret laid a hand on her shoulder, her face lined with concern.

Not possible, Grace told herself. Her mind was simply substituting a terror she couldn't understand with one that she understood all too well. She pushed away thoughts of Alex and tried to find the words to explain what she'd seen. Haltingly, uncertainly, she described the shadow that had attacked Natasha, and the sudden appearance of so many wolves. "I have to be hallucinating," Grace told her, half-hoping Margaret would assure her that she was.

Instead, Margaret looked grimly resolved. She nodded

and looked over to Jess. "That square up with what you saw?"

"Yeah. I mean... what little I did see." She shrugged.

Grace's eyes drifted shut as Jess and Margaret continued to speak in low tones. Sleep tugged at her, blurring their voices into a meaningless hum. Exhausted, she let herself slip into the darkness.

CHAPTER 18

A long creak startled Grace into half-awake confusion. She blinked into the darkness of her room just as her door clicked shut. How long had she been asleep? It felt like only a second had passed, but her lights were all turned out and the hot water bottle at her feet was no longer hot.

"How is she?" Caleb's low voice came from the hall, just outside Grace's door.

"She'll be fine," Margaret answered. "She's sleeping."

Grace expected to hear the sound of their departing footsteps, but instead, there was a prolonged silence.

Caleb broke it first. "Tougher than she looks."

"Maybe." Another silence. Then Margaret spoke again, "I worry we haven't done right by her."

"You mean me."

"I mean all of us. She's been hurting since she got here. We invited her here, asked her to live with us, teach our children, care for us... what's she gotten in return for it?"

"We look out for her, just like any—"

"You ever notice she never talks about her parents? That she gets embarrassed when Natasha mothers her? That she doesn't know how to take a compliment? That's a woman who's not used to being taken care of by anybody. She's not going to take the risk of putting herself out there—because it hasn't paid off in the past."

Caleb said nothing.

"She knows she's being held at arm's length," Margaret said softly. "And we're all waiting for her to take the final step. But why should she trust us, when we haven't trusted her?"

"What are you suggesting?"

"I'm not even sure." She sighed. "Just that something needs to give with her. And I think the give is going to be on our end."

"You want to tell her."

"Not yet. I need to think. Talk to some people." Her voice hardened a bit. "And in the meantime, you better fix your attitude. I still claim wardship over her, even if Natasha's been staking out my claim, and if I hear you've been—"

"I know, Margaret. I told you I was wrong about her."

"You were wrong about yourself, too, pup."

"No, I admitted the wolf wanted her. But—"

"You're full of shit. The man wanted her as much as the wolf."

A low growl rumbled.

"Fine, lie to yourself."

The growl faded into a sigh. "Mags. Look what happens with my family and their mates. Look at the mistake *I* almost made..." He trailed off into silence.

"Honey, both your mom and your sister were young—

maybe too young—and they trusted the wrong people. You missed warning signs you maybe should have picked up on. It happens to the best of us. But age brings wisdom. And you're not exactly a puppy anymore. Have a little faith in yourself."

The sound of their voices, so low and steady, lulled Grace in and out of sleep. As soon as she heard the words, she forgot what was said. She drifted off again, unsettled and confused, but mostly just exhausted.

"I miss you, Grace."

She opened her eyes to see Alex sitting on the railing outside her window, staring at her glumly.

She sat up, fighting her way from beneath a mound of blankets. "I told you to leave me alone." There was an embarrassing quaver in her voice.

"Don't say that. You never even gave me a chance. I was going to give you something wonderful, Grace. And you just threw it away."

"I don't want anything from you."

"I want to give you *eternity*. I want to be with you forever."

She shook her head. She tried to look away from the piercing intensity of his beautiful eyes, but she couldn't bring herself to do it.

"Alex—"

"Come with me, Grace. I'll take care of you."

She tried to tell him no, but she couldn't make a noise. Her entire body trembled with the need to get out of bed, to go outside, to find Alex.

"Come on, love," Alex coaxed.

Grace slid her legs out of bed but clung to the edge of the mattress with white-knuckled fists.

"That's it. Now stand up."

She tried to scream, but all that emerged was a whimper. She pushed off of the bed.

"There's my girl. Come on, Grace. Out the door. Come out to me."

On shaking legs, she walked to the door. Screams died in her throat as pathetic whines. She fought to turn back, to resist his command, but her legs carried her into the hall.

"Please no," she begged, but the words emerged only as hissed breaths. Hot tears streamed down her cheeks. She reached the top of the stairs. Her feet shuffled on the hard-wood planks as she fought not to descend. But her will was no match for Alex's. She took one wobbly step, and then another.

She tried to take a third step, but she was trapped in place. Her feet slid uselessly over the smooth floorboards, bringing her nowhere.

"Come outside, Grace. Come to me." Alex's voice echoed in her mind at the same time as another man's voice sounded in her ear.

"Wake up. Grace. Stop fighting me—*ouch!* Grace, wake up. Grace. *Grace!*"

She blinked and, suddenly, there was Caleb. His big hands had her shoulders pinned against the stairwell wall.

"Caleb?" The tension immediately ebbed from her body, the compulsion releasing her.

Caleb loomed over her, holding her in place. His face, so starkly, ruggedly appealing, was close enough to hers that she could see each individual eyelash framing his dark, hooded eyes.

She reached up and pressed her palm to his cheek, reassuring herself that he was actually there, that she wasn't still trapped in a dream. He sighed, his eyes falling shut.

"You're here," she rasped through a throat sore from trying to scream. His skin was hot against her palm, his beard coarse.

His eyes opened. They were pale as amber.

"Are you a werewolf?" she asked.

Caleb said nothing, just watched her.

"Tell me I'm imagining things," Grace pleaded. "There's no such thing as werewolves. Tell me I'm recovering from a traumatic—"

He kissed her. His mouth was hot and hard. His beard scraped against her skin. Grace slid her hand from his cheek to clutch the back of his neck. His arms encircled her, hauling her body flush against his.

"You're imagining things," he growled against her mouth. His tongue traced the seam of her lips, and she opened for him, tasted him. After a long, deep kiss, he broke away. "You're recovering from a traumatic experience." And then he was kissing her again. His lips trailed hotly along her jaw, her neck, her throat. "There's no such thing as werewolves," he said, before taking her mouth again, using his big body to pin her against the wall.

Once again, his heat sank into her, melting the ice, turning it into steam. Grace clutched him, pressing her body against his. She needed that heat, needed him to burn away the cold forever. He nipped her bottom lip, her jaw, her throat. He bit down on the muscle between her shoulder and her neck, the pressure just shy of really hurting.

"Wait—" Grace gasped.

His teeth released her, and she felt the touch of his tongue soothing the spot he'd bitten.

"Hang on—" she pushed at his shoulders.

He drew back, watching her with that unusual golden gaze.

Grace frowned. "You don't like me."

Caleb grinned. "Aw, Gracie, come on. You can figure out werewolves, but you can't figure *this* out?"

"You were a jerk tonight."

His smile faded. "I—" He hesitated. His jaw clenched with resolve. "I was jealous," he said flatly. "You were dancing with every man in the room, but you ran from me like—"

"You make me nervous," she blurted.

His wicked grin returned. "Oh, really?" He bent forward suddenly, catching her behind the knees, and scooped her up into his arms.

"Ack! Caleb!"

He carried her down the hall.

"What are you—where are we—"

He carried her past her room, to his own. He nudged his door open with his foot and brought her inside.

"*Your room?*"

"Relax." He dropped her onto his bed like an armful of laundry. "I'm not going to do anything to you. You need to sleep. And I need you to do it where I can keep an eye on you."

"Why?"

The golden gleam in his eyes was receding, returning to his usual midnight gaze. "Because apparently you're a sleep-walker. And that's a real liability when there's a predator roaming around." He caught the edge of the comforter and flipped it over her. "Get some sleep. I won't touch you."

He settled into the armchair next to his dresser, sinking deeply against the backrest and toeing his boots off. Somehow, they'd gone from making out against the wall to some kind of sexless sleepover. As she settled back against his pillows, Grace became aware of his scent surrounding her. Her face burned pleasantly where his beard had rasped against her. He was on the other side of the room, but she could almost feel the warmth of his body enveloping her.

He watched her shift beneath the covers, his gaze feverishly intent. She heard a sound so low, she couldn't be sure she wasn't imagining it—a rolling growl, resonating deep in his chest. When she looked back up at him, the growl died away.

"Go to sleep, Grace," he commanded. His voice rasped over her skin like calloused hands. A delicious shiver chased up her spine. She turned away from his heated gaze before she did something really stupid.

Before she knew it, the comfort of his scent and the warmth of his bed had lulled her. She fell asleep.

CHAPTER 19

Grace woke up the next morning in her own bed. She lifted her t-shirt to her face, inhaling deeply. There was no scent of Caleb. Her cheeks and neck were cool and smooth, with no beard burn. Her door was locked from the inside.

Had she dreamt it all? Alex *and* Caleb? The werewolf conversation?

As soon as the word "werewolf" crossed her mind, she laughed at herself. Of course it had been a dream. If Caleb kissing her and bringing her into his room weren't fantastical enough, the absurdity of *werewolves* certainly brought reality crashing down.

Damn. She slid out of bed, smiling ruefully. Even in her dreams, she wasn't getting laid. Dream Caleb had been a perfect gentleman, dozing in his chair while Grace slept in his bed. In the dream, his room had been tidy and sparse, with a green and blue quilt on the bed. Unlike the irregular shape of her room, his had been a perfect rectangle. Just like hers, the ledge below his window was stuffed with books. In the dark, she hadn't been able to read most of the spines, but she'd noticed a copy of Julius Caesar's *The Gallic Wars* and a big hardcover entitled *Montezuma*. Clearly, the sight of him reading had left a big imprint on her subconscious.

When Grace made her way down to the dining room, half of the town seemed to be packed in there. Every head swiveled towards her. She froze in the doorway, mid-step.

"Alright, alright," Harry Lance's voice cut through the buzz of conversation, impatient and gruff. "Leave the girl alone. She just wants some breakfast." He leaned away from the counter, waving her over. "Come on, Grace. Get some food in your belly."

Was she still dreaming? Was that really *Harry* being protective of *her?*

There was an open seat at the counter between Jess and Wade. It had to have been intentionally saved for Grace, judging by the crowd in the dining room. Every other seat was occupied, with spare, mismatched chairs having been pulled out of storage and crowded around tables.

"Hey, Grace." Jess nudged her, shoulder to shoulder.

"Morning," Wade said, giving her forearm a friendly squeeze.

She hadn't been sitting for even thirty seconds when a deep male bass rumbled behind her, "Grace."

She turned to see Arthur. Before she could speak, he pulled her into a lung-crushing hug.

"Thank you," he said hoarsely, crushing her even tighter. "You saved her."

"No I didn't," Grace wheezed. "I couldn't get to her."

Arthur released her, only to grab her shoulders. Holding her at arm's length, he looked fiercely into her eyes. "If it hadn't been for you, we'd have lost Tasha." He looked stricken. "You were brave and selfless and I owe you my life."

"Arthur, no you don't," Grace mumbled, embarrassed.

"I do." He held her gaze for a moment, then clapped her on the shoulders and released her. Natasha emerged from the kitchen's swinging door and Arthur hurtled over the counter with astonishing grace, pulled her into his arms, and kissed her deeply. After a second of stiffened surprise, Natasha melted into his arms. When at last they broke apart, Arthur bent his head and bit at her shoulder playfully.

Hoots and wolf-whistles went up and down the length of the dining room. Natasha blushed like a schoolgirl, swatting at Arthur's chest. "Go on, you," she told him with an unconvincing attempt at sternness. "The water heater is still leaking."

He flashed her a grin that nearly made *Grace* blush, and disappeared down the hall.

Natasha smoothed her hair, looking at a loss for just a second before she noticed Grace sitting at the counter. "Gracie! You need breakfast." She pushed into the kitchen and reemerged a minute later with a heaping plate of eggs and fried caribou steak.

As Grace ate, people drifted over, one by one. They greeted her with little touches to the shoulder, squeezes on the arm. She'd gotten accustomed to those friendly touches from certain people, but it was strange to receive them from so many others. There was a vaguely ceremonial feel to the flow of people, touching her, greeting her, then leaving The Spruce. By the time she finished her breakfast, the dining room was mostly empty. Harry, Wade, Jess, Harlan, and Eric were the only remainders. She glanced at all the empty chairs.

On the far side of the dining room, the rear door opened. Natasha's son Max stepped in.

Max spotted Grace and crossed the room immediately. He caught her by the arms, just as his father had done, and gazed down at her with grave intensity. "I didn't get the chance to thank you last night."

"There's nothing to thank me for. Really. Anybody—"

"Not anybody," Max objected. "You. *You* risked your life to save my mom. Thank you, Grace." He squeezed her arms and released her.

She suddenly noticed Caleb had entered behind him, dressed for the cold just as Max was.

"Oh. Caleb. Hi," she said faintly, suddenly overwhelmed by the memories of last night's too-real dream.

"Morning, Grace. You alright?"

She nodded. "You were out searching this morning?"

"We were out all night," Max told her. "Caleb and I just got in. Could use a meal and some sleep."

He'd been out all night. Any hope she'd harbored that last night *hadn't* been a dream was instantly quashed.

"Sleep sounds good right now," Caleb agreed, looking past Grace.

She swallowed, shoving away the disappointment. "Did you find anything?" she asked them both.

Max and Caleb exchanged another glance, this one grim. "Just prints that led nowhere," Max said, disgusted. "No scent trail."

"No *scent trail?*" Grace echoed suspiciously.

"Nothing for the dogs to pick up," Caleb explained.

"Oh. Right. Of course." She was truly going insane. She actually *wanted* Caleb to be a werewolf if it would mean that they'd kissed—that he'd spent the night guarding her. She was pathetic and delusional. "Well... get some rest."

Grace spent the rest of the day sitting in the dining room and catching up on grading. Arthur hovered near Natasha all day. If she was in the kitchen, he needed to fix something on one of the faucets in there. If she was in the dining room, he needed to tighten the screws on the chairs and tables. She'd walked down the hall towards the short-stay rooms, and Arthur had dropped his wrench and cracked his head on the table before bounding after her.

Other people came and went, getting meals from Natasha, and dropping off bits of news—all of it inconclusive. They hadn't found anything, nobody saw anything, the tracks just vanished, and there was no scent trail. Every time somebody new came to report, Grace couldn't help but replay the events of the previous night. Hectic memories flashed in her mind, spliced together in a confusing, incomplete reel. Natasha being taken. A knife in Grace's hand. So many wolves appearing from nowhere. Moonlight gleaming over the shadow attacker, revealing...Alex.

She flinched and shoved it all from her mind. That way lay madness.

CHAPTER 20

After the subdued tension of Sunday, Monday seemed largely back to normal. A late February snowfall was drifting down in big, fat flakes. The dining room was filled with the usual hum of conversation and the clatter of plates. Except for Jess and Connor, the usual regulars were in the dining room when she went down for breakfast. Arthur was sitting at the counter, pretending not to be guarding Natasha. Grace took the seat next to him. Without lifting his gaze from where Natasha was fiddling with the coffee maker, he reached over and gave Grace's shoulder a brief squeeze.

"Morning, Arthur."

"Morning. You tell your family what happened?" he asked, picking up his cup of coffee.

"No." They wouldn't care. If Grace had been seriously hurt, they would've worried. But since she was fine, her mom would only be interested in hearing about the wolves, and her dad would just subside into one of his skeptical silences, the way he did whenever Grace had tried to tell him something bad had happened to her. It wasn't that he thought she was a liar. It was just that he was so low-key and unexcitable that he found it hard to believe that disasters and traumas actually did happen to people. Or so her mom said.

"You don't want them to worry?" Arthur asked.

"They wouldn't be worried." She spoke before she realized how odd it would sound to someone like Arthur, whose love for his family radiated from him like a constant, calming glow.

He frowned at her. "Why wouldn't they worry?"

Grace shrugged off the uncomfortable heaviness that had settled over her. "They're pretty laid-back, I guess."

Arthur's thick, salt-and-pepper eyebrows climbed nearly to his hairline. "Laid-back?"

She shrugged again. Natasha appeared with a coffee carafe, and Grace tried to shift the conversation to her. "How are you doing?" she asked.

Natasha's expression turned thunderous. "Nobody is allowed to ask me that question anymore! I am perfectly fine!"

Grace froze with her hand halfway to her coffee mug. "Oh. Uh. Glad to hear it."

Arthur hid a grin with a sip of coffee.

Natasha softened as she searched Grace's face. "And how are you, then?"

"No fair. You can ask me, but I can't ask you?"

"A mother's privilege."

"I think that only applies to your own children."

Natasha gave her an impatient look. "I am your Alaskan mother."

"Sounds like she could use one," Arthur muttered.

Grace flushed. "I'm fine," she said firmly, to both of them.

She finished her breakfast without any more questions about her emotional state or her family issues. On the way out, she caught sight of Caleb sitting at a table with Harry Lance. He wasn't as polished as he'd been the night of the party, but the haircut and beard trim were very much in evidence, and they were doing the same things to Grace as they had two nights ago. Unfortunately, she had to walk past his table to get to the door. She straightened her shoulders and made herself go. As she passed by, he didn't so much as glance in her direction.

Harry, on the other hand, said, "Morning, Grace."

Grace faltered, caught off guard by his pleasantness. "Oh —uh, good morning, Harry." She flicked a glance at Caleb. He was staring out the window, resolutely ignoring her.

Well fine, then.

She went out to the garage, started her truck, and headed to school. When she got to her classroom, she flipped on the light and froze in the doorway. Her desk was covered—absolutely *covered*—in blue yarn. Everything on top of her desk was strapped down by crisscrossing wefts of yarn—her stapler, her ceramic pen holder, the school laptop, her lamp. All the drawers were wrapped shut.

Grace stared at the mess with a slow smile spreading across her face. Cursing on a breath that came perilously close to a giggle, she crossed the room and began peeling the yarn off her desk. When her first period freshman started drifting in, she had a massive heap of tangled blue yarn sitting on her desktop, and she was trying to extract the laptop cord from it without making the tangle worse.

"Uh, Ms. Rossi? What's this?" Leo Daaldinh asked.

"The work of a madman." She gathered the whole heap and stuffed it into her bag. "Don't worry, it's not for class."

The day passed so slowly, she thought she'd scream. Every time she glanced towards her bag and saw all that blue yarn overflowing the top, she thought of Caleb. She wondered when he'd done it. What he'd been thinking. Had he been smiling? Laughing? Is that why he wouldn't look at her this morning?

When her last class emptied out, she gathered her things and all but sprinted to her truck. Snow had been falling steadily all day, and she had to put the Jimmy into four-wheel-drive to make it out of the parking lot. Once back at The Spruce, she found Arthur in the dining room, repairing a tabletop he'd cracked on Sunday.

"Where's Caleb? I saw his truck in the garage."

Arthur shrugged. "He was helping with the searches this afternoon. He might still be out there. Otherwise, he's probably in his room."

Grace turned and bounded up the stairs. One flight. Two flights. She hit the landing on silent feet and stalked down the hallway. She dropped her bag by her door, fished the heap of yarn out, and then pounded on Caleb's door.

A second later, it opened, revealing a sleep-mussed Caleb. Grace threw the yarn against his chest. He caught it, staring down in confusion. After a second, he looked up, comprehension in his eyes, something wicked in his smile.

"Where'd all this come from?" he asked innocently.

Before she even knew she was moving, Grace was on him. He met her halfway, hauling her body hard against his as she wrapped her legs around his waist. She grabbed a fistful of hair and yanked his head back. And then they were kissing—really kissing. It was as good as it had been in her dream. Better, because this time it was real. The taste of him, the touch of his lips, the feel of his big hands running down her back—it was all real. His heat sank into her like a series of timed explosions, making her hotter and hungrier and more out of her mind with each stroke of his tongue, each nip from his teeth, each squeeze of his hands.

Caleb kicked his door shut and carried Grace into his room. Suddenly, there was the bed, and she was on her back with Caleb's big body pinning her down. His mouth trailed fire from her ear to her throat. She wrapped her arms around his neck, pulling him closer. She twisted her fingers into his hair and tugged, making him growl. He nipped her throat and she gasped, hips arching against his. He brought his mouth back to hers, kissing her with hungry desperation.

It was overwhelming. Grace hadn't been touched this way in so long—hadn't felt desire like this for even longer. She felt every single sensation at once—the firm, hot press of his lips and tongue. The scrape of his beard. The weight of his body. The strength of his hands and arms. The rise of his erection, pressed against her hip. Instinctively, she shifted, wrapping her legs around his waist, pressing the needy hot core of herself against the hardness of him. He worked his hips, thrusting that rigid length exactly where she needed it. White-hot pleasure lanced through her, and she tore her mouth from his with a sharp gasp. Caleb sagged against her, panting for breath. The yarn was caught between them, a hopelessly tangled mess.

Still clinging to him with both arms and legs, Grace lay still for a moment, catching her breath. Caleb's room was dim, but something about it seemed strange. Struggling to comprehend through the fog of lust, she looked around. Unlike the awkward L-shape of her room, with the slanted ceilings, Caleb's room was a perfect rectangle, with normal ceilings. He had a ledge beneath his window like she did, and he'd filled it with books, like she had. A big one at the end caught her eye, *Montezuma*.

Why did that seem familiar?

"Grace?" Caleb must've sensed her confusion. He eased off of her. The yarn stretched between them, tangled around both of their arms, looped around several of the buttons on Caleb's flannel. Grace looked down and saw his quilt bunched beneath them. A blue and green pattern.

It hit her like a gong—the dream. His room had looked exactly like this in her dream. *Exactly* like this.

Caleb searched her face. "Shit," he swore softly, pushing away from her entirely. He sat on the edge of the bed and tried to untangle the yarn from his shirt.

Grace sat up, looked around his room again. There was his dresser, shaped exactly how she'd dreamed. And the chair he'd slept in that night, while she'd taken his bed.

"It wasn't a dream," she said. They'd kissed, and he'd tried to make her think it'd never happened. The dream that wasn't a dream replayed in her mind.

His hands all over her, his lips on hers.

"Wait—hang on—you don't like me."

Caleb's unrepentant grin. "Aw, Gracie, come on. You can figure out werewolves, but you can't figure this out?"

Oh god. She'd been so pathetically obsessed with the kiss that she'd forgotten what had started this all.

He was a fucking werewolf. They all were. That's how the wolves had come from nowhere that night. That's how Arthur had suddenly appeared, naked, in the distance. That was why nobody wanted her to know about Caitlin's "health condition." It was why Caleb and Jess did that sniffing thing.

It was why Natasha was feeding wolves at the kitchen door. And it was why the wolves came into town so often. Because they *lived here.*

Grace shifted to look at him. Was she insane? She had to be. And yet... "Why did you make me think I dreamt that?"

Caleb said nothing, searching her face with a pained expression.

"Please, Caleb. I won't say anything to anybody. Just tell me I'm not crazy."

He wouldn't speak. Wouldn't even look at her. He sat on the edge of the bed, staring down at his hands.

She got to her feet, pulling the yarn off of her arms and tossing it on his bed. "Fine. Don't tell me."

She left.

Grace stood in front of her first class the next day thinking, *werewolves. Each and every one of you is a werewolf.* Or were they? Linnea had said Caitlin's "condition" ran in their family. So maybe only some of the locals were werewolves. But even if that were the case, the rest of them obviously knew about it. How else would the whole class have known to react to Caitlin's episode so immediately?

The fourteen-year-old werewolves stared back at Grace, clearly wondering what the hell was up. She'd been silent for too long. Jarring back into motion, she cleared her throat. "Okay, so yesterday we left off with..."

Every hour, every class, she wrestled with the same negotiation between reality and logic. *Werewolves. I'm teaching werewolves how to identify metaphors.* Even when she was speaking to the class, a constant stream of questions was flowing through the back of her mind. How many of them were werewolves? Did they retain wolf-like qualities when in human form? More acute hearing? A craving for raw meat? She'd already seen Caleb, Jess, and Elena smelling the air, and suddenly remembered Connor telling her *"You smell like him."* An uncomfortable suspicion crossed her mind—could her students smell Caleb on her? She'd showered this morning, so hopefully his scent was gone.

"Ms. Rossi?" Mia Lance waved her hand around impatiently.

"Huh?" Grace realized she'd zoned out again. "Sorry, I was... What's your question, Mia?"

By the end of the day, she'd mostly come to terms with it. Maybe some of them were werewolves. Maybe all of them were. But they were still kids. They interacted with books just like anybody else did, they liked good stories just like anybody else.

Her last class ended and Daniel Gray—possible werewolf —hung back as the rest of the students filed out. He'd finished the last book Grace had loaned him, and set it on her desk.

"What did you think?" she asked, turning in her chair to shelve the book.

"It was good," Daniel answered with his usual reserve.

"Do you want the next book in the series?"

He shrugged, which Grace took as a no.

"Are you looking for something different, or something similar?" she asked, scanning the spines on her shelves. She'd figured out that Daniel was more likely to open up—just a little—if she wasn't looking at him, and if the conversation remained brisk.

"I want something..." He hesitated, and Grace resisted

the urge to turn to face him. "Um... something where the parents are gone."

She nodded casually. Her emotional-landmine radar was pinging, but she kept her focus on the book spines. "The orphan trope is pretty common in young adult fiction, I've got quite a few—"

"Not an orphan," Daniel cut in. "The parents just...aren't there."

The radar went crazy. Keeping her tone even, Grace said, "Well, that narrows it down. Give me a second here." She pulled a couple books and finally turned to face Daniel. Keeping her focus on the books, her face impassive, she laid them out. "Have you read *A Wrinkle in Time?*"

"Yeah, a long time ago for school."

She picked up *The Golden Compass*. Her juniors had been reading it earlier this year, and it was a little more dense than what Daniel had read so far, but he'd been mowing through books at a breakneck pace, so she decided to give it a try. "This one takes a little while to get going, but once you get into it, it's amazing. It's set in a world like our own, but just a little different. Everybody has an animal familiar—" Grace almost choked on her own words, but managed to keep it together. She cleared her throat. "They have animal familiars. And the main character *thinks* she's an orphan, but... well, it's a good story."

"Sure." Daniel took it and slid it into his backpack. "Thanks, Ms. Rossi."

She watched him walk out. When the sound of his footsteps faded away, she got up and made her way to Margaret's office. Margaret looked up when she knocked on the door, phone pressed to her ear, and gestured for Grace to come in. Grace sank into one of the chairs across from Margaret's desk while she wrapped up her call.

"Well, of course," Margaret said impatiently to whoever was on the other end. "That goes without saying." She listened for a moment. "Okay. Keep me updated." She hung up. "Gracie. How are you?"

Is Margaret a werewolf, too? Grace remembered her change of clothes after the shadow attack, the way she called younger people "pup," and concluded that she definitely was.

"Uh, I have a question that maybe isn't my place to ask."

Margaret folded her hands together, regarding Grace for a moment over her desk. A heavy weight seemed to settle between them. "I can't guarantee I'll answer," she said. "But why don't you ask, anyway."

She thinks I'm going to ask about werewolves. She must've been wondering how much Grace had seen the night of the attack, how much she'd figured out. And if Caleb had spoken to her...

"It's about Daniel Gray."

Immediately, the heaviness faded. Margaret sat back, her expression softening. "Is everything okay?"

"I don't know. That's my question. Daniel's so much more reserved than the other kids. He has this...guardedness that he's too young for. He's been borrowing books, and today he asked me specifically for a book where the parents aren't *dead*, but are *gone*."

Margaret nodded. She was quiet for a moment, contemplative.

Grace steeled herself to be shut down with yet another "Valley business" dismissal. But instead, she said, "Daniel's father left him and his mother about a year ago. Left the Valley, left Alaska. Obviously, that's hard on a child."

Grace's stomach twisted. "Okay. That explains some things."

"Daniel's having a tough time right now, but he'll come through it. He has the entire Valley standing behind him. His mother's a little lost in grief right now, but she'll recover. The same thing happened to her mother, and Meredith came out the other side, whole and capable."

"Meredith Kinoyit?" Caleb's mother? Had Caleb been abandoned by his father?

Margaret's expression flattened. "Damn me. That wasn't my story to tell. I trust you'll keep that knowledge to yourself."

"Of course I will."

"I know." She contemplated Grace for a moment. "How have you been doing, Grace?"

Grace shrugged, uncomfortable. "I'm fine. Same as always."

"After the attack?"

She laughed. Between Caleb and Daniel, she'd almost forgotten about it. "Oh, that. I'm..." Alex's face flashed into her mind again, and she somehow managed not to flinch. "I'm totally fine. No frostbite."

"No frostbite."

"Yep."

Margaret rested her chin on one hand, considering Grace. "You haven't asked much about that night."

Did she *want* Grace to ask about werewolves? "Nobody seems to have any answers," she said, observing Margaret's expression carefully, but Margaret betrayed nothing. Another silence stretched between them.

Margaret shifted, leaning back. "Does Longtooth feel like home to you?"

The change of topic caught Grace by surprise, and she didn't know how to answer. She didn't want to reveal too much. The crushing loneliness hadn't been quite so crushing lately, and she didn't want to think about it too much, for fear of reviving it.

"I don't know if…" Grace hesitated. Margaret watched patiently. "I don't know if anywhere has ever felt like *home*, you know? I've moved around a lot."

"Don't you have a hometown?"

"Yeah, but I don't want to live there."

"Even though your family is there?"

Grace shrugged. "I was only ever close to my grandma, and she died when I was sixteen." Her wedding ring was the only memento Grace had of her and it had been stolen by Alex.

"What about your parents?"

Grace shrugged again.

Margaret continued to watch her.

"They're not bad parents. They didn't abuse me or anything. We just…" She trailed off, trying to find the right words. "Some families aren't close."

Margaret considered that for a moment. "Grace," she began gently, "people need family. They don't have to be your blood relatives, but everybody needs people they can depend on, people who love them."

Grace said nothing. Her stomach was twisting again. Living in Longtooth, seeing the tightly interwoven community, the strong bonds between friends and family and lovers, made her acutely conscious of how little of that she had in her life.

"People here care about you a lot. If you wanted to make your life here, you'd be welcomed with open arms." Margaret paused meaningfully. "There are things about the Valley that we don't talk about with outsiders."

Werewolves, Grace's mind whispered. She said nothing. She and Margaret regarded each other quietly, caught in a mild stalemate.

Grace started to rise from her chair. "Okay, well—"

"Did you know," Margaret said, pulling her reading glasses off to check the lenses, "that when your truck broke down and we realized you were missing, two dozen people went searching for you?"

Grace cringed into her seat. "I'm sorry, I didn't—"

"Caleb was the first one to notice you weren't back when you should have been." She picked up the hem of her sweater and rubbed at one lens.

"Caleb?"

"He asked Natasha to call you. When you didn't answer, he badgered her to call Sheryl Toonikoh, up in Eagle Ridge. Sheryl told her you'd left hours ago. As soon as Caleb heard that, he was out the door." She switched to clean the other lens.

"Caleb?" Grace repeated, incredulous. He'd been so pissed at her when he'd found her.

"The rest of us weren't too far behind—though we did take a few minutes to form a search plan." She slid her glasses back on and smiled. "We care about you, Grace. All of us."

CHAPTER 21

When Grace got back to The Spruce, Caleb was standing in the dining room, speaking to Arthur. He was still wearing his outdoor gear, and his cheeks were flushed with cold. Grace stopped when she saw him, overwhelmed by the memory of his heated touch and thrown off-kilter by what Margaret had told her. He'd worried about her. He'd been the one to start searching for her.

As if he could feel her gaze, Caleb suddenly looked up. Like an awkward teenager, Grace spun away from him and hurried towards the stairs.

She was halfway up when she heard Caleb's boots pounding behind her.

"Grace, wait up."

"No." She didn't know what to say to him, or even what she wanted from him. She ran up the stairs.

Behind her, Caleb chuckled, and it sounded eerily like a growl. His big body hit the landing a split-second after hers.

Grace yelped and sprinted up the next flight. She felt him at her heels, his fingers teasing the backs of her legs.

"You shouldn't run from me, Gracie," he warned in a low voice.

Werewolf.

But Grace wasn't scared. Somewhere between the dining room and the second flight of stairs, it had become a game. She skittered around the corner on the final landing—letting out a small scream when Caleb's hand closed around her ankle. She kicked free and sprinted down the hallway. She hadn't taken more than two steps when Caleb tackled her from behind. They went to the floor in a tangle of limbs, but Caleb wrapped his arms around her and rolled so that she landed on top of him.

Panting for breath, she lifted her head to look down at him. "That was unnecessary."

"Was it?" Caleb grinned. It was such a self-satisfied, unrepentant expression. But it also so wholly and unreservedly happy—and directed at Grace. Lightness like she hadn't felt in a long time made her chest ache.

She couldn't hold back any longer. She cupped his smiling, cocksure face between her hands and kissed him. There was a split-second of fear where she thought he wasn't going to kiss her back, that he was going to shove her away like he had in the past.

But she worried for nothing. His arms tightened around her, pulling her close, and he kissed her like she was the only thing keeping him alive. Grace had started this, but Caleb quickly wrested control from her. His mouth was hot and hard against hers, devouring her with the focused hunger of a predator.

She broke the kiss for a second. "Caleb—"

He kissed her jaw, the tender skin on her neck. She gasped with each explosive bloom of heat beneath her skin.

"Caleb—*ah!*—" he bit her collarbone "—not in the hallway!"

Without breaking away from her, Caleb managed to get to his feet and hoist Grace up in his arms. He kicked his door open, carried her inside, and kicked it shut again. He dropped her on his bed and followed her down, covering her body with his. Grace wrapped her arms around his neck, pulling herself harder against him. They were both still wearing their parkas, and it was too much between them. Grace wriggled against him, frustrated by layers of goose down and gore-tex. Caleb went for her zipper, opening her jacket and peeling it off. Their hands clashed as she tried to do the same for him. Between groping kisses and muttered cursing, they managed to get their coats off.

"I have to tell you something," Grace gasped when they broke apart for air.

"Later." Caleb moved to kiss her again.

"No." She hooked her heel behind his right knee at the same time as she shoved against his left shoulder. If he'd been expecting it, Grace doubted she would have budged him. But, to her advantage, he was more than a little distracted. Caleb collapsed with an *oof* onto his side. Grace shoved him onto his back and straddled his hips. "Listen to me."

He gripped her hips and rolled, flipping her onto her back. Still cradled between her thighs, he grinned and ground his hips against her heated core.

"Oh!" She arched against him with a ragged gasp.

Caleb looked slightly undone himself, breathing roughly, head bowed.

"Look," Grace said breathlessly, "Not to kill the mood but I just need to tell you something—I talked to Margaret about what I saw that night, at the party."

Caleb groaned. Not a sexy groan. An annoyed one. "Grace—"

"Just listen. I want you to know that you don't have to tell me anything, okay? I won't ask about things you can't talk about. I'm not family. I don't belong here. I get that."

Caleb frowned down at her, the heat in his gaze cooling to confusion. "Margaret said you don't belong here?"

"She said that there are certain things you guys don't discuss with outsiders. I know I'm an outsider. I can do the math."

"You don't have to be an outsider," he said softly, dipping down to kiss her again. This one was soft, gentle. "The pack would take you in."

"The pack?"

"Goddamn it, Grace! Quit using your feminine wiles to pull information out of me."

"I'm just laying here!"

"And you're very good at it." He sank back down against her, letting all of his weight press her into the mattress. She savored the pleasant crush of his powerful body, wrapping her arms around his neck and arching her hips against his. There was a big pink elephant in the room—it was covered in fur and looked a lot like a wolf—and without a word, they agreed to ignore it.

Grace reached for the hem of Caleb's shirt and pulled it up, pressing her hands against the taut skin on his pelvis, roving higher, over a hard stomach and a broad chest, exploring all that hot skin and thick muscle. Caleb made a pleasured sound deep in his throat—a sort of groan-growl-sigh. He pushed up, taking his weight off of her so that he could yank his shirt over his head and fling it to the floor, laying his glorious torso bare for her eyes and hands.

"Your turn," he growled, reaching for the hem of her sweater. Grace lifted her arms and let him pull her sweater up. her camisole came with it, leaving her in just her bra.

"Ah," Caleb breathed, his gleaming eyes arrested by the sight of her breasts overflowing her slightly-too-small bra. After a few months of good meals, Grace was filling her clothes back out—some places more than others. Caleb leaned in, pressing his lips to the soft upper curve of one breast, then the other. His touch felt so good, so warm, so electric. Grace reached for the clasp and tugged her bra off. Caleb's lips went immediately to one peaked, aching nipple and sucked.

"Oh!" Her hands fisted in his hair, clutching him to her.

He laughed softly, a low rumble against her skin, and turned his attention to the other nipple.

"Mmmm... Caleb..." She arched against him, helpless under the onslaught of delicious sensations sparking through her body. His teeth closed around her nipple, and a jolt of pleasure nearly tipped her into orgasm, even though she hadn't even taken her pants off yet. "God, I want you inside me," she gasped.

Her words clearly unleashed whatever restraint Caleb had been imposing on himself. He ripped Grace's jeans off her legs like a magician doing the tablecloth trick. Her underwear came next. He shoved his own jeans down his hips, and then he was between her thighs, his cock pressed against her, hard and hot and big. Taking himself in hand, he swiped the head of his cock through her folds and Grace moaned as he glided over her clit.

"Oh, god, Grace. You're so wet for me."

"Caleb—I need—"

He dropped his weight back down on her, and then the blunt pressure of his cock was pressing inside of her, stretching her. She was soaking wet, but it'd been a while since she'd had sex, and Caleb was not a small man.

"Oh!" She flinched as the stretch became too painful. "Just, wait a second... *Eeeeee*—nope, wait—"

Caleb held stock still, panting against her ear. "It's alright, Grace, we can stop. I can—"

She wrapped her legs around his waist. "I don't want to stop. I just need a second." She froze. "Unless you want to stop?"

A pained laugh escaped him. "Would rather not—but if you're hurting..."

"I'm okay." She flexed her legs wider, rolled her hips. Caleb slipped deeper inside her, just an inch, but it felt like a yard. They both groaned, bodies trembling.

"You alright?" Caleb asked raggedly.

Grace nodded. "Go a little deeper."

He shifted his hips carefully, pressing another thick inch inside of her. She felt her inner muscles relaxing, yielding. He gained another inch. And then another. And another, until he was buried all the way inside of her, filling her so good her head lolled back and her hips rocked up.

"Jesus, Gracie," he moaned, his mouth moving hotly against her ear. "Fuck, you feel so good. Can I move? Please tell me—"

"Move," she urged, rocking against him.

He drew back slowly and pushed back in with the same trembling restraint. "Okay?" he asked.

"So good," Grace breathed, tightening her legs around his waist. "Faster."

He gave her swift, shallow strokes, his breath coming in grunts with each thrust.

"Harder," she gasped.

He made a pained sound in his throat, but his body was eager to obey, thrusting into her with a hard, fast, punishing tempo that matched the ragged beat of their breaths. Grace clung to him, hips rolling to meet his, riding the powerful movements of his body. He was on top of her, fucking her hard, but she felt like the conquerer—the one who'd taken a powerful beast and bent him to her will. He was so big and strong, but he was giving her exactly what she wanted, paying such careful attention to the cues of her breathing and the shift of her body.

She wanted to ride him all night, use him, enjoy him, stretch out this heady pleasure for hours, but she could feel the strain in his clenched muscles, the fine tremors in his arms. He needed to come, but he was waiting for Grace. She reached her hand between their bodies and circled her clit with one finger.

"Oh, fuck, Grace. Yes. Touch yourself. Let me see you come. Please—"

She was so close to the edge and his ragged pleas tipped her over. Her legs tightened like a vise on his big, charging body, and she shook and trembled as her climax seized her. Caleb growled in her ear, thrusting desperately, losing his rhythm, giving her a few more surging thrusts, until he shuddered hard. He groaned like a dying beast as his cock pulsed inside of her and she felt the hot flood of his release.

He collapsed on top of her. His weight was... well, it was a lot. But Grace liked the heavy, warm crush of him. She kept her arms and legs wrapped tightly around him as they both gasped for breath. When he was able to move again, his cock had begun to soften inside of her. He pulled out gently and lay beside her, his face pressed into her hair, inhaling deeply.

"Are you smelling me?" Grace asked.

"Can't help it if you smell so fucking good," he answered, sounding a bit annoyed.

She smiled. A moment later, panic hit her. "We didn't use any protection!"

Caleb's hand slid to her arm, giving her a comforting squeeze. "I can't carry anything you have to be worried about," he said. "Can't catch it, can't pass it along."

Is that a werewolf thing? she almost asked, before she realized that first of all, he couldn't tell her if it was, and second of all, of course it fucking was. Every weird thing about the Teekkonlit Valley was a werewolf thing.

"Oh," she said, relaxing. She knew she could believe him, even if the answer made no logical sense. "Well, I've got an IUD, so you don't have to worry about a surprise in nine months."

"I wouldn't be worried," Caleb said quietly.

That was a conversational avenue that Grace wasn't even remotely ready to discuss. So she changed the topic in the easiest way possible—she turned to face Caleb, wrapping her arms around his neck, and kissed him.

Several hours later, they'd missed dinner, but they'd made each other come three more times. They lay drowsily in bed together, neither one of them talking. Grace was content with the silence. It felt good. And besides, talking meant asking—and answering—uncomfortable questions. Like *what are we doing? Where is this going?* Things had changed between them. But how much they had changed, and how exactly, was a question she was too scared to ask. So instead, she lay quietly with Caleb's strong arms wrapped around her, pressed against his heavy, warm body.

"Gracie," Caleb said, late in the evening, sounding contemplative.

"Hm?" She tried not to tense. There was a big question coming, she could feel it. But she didn't know if she was ready to answer it.

"We should—"

A scream shattered through the peaceful silence of the night. Caleb and Grace sat bolt upright. He went to the window, staring down at the street. In a flash, he was off the bed.

"What's going on?" Grace looked out the window. A huddled mass lay in the middle of the street, dark and unmoving.

"I don't know. Stay here." He ripped the door open and vanished into the hall, slamming the door behind him.

CHAPTER 22

The huddled shape in the middle of the street was Elena Morris. She was naked, splashed with gore, and as still as death. By the time Grace made it outside, a small crowd had gathered around her. Grace reached them in time to see Max Freeman gather Elena into his arms and lift her limp body from the street.

The snow-packed street was splashed with vivid red where she'd been laying. That same red—shiny and slick and still steaming in the frigid air—coated the front of her naked body.

Caleb, Jess, and Connor were in the process of peeling off their jackets. Grace stared, dumbfounded as they dumped them on the ground and began pulling off their shirts as well.

Caleb stiffened suddenly, turning to face her. His face blanched, and he surged towards her. "Get inside, Grace. Hurry." He caught her around the waist and all but carried her back into The Spruce.

"Caleb, what's—"

"I can't explain right now. But I need you to stay inside, okay?" He carried her across the threshold of The Spruce and deposited her back on her feet, visibly relaxing. "Tell me you'll stay inside."

"I'll stay inside," she said, a frisson of fear winding up her spine. "Just tell me—"

"You wouldn't believe me. Stay inside and I'll explain when I get back, okay? And if any strangers come to The Spruce, asking to be let in—*do not* let them in. Even if they're injured, or freezing, or begging for help. Even if it's a child. *Do not* invite them in."

"What if they just walk in?" The entry doors to The Spruce were never locked, as far as she knew.

He held her gaze, a grim apology in his expression. "They won't. Not without an invitation."

Grace stared at him, horrified by the dawning realization of what he was telling her.

"I have to go." He frowned, his gaze searching hers worriedly. "Stay inside," he said one last time.

Grace nodded, still speechless. Caleb went back outside, and the door thudded heavily in his wake.

Had Caleb been trying to warn her about a... *vampire*? She'd already accepted the existence of werewolves, why should vampires be any harder to believe? And more importantly—why did the word tickle at her mind in a strange way? It was like a whisper of a memory she couldn't quite recall.

Grace turned away from the door. Max was carrying Elena down the hall towards the guest rooms. Grace followed, swinging into the room as Max laid Elena in the bed. Natasha was there with a heap of towels, wiping gently at Elena's skin. Elena's throat was a torn mess, her normally warm tan skin bleached of color.

"She needs a doctor," Grace said, feeling faint at the sight of the gristle of her throat. "Is she even—"

"She's alive," Max said grimly. He looked to his mother. "I have to go. Grace shouldn't be here, in case she..."

In case Grace... what? Or did he mean Elena? In case she... died?

"Go," Natasha told him. "I will take care of them both."

"She needs a doctor!" Grace objected as Max strode from the room. "Look at her. We need to get Harlan or—"

"Anna is on her way," Natasha said calmly.

Anna Daaldinh was the other doctor at the Valley clinics. Grace had never met her, since she tended to rotate her time between Eagle Ridge and the villages while Harlan mostly remained in Longtooth. But she knew Anna had been practicing medicine in Longtooth since the early eighties, and had attended almost every birth in the Valley since then.

Grace hovered nervously while Natasha gently cleaned blood off of Elena. Her chest moved with shallow, rapid breaths. "God, her throat," Grace said fretfully.

"It looks worse than it is," Natasha said calmly.

"Is there something I can do to help?"

"You should go knock on the doors upstairs and make sure everybody knows not to leave The Spruce."

Grace nodded. It was clear Natasha wanted her out of the room. She turned to leave when something caught her attention—a twinkling diamond ring on Elena's left ring finger. Grace had never seen her wear jewelry before. But more alarmingly, she recognized the ring.

The diamond was a small tear-drop shape, not even half

a carat, flanked on each side by tiny opals. The band was yellow gold, with a thin channel engraved along the center.

Her grandmother's wedding ring.

She'd forgotten how brutal the cold inside of her had been. Over the last few months in Longtooth, she'd been slowly thawing without even realizing it. But now, at the sight of Grandma's ring on Elena's blood-soaked hand, ice splintered through her with such force that she doubled over. It was so cold it burned. Her bones became brittle as glass. Burning-cold knives stabbed at her skin.

"Gracie?" Natasha turned to her, alarmed.

"Her hand—the ring—"

Natasha looked down and frowned. She reached for it.

"No!"

She recoiled, looking to Grace with wide eyes.

"Gracie, what—"

"He found me," Grace told her hoarsely. The last time she'd seen the ring, it'd been in the chest with all her other mementos—including Freya's collar and her middle school friendship bracelet.

"Who?" Natasha asked.

"Alex. He did this." Grace went to the bed and gently removed the ring from Elena's finger. Her hand was cold and stiff, and Grace nervously felt for a pulse. Thready, faint, but still there.

"Who's Alex?"

"He's the reason I came to Longtooth. I was in a relationship with him, and I tried to end it. But he wouldn't let me go. So I ran away." She spoke flatly, feeling oddly detached as she examined the bloodied ring in her fingers. "This was my grandmother's wedding ring. He stole it from me." The ring was a message. Alex was telling her that he had found her. The dreams were real. And if she didn't come to him, he would hurt the people she cared for.

Natasha was quiet for a moment. Finally, she said, "You should go tell the others they need to stay inside."

Grace nodded. Her blood turned to solid ice in her veins. "Okay."

She stayed up late into the night, sitting on the edge of her bed and staring out her window at the street. Elena's blood was a scarlet flag. Grandma's ring bit into her palm, clutched in her shaking fist. Her entire body trembled with the painful cold. She hunched over until her forehead rested against the wooden sill.

She wanted to go downstairs and ask how Elena was doing, but both Max and Natasha had told her to leave the room. As well they should have. It was her fault. Elena was hurt because of her.

"*Gracie.*" The voice sounded like it came from inside her own head, but when she looked up, Alex was perched on the Juliet balcony outside her window. His beautiful golden face was taut with grief, his glacial blue eyes bleak with sorrow.

Alex. Her lips moved around the shape of his name, but no sound came out.

He smiled sadly. "Will you come to me now, Grace?"

"I don't have much of a choice, do I?"

"I didn't want it to come to this. I tried asking nicely."

Grace nodded. Tears welled in her eyes. "What's going to happen to me?"

"I would never hurt you, Grace. You're mine," he said earnestly. "Forever mine. Put the ring on, love."

She slid it onto her left ring finger. Elena's blood streaked her skin.

"There you go. Now, come outside. Don't let anybody see you."

She got up without a fight. She slipped her boots and her jacket on. She turned back to the window. Alex was watching her intently.

"Will Elena be okay?"

"Probably," he said with a note of disdain in his voice. "Their kind are hardy. Now, come outside, darling."

Her body moved at Alex's command, and she didn't resist. It felt like she was observing herself from the outside as she opened her door and walked quietly down the hall. At the bottom of the stairs, she stood still, listening. There was only silence. Moving quickly, quietly, she crossed the dining room and went to the back door. Easing the door open gently so that the hinge wouldn't squeak, she slipped out into the cold.

"*Into the woods,*" Alex's voice guided her. He was nowhere in sight. Grace shivered and followed his directions. She walked along the edge of the garage, keeping to the shadows so anybody looking out their windows from the Spruce would be unlikely to notice her. She reached the edge of the forest on legs shaking so badly, she could hardly walk.

"*Just a little further, Grace. I'm waiting for you.*"

She stumbled in the deep snow, crossing into the cover of the trees. The snow-covered boughs blocked the moonlight, plunging her into total darkness. She groped blindly, feeling her way between needled branches. She was strangely unaffected—her pulse was steady, her breathing even.

"*Almost there, Grace.*"

The tree cover thinned and she stepped into a rocky clearing. She stood blinking in the moonlight, letting her eyes adjust. Slowly, a figure on the opposite side of the clearing came into focus—a shadow in the form of a man. Grace couldn't see his face, but she knew now. There was no way to rationalize it away anymore.

"Hello, Alex."

She walked towards him, but the shadow would not show his face.

"*I told you to come alone, Grace.*" His voice echoed inside her skull, foreboding and impatient.

"I did." The words emerged as a soundless puff of vapor. Tears spilled from her eyes, freezing to her cheeks.

"*You were followed.*"

She squeezed her eyes shut and shook her head. "No." Her voice was a croak. "I—"

A deep, animalistic growl reverberated through the clearing. Grace stiffened as a massive silver-gray wolf emerged from behind her. That menacing growl continued to rumble in his chest as he positioned himself between Grace and Alex.

Alex sighed. "*Grace.*" His voice was heavy with accusation.

Two more wolves emerged into the clearing, flanking her on either side. One was snowy-white, the other russet-brown. Their snarls joined with the first wolf, creating a vicious, hair-raising harmony.

"*You will come to me, Grace,*" Alex's voice echoed in her mind, and then with impossible speed, the shadow vanished into the trees.

The wolves chuffed and whined, circling restlessly around Grace, eyes scanning the darkness of the forest. The big silver one nudged his head against her hip, gently at first, and then more insistently.

"Ah," she realized. "You want me to go back to The Spruce." Her voice sounded flat and far away, like she was listening to somebody else speak in another room. Numbly, she turned and began walking.

She hadn't realized how far she'd walked from The Spruce. Journeying into the woods under Alex's command had felt strangely timeless, dreamlike. On the walk back, she was acutely aware of every plodding step through thigh-deep snow, ducking beneath scratching spruce boughs, stumbling in the dark over snow-covered rocks and stumps. When she finally broke free of the cover of the forest, she was sweating and breathing raggedly. The three wolves circled her restlessly, herding her forward.

When she reached the back door, the silver wolf followed her inside, and it seemed oddly natural.

And then suddenly, there was no wolf. Caleb's hands were on her, gripping her shoulders like he wanted to shake the life out of her. His eyes were frantic, his face a mask of terror.

"*Why?*" he demanded angrily. "I told you to stay inside. Why would you—" Words failed him, and with a hoarse exclamation, he hauled Grace against him, his arms wrapped around her in a crushing embrace.

"I'm sorry," she whispered. "I had to." She wrapped her arms around his torso, meaning to comfort him, and found herself touching his bare skin. The searing heat of his skin bloomed against her palms, snaked slowly up her arms, and spread through her entire body with a comforting radiance. "Caleb?"

"Hm?"

"You're naked."

"Am I?" He bent and scooped her into his arms, carrying her towards the stairs. She held onto him as he maneuvered up the narrow staircase, his bare feet ghostly silent upon the treads.

He brought Grace to his room and laid her on his bed. He pulled off her boots and helped her out of her jacket. But he didn't join her on the bed. He sank into the chair beside his dresser with a complete lack of self-consciousness for his nudity. Despite all the events of the last several hours, Grace was apparently still capable of being flustered. She blushed and turned away from him, examining the spines of the books lined up on his window ledge. Behind her, Caleb let out a heavy breath. She risked looking at him to find that he'd dropped his head into his hands. Every line of his body sagged with weariness.

"*Why* did you leave The Spruce, Grace?" He lifted his head, pinning her with his gaze. His eyes burned with emotion, gleaming amber bright in the dimness of his room. "He nearly had you! He could've—"

"It was Alex. He's the..." She couldn't say it out loud. "He's here because of me."

Caleb lapsed into silence, watching her with an inscrutable look.

"He gave me my grandmother's wedding ring back." She held up her hand, the bloodied ring still on her finger. "He left it on Elena's finger. He knew I'd get the message." The cold inside of her deepened into a knife-sharp ache. She curled in on herself, making a futile effort to warm herself.

Caleb made an inarticulate sound, and then the mattress depressed beneath his weight. He slid beneath the blankets and pulled her into his arms. The warmth of him seeped into her, leeching away the cold. She sighed, closing her eyes and leaning against him.

"What do you know about him, Grace?"

"I didn't know what he is. Not until today." She still couldn't say it out loud, but the word echoed in her mind.

Vampire.

She shivered and Caleb's arms tightened around her.

"I've been having dreams about him, ever since I got here. He was looking for me, telling me to come to him. I thought they were just dreams, but..."

A low growl reverberated in Caleb's chest. "That's something they can do," he said darkly. "I should've put it together—you were sleepwalking, saying his name. It's why your scent was so confusing when you first got here."

"My scent?"

"You smelled like... like one of them. Just the faintest hint. But, by the time we landed in Longtooth, the only other scent anybody could get from you was mine. They all thought I was paranoid." He nuzzled his face against her neck and inhaled deeply. "Should've pushed harder about that. We might've gotten the fucker sooner."

Pleasant shivers radiated up and down her body, but the fear was stronger. She couldn't relax, couldn't enjoy Caleb's touch. "I have to go to him, Caleb. If I don't, he'll just keep hurting people until he gets to me."

Caleb's hold tightened to a nearly painful degree. "No."

"I don't think he wants to hurt me. He just wants to... have me."

"Grace, no." Caleb pulled away, turning her so that she faced him. "He'll make you like him. You'll never see daylight again, never feel warm again. You'll become a killer. Like him."

Grace stared at him. "Say it bluntly, Caleb. It doesn't seem real when you keep tip-toeing around it."

He sighed, head dropping. "We have laws. If I explain these things to you without pack approval…"

"*Pack*," she repeated in a whisper. "What if I just figure it out on my own? Does that break your laws?"

Caleb lifted his head. "What have you figured out?"

"You're a werewolf."

"That's not what we call ourselves."

"Quiet, you law-breaker." She laid her fingers over his lips. They curved in a smile against her touch. More warmth flooded her. "You can all shift into wolves. Or maybe just certain families can. I haven't figured that out yet."

"Hmmm," Caleb murmured noncommittally. "Does that scare you?"

"It did at first." She cupped his face, stroking her thumbs along the wind-burnt crests of his cheekbones. "But only because I thought I was going crazy."

Caleb's eyes shadowed with guilt. "What else have you figured out?" he asked grimly.

"Alex is a vampire. Isn't he?"

"That's not what we call them," Caleb said, which was as good as a yes.

"Are they all evil?"

Caleb considered the question for a moment. "Is a grizzly evil for killing? They need to do it to survive. But if one came into your community, endangered your people, you'd destroy it in a heartbeat." He lapsed into silence.

"He hurt Elena. Not to survive. Just to make a point."

Caleb nodded. "I guess it's not fair to compare them to grizzlies. Grizzlies were never human. They don't have human notions of right or wrong. Either way, he'll die. The minute he set a foot on Teekkonlit territory, he signed his own death warrant."

Caleb's surety eased her fear a little. She turned towards him so that she could wrap her arm around his waist, press her face into his chest. Holding onto all that strength gave her comfort. He was here with her. He would fight with her. She didn't have to be alone.

"Is Elena going to be okay?"

"I don't know," he answered honestly.

Guilt tore at her. "Why aren't you flying her to a hospital?"

"Injuries from his kind aren't treatable with medicine. Not modern medicine."

A convulsive shiver ran down her spine. "It's my fault," she said hoarsely. "I brought him here."

Caleb's arms tightened around her. "He brought himself here. He made his own choices. You're not responsible for him."

She wanted so badly to believe him.

He pressed his lips to the top of her head. "Sleep, Grace. You're exhausted. Things will look better in the morning."

CHAPTER 23

Grace woke half-crushed beneath the warm weight of a male body. It was the second time she'd woken in Caleb's arms, but this time, it felt right. His face was pressed against her neck, his breath gusting humidly against her skin. The last time she woke up like this, he tried to bite her. Would he do it again?

Why did she want him to?

She shifted slightly, easing out from under his bulk so that she could breathe more easily. His arms tightened, trapping her against him.

"Where are you going?" he growled, lips moving against her neck, beard rasping her skin. A delicate, delicious tremor chased over her. Caleb sensed it, his lips curving into a smile. He nipped her—not a real bite—but enough to make her gasp. A self-satisfied laugh rumbled in his chest.

"Careful," Grace told him, forcing herself to breathe evenly. "I bite back."

"I wish you would."

Held tightly against him, she couldn't miss the rigid press of his arousal. She rolled her hips back, teasing that hard length. Caleb groaned, rocking against her.

"Grace, you witch." His hands coasted down the front of her body, tracing her stomach to her hips and back up to cup her breasts. "I want to kiss you, but I can't remember the last time I brushed my teeth."

She arched into his caress. "Gross."

He chuckled and smacked her on the ass like he was sending a horse off to the races, then pushed away from her. He got out of bed and whipped the blankets off.

"Hey!" Grace objected, curling up against the sudden cold. Caleb stood over her, completely naked.

Oh. She took in the sight with wide eyes. *Whoa ho ho.* He was big and broad and hairy and she couldn't look away. *Woof.*

Caleb gave her a smug look and wrapped the blanket around his hips. "Go on, pervert. Get cleaned up. We'll go down for breakfast. Margaret will want to talk to you about what happened last night."

Until then, Grace had forgotten about the rest of the world. Suddenly it all came crashing back down on her— Alex, and Elena, and the danger she'd brought to Longtooth. She sat up uneasily, suddenly filled with dread.

"Hey." Caleb crouched in front of her. "It's going to be alright. Elena's still with us."

"How do you know?"

Caleb hesitated.

"Oh—right. You don't have to tell me. Sorry I asked." She started to get up, but Caleb caught her by one ankle. She stumbled and sat back down on the bed.

"I trust you, Grace," he said solemnly.

"It's not a big deal, Caleb. At breakfast I'll just—"

"The pack has a mental connection with each other."

He was telling her things he shouldn't be. "Caleb, you don't have to—"

"It's not like telepathy. We can't speak to each other. But we have a general sense of the others—to an extent. When I fly out of the Valley, the rest of the pack loses that sense of me. They know I'm still alive—still in the pack—but they don't know where I am." He released her ankle and took her hands. "Elena's still in the pack."

"Oh." Grace dropped her head, letting the relief of that wash over her. "Thank you for telling me."

Caleb stood up. "Go on and get ready for breakfast. We'll get the news downstairs." He glanced out the window at the rising sun. "You're safe in the daylight. So as long as you are back at The Spruce before sunset, we can keep you safe."

That made sense. In the entirety of their relationship, Grace had never seen Alex during the day.

Grace went to her room to shower and change into clean clothes. When she emerged, Caleb was waiting in the hall. She suddenly felt a bit bashful as they walked down to breakfast together. A nearly-forgotten memory flashed into her mind. Connor Ankkonisdoy telling her, *You smell like him.* She stuttered to a halt halfway down the stairs. Caleb looked back with a confused frown.

"They're all going to know we slept together."

His expression cleared, and he flashed her a feral smile. "Yeah."

When she didn't move, he leaned lazily against the wall, arms crossed against his chest.

"I hate to break it to you, Gracie, but you've had my scent

for a while now—and I've had yours. The whole pack knows we've been circling each other for weeks."

Her ears went hot. "They do?"

"To be honest, most of them knew before I did." He shrugged. "So, for them, the only change will be that we're not ignoring each other anymore."

"How can they have known for weeks? We never even touched each other until pretty recently."

Caleb's smile turned slightly sheepish. "I may have been...inadvertently...scent marking you when we passed in the hall."

Grace gasped, both in dawning realization and refreshed outrage. "*That's* why you never moved aside for me! I thought you were just an asshole!"

"Ah, Grace, I'm definitely an asshole." He walked back up the stairs, closing the distance between them, and pulled her into a heated kiss. When he broke away, it took her a second to get her bearings again. Caleb gave her that cocky, wolfish grin. There was something about it that filled her with delight, while simultaneously making her want to rip the rug right out from under him.

"Thank you for brushing your teeth," she said, patting his cheek. She turned away and trotted down the stairs.

Caleb chuckled darkly behind her. "Witch."

The mood in the dining room was subdued when they entered. But as people saw Caleb and Grace walk in together, knowing smiles were cast their way. Grace's burning ears spread to burning cheeks, and she couldn't make eye-contact with anybody.

"Gracie. Caleb." Natasha appeared with mugs and a coffee pot. She smiled at the two of them like an angel observing a good deed. "Good morning."

"Morning, Tasha." Caleb watched her pour coffee. "How's Elena?"

"She's awake. She's speaking."

Some tension lifted from Caleb's shoulders. "Has she... changed?" He said the word carefully enough for Grace to understand that he was trying to refer obliquely to something else. She could pretty easily guess what that something else might be.

Natasha glanced uncertainly at Grace. "Not yet," she said, a question in her eyes as she looked back to Caleb. "Margaret wants to speak to you—both of you."

"We'll go see her after breakfast," Caleb said.

CALEB AND GRACE met Margaret in an empty short-stay room, next-door to where Elena was resting. Stomach churning, back sweating, Grace explained everything—how she'd met Alex in Chicago, how he'd stalked her after the breakup, and how she'd continued to see him in her dreams in Longtooth, how she'd realized he'd followed her when she found her grandmother's wedding ring on Elena's finger.

"I'm so sorry for everything. I had no idea what he was," she finished hoarsely.

"How could you have known?" Margaret asked.

Grace had to force herself not to cringe away from the anger in Margaret's voice. But when she managed to lift her gaze to Margaret's, she realized that anger wasn't directed at her. Margaret was angry at herself.

"You haven't been told anything that might have helped you. At worst, you've been actively lied to." Margaret's gaze went to Caleb. "You're exempted from the law of Silence. Tell her everything. But get her out of here."

Grace's heart dropped into her stomach. Margaret wasn't blaming her for what had happened, but she wanted Grace gone all the same.

"There are too many vulnerabilities at The Spruce. Too many occupants, too many entrances. Take her to the old ranger station. There's only one door, and it'll just be the two of you."

Grace frowned, confused. "Just the—what?"

"I'm sorry, Grace," Margaret said with a sigh. "Your students are going to have to do without you until we hunt this thing down."

"You don't want me to leave the Valley?"

Margaret's eyebrows flew up. "Why would I want that?"

Grace looked askance at her and Caleb. "Oh, I don't know, maybe because I brought a vampire into your home?"

"We don't call them that," Margaret said. "And you didn't bring anything. You were followed by something that's old enough to know better than to enter wolf territory."

"Wolf," Grace repeated faintly.

Margaret gave her an apologetic smile. "Caleb will explain everything. You need to pack your things. Give me whatever lesson plans you have. We'll see if Julie Angwin can take your classes until this is settled." Margaret got up from her spot on the edge of the bed, looking decisive.

"I don't understand." Grace stood as Caleb did. "Why do I have to leave? Why can't I keep teaching? The days are long enough now that I can get to and from school during the daylight."

"During the daylight, huh?" Margaret slid a sour look at Caleb. "Been getting a jump on that Silence exemption, pup?"

Caleb tried, and failed, to look innocent.

Margaret sighed. "You can't go to school, Grace, because it's too much of a security risk. There are too many doors, too many people who don't know what to look out for. It only takes one person to unknowingly give him an invitation inside. Absent-mindedly holding a door open for him is enough of an invitation."

"That might have already happened," Grace said in a small voice. "He left something in one of my desk drawers."

Margaret sighed, rubbing at her temple. "We'll have to put signs on every door revoking his invitation."

"Are you going to tell the others?" Caleb asked, and Grace realized he meant the other outsiders.

Margaret spread her hands helplessly. "We have to tell them something. How much of this mess could have been prevented if we'd told Grace everything from the start?" Margaret dropped her hands and let out a frustrated huff. "Anyways, you might as well know, Gracie... we're using you as bait."

Both Caleb and Margaret regarded her grimly. The heavy silence that followed the declaration seemed to hum in Grace's ears.

"That's why we need to get you away from Longtooth," Margaret said. "We need to draw your old friend out where there are fewer people for him to hurt, and fewer places to hide. As long as you stay in the station—and *don't* invite him in—he can't get you."

"Won't stop him from trying, though," Caleb said, a low growl in his voice.

"Which is why Caleb will be with you," Margaret said. "So get upstairs and pack what you'll need for a week. Hopefully it won't take that long, but it doesn't hurt to be prepared."

Strangely, Grace wasn't as terrified of being used as vampire bait as she was of spending a week alone with Caleb. Just the two of them.

She looked up at him. He met her gaze, and his dark eyes shone with the faintest gleam of amber.

CHAPTER 24

The Ranger Station was an old cabin in the mountains overlooking the meandering flow of the same tributary river that ran through Longtooth. Caleb brought Grace inside and then left her there while he scouted the surroundings.

The cabin was small, but unlike the tiny shack they'd stayed in when her truck broke down, this place had a narrow kitchenette, a table with four chairs, and an indoor composting toilet. The sleeping space was lofted above the kitchen, accessible by a wooden ladder.

Grace stared up at it, thinking. There was only one bed. And you'd think that, after sleeping in Caleb's bed last night and kissing him this morning, it'd be easy to assume they'd be sharing the bed. But it wasn't in Grace's nature to assume that she was wanted, and Caleb hadn't exactly made any declarations to her. In fact, all he'd said was that they weren't ignoring each other anymore. Which made things about as clear as mud. With a sigh, she dropped into one of the chairs and stared out the window at the river.

She was still lost in thought when she heard something scratch against the door. Startled, she twisted around to look at the door. That scratch sounded again.

"Hello?" she called nervously.

Another scratch. Right outside the door, a wolf howled.

"Caleb?"

A canine whine answered.

Grace went to the door and opened it a crack, peering out nervously. A massive silver-gray wolf stood at the threshold, looking up at her with bright, amber eyes. Awareness and familiarity shone in those eyes. Hoping she wasn't a complete and total idiot, she pulled the door open. The wolf trotted inside, tame as a poodle. Grace shut the door, and when she turned around, Caleb was there, stark naked and grinning. His hair was mussed and windblown, his cheeks ruddy from the cold.

"Where are your clothes?"

"Left them in the truck when I shifted, and then I couldn't get them when I made it back." He held up his hands, fingers wiggling. "Wolves don't have thumbs. And I wasn't going to shift outside."

"Shift," Grace repeated contemplatively.

Caleb's expression sobered. "Right. Explanations." He ran a hand through his hair, mussing it further. "Let me get some pants on."

"That'd be good," she said, face flushed.

He grinned and then turned away from her to rummage through his bag. He pulled on a pair of gray sweatpants. Grace returned to her chair at the table, and Caleb pulled out the one across from her. He hadn't put a shirt on, and his broad, muscular, hairy chest was immensely distracting. It took all her effort to keep her eyes on his face.

"So," he said, rubbing at his beard. "I don't know where to start."

"You're a werewolf," Grace said, "Start there."

He nodded. "We call our kind wolf kin. Here in the Valley, our pack is the Teekkonlit. It's what neighboring tribes called the First People of our pack. It means 'wolfskin.' Wolf kin from other parts of the world, from other traditions, have joined our pack over time, but we are still the Teekkonlit. The blood of the First People still flows in all of our veins."

Grace suddenly remembered her first night in Longtooth, when Wade had given her an extremely detailed explanation of the Valley's history. She'd been exhausted and numb at the time, but everything she could remember him telling her lined up with what Caleb was telling her now. Wade had just conveniently left out the part about wolf kin and packs.

"We can shift into our wolf form and back into our human form at will," Caleb continued. "The moon doesn't force the change."

"Could you live as a human and never shift?" Grace asked.

"No. We need to shift. We can hold off if we have to—although younger kids sometimes have trouble controlling it—"

Caitlin, she remembered.

"—but staying in one form forever would be like spending the rest of your life locked in a windowless room. Technically, it wouldn't kill you, but you'd be miserable. You'd lose your mind."

Grace nodded. Chicago hadn't been a windowless room, exactly, but Grace hadn't realized until she left how much she'd felt boxed in and claustrophobic there. Thinking of

Chicago made her think of Alex—though she hardly needed the reminder, considering the circumstances.

"So Alex is... what, exactly? Margaret said you don't call them vampires."

"We call them strigoi."

"But they're basically like vampires? Drink blood, hide from daylight, can't come inside without an invitation..."

"Well, yes. But they aren't repelled by garlic or holy water or Christian symbols. They can dematerialize and move at speeds that even wolves can't keep up with. A single wolf is no match for a strigoi. You need a pack to take one down."

A thought suddenly occurred to her. "Do you think Alex is the one who cut my fuel line?"

Caleb's expression turned grim. "Now I do. Fucker was trying to get you stranded until dark so he could snatch you when nobody was around to protect you."

Grace was quiet for a moment, absorbing that. Dread settled in the pit of her stomach, and she couldn't think about him anymore. She turned her thoughts back to the wolves. "So, all of the locals are... wolf kin?"

"Yes."

"Is Natasha?"

"No. Natasha's skinlocked."

"Skinlocked?"

"Can't change skins. Regular humans."

She tried to think of other people she knew who'd come from the outside and married a local. "What about Joanne Lance?" Harry had met his wife in Wyoming.

"Joanie's kin. She came from the Yellowstone Pack. Tom Tremaine's kin, too. He was a loner before he came to the Valley."

"What about the other outsiders? Lucia? Eric? Harlan?"

"All skinlocked."

"What about your father?"

Caleb went totally still.

"Oh, god, I'm sorry Caleb. I don't know why I blurted that out." Except that Grace couldn't stop thinking about what Margaret had told her—that Caleb's father had ditched their family when he was a kid, and that his sister's husband had recently done the same. "Never mind. Forget I—"

"No," he said curtly. "It's fine. My father was skinlocked. It was part of the reason he left."

There was an awkward tension between them, and Grace didn't know how to fix it. She tried desperately to think of a new question, to steer the conversation back to safer ground.

"He left right after I had my first change," Caleb said, breaking the stiff silence.

His admission took her by surprise. "How old were you?"

"Fourteen." His gaze had drifted to the window, staring out over the river. "I blamed myself for a long time. Before I changed, my dad was my idol. He taught me to fly—started when I was way too young. I wanted to be a pilot just like him." He sighed. "But then, one day, we were all sitting at the dinner table, and I started feeling overheated and itchy... and then I was in my wolfskin. He looked at me like I was a monster. Like I'd betrayed him. He thought I'd be like him—skinlocked. Everyone kept telling him that kids from inter-marriages always end up shifting, but he kept hoping. He hated feeling weak. He liked having somebody like him, who depended on him, looked up to him. And then all of a sudden his kid had this power that he didn't..." He trailed off, his gaze distant.

"I'm sorry Caleb." The words were inadequate, but Grace didn't know what else to say.

"He *was* weak," Caleb said with a shrug. "But not for the reason he thought. Nobody cared that he couldn't shift. But he let it eat him up. He let it ruin his family."

Grace reached out and laid a hand on his crossed forearms. He looked down at her touch, and the darkness eased from his features. His gaze came back to her.

"I was born Caleb Whitaker," he said.

"Your dad's name?"

He nodded. "Mom wouldn't let me change it after he left. I think she kept hoping that he'd come back. But when I turned eighteen, I went through all the legal hassle of changing it to my mom's."

"Caleb Kinoyit," she said softly.

His eyes warmed as he looked at her. "Anything else you want to know about wolf kin? About the pack?"

For a second, Grace was tempted to ask Caleb about the woman Jess and Elena had told her about—the one who'd used and left him. But she decided she didn't need to know. Maybe someday they'd talk about it, if Caleb wanted to. But Grace didn't want to hear the ugly details of his past relationships anymore than she wanted to share hers.

She thought for a second, pulling her hands back to herself. Caleb moved as if he might reach for her, but whatever he intended, she never found out. He pulled his hands back right away, crossing his arms over his chest.

"Uh... what about when you're in human form? You're not the same as other humans, are you?" Grace could already guess the answer.

"No. We carry some wolf characteristics with us. We have a stronger sense of smell than skinlocked humans. We can hear higher sound frequencies than most humans. We're omnivores, but need much more protein in our diet than ordinary humans. And—" his gaze intensified on Grace, flickering with a subtle golden gleam "—we form very strong bonds with... our people."

It felt significant, what he was telling her. But it could mean so many things, "our people." In the singular it could be *my person*, as in, that one special person that everybody wants to find. But he could also mean it in the broader sense, *my people* being the entire pack.

"Oh," Grace said softly, wishing she had the courage to ask him to clarify. But she couldn't. If she asked him which one he meant, he'd know which one she was hoping for. And if the answer wasn't the one she wanted, he'd feel bad for her, and things would get awkward between them. "I wish I had that," she said, and it was as bold as she could make herself be.

"You could," he answered, the golden gleam in his eyes deepening. "The pack—"

Of course it was the pack. Not him and Grace. But *his people*. All of them. She kept the disappointment off her face.

"—would have you, Grace. You could be one of us."

She smiled sardonically. "I think we both know that's not really true."

Caleb's expression darkened, his brows drawing together. "Because you can't shift?"

She realized she was poking at old wounds with that one, but she wasn't going to lie to him. "I don't have a problem being 'skinlocked,' but I don't think I'll ever really be one of you because of it. Margaret basically told me as much."

His frown shifted from anger to bafflement. "You said

that the other day—that Margaret told you that you don't belong here?" He tilted his head in question, the gesture distinctly canine.

"That was the gist of it, more or less. And it's fine, really. I get it. But you can't tell me—"

"What were her exact words?"

"We were sort of talking in circles around the whole werewolf thing—"

"Wolf kin."

"—*wolf kin* thing, and she told me that there are certain things you guys don't discuss with outsiders." She kept her hands perfectly still on the table, even though she was tempted to pick nervously at the wood planks. "I can read between the lines. I'm an outsider. She wanted me to stop asking questions and just accept—"

Caleb's expression shifted to one of amusement.

"Don't look at me like that," Grace said, annoyed by his patronizing smile. "I'm telling you exactly what she said to me."

"Gracie," Caleb said fondly, that irritating smile still on his lips. "For such a smart woman, you sure do misread a lot of signs."

She frowned. "It was pretty unambiguous."

Caleb reached out, grabbing her hands. The heat of his touch bloomed beneath her skin, as heady and intoxicating as always. "Grace. Margaret wasn't telling you that you'd be an outsider forever. She was telling you that she wanted you to choose *not* to be an outsider so that we could tell you everything."

"Uh... what?" How does a person just *stop* being an outsider? Isn't that kind of dependent on the community?

Natasha's advice suddenly echoed in her mind—*you have to demand what you want.*

"I told you that there's a connection between pack members. That we can sense each other in our minds."

"Yes."

"When someone leaves the pack, they drop out of our sense. When my dad left, everybody knew. When my sister's —" he cut himself off. "Anyway, the opposite is true, too. When Tom Tremaine joined the pack, we all felt it."

Grace shook her head, confused. "Caleb, I'm not wolf kin. I don't have this wolf telepathy thing. I don't know what you expect me to do."

"You have to want to join the pack, Grace. You have to believe that you are a part of it."

"That's it?"

He nodded. "That's it."

"It can't be that easy."

"It is. The pack has already accepted you, Grace. Everyone's just been waiting for you to take the last step." His grip tightened on hers.

Hopeful, doubtful, she closed her eyes and with every fiber of her being, she thought, *please.* After a moment, she opened her eyes and met Caleb's intent gaze.

"Did it happen?" she asked.

He shook his head, his grasp easing from hers. "You would have felt it. You still don't think of yourself as one of us."

Because she *wasn't* one of them. "I... I think I need a little time. This is a lot of new information."

The intensity left his gaze, and he leaned back in his chair, crossing his arms over his chest again. With a quiet sigh, he said, "Don't take forever, Grace."

CHAPTER 25

The sun went down, turning the cabin's only window into a black mirror. It made Grace nervous, so she pulled the dusty curtains shut. There were no overhead lights in the cabin—just a few dim lamps. It would have been cozy and romantic if it weren't for the crazed vampire trying to get ahold of her.

Caleb had put on a shirt and shoes and brought in food packed by Natasha. The two of them sat at the table again, eating cold caribou pierogis straight out of the container. After their conversation about joining the pack, Caleb had been a bit distant with her. The coolness eventually faded, and they were back to talking again. But the easy intimacy they'd shared in his bed was gone, replaced by the sort of forced friendliness you share with a second-cousin that you only see at Christmas.

"So," Caleb asked, licking tallow from his fingers. "Why did you want to be a teacher?"

Grace tore her gaze away from the sight of his lips closing around his thumb. "I didn't. I only got my teaching license as a backup plan. My original plan was to be an award-winning, history-making, investigative journalist."

"So what changed your mind?"

"Reality. Turns out, you don't show up on your first day as a beat reporter and immediately break stories about high-level government corruption and political conspiracies."

"No?" Caleb pretended at surprise. "You had to start with mid-level corruption?"

"No." Grace suppressed a smile. "I had to start out by covering town council meetings, and changes in municipal zoning laws, and school board elections."

Caleb tilted his head, considering. "Everyone starts at the bottom. You would've eventually gotten to cover bigger stories, right?"

"Right. But I was miserable covering the smaller stuff and it made me realize I hadn't gone into journalism for the right reasons. Those little stories still matter, and the work involved is still the same as the big stories—investigate, interview, gather information, then compile it into clear and compelling copy. I realized what I wanted was the intrigue, the adventure, the glory. I wasn't passionate about freedom of the press or the importance of the Fourth Estate. I just liked stories. Big stories."

"Like in books."

That he'd picked up on something so fundamental to her filled Grace with an unnameable brightness. It took her a second to respond. "Yes, exactly like books." Swallowing, she tried to gather her wits. "Shortly after that epiphany, a friend called up and told me the school where she was teaching was desperate for English teachers. I hadn't enjoyed student teaching, but I knew journalism wasn't the right fit, and Milwaukee had never really felt like home. So I interviewed, got the job, moved to Chicago, and started teaching. I was only a few weeks in when I realized that this was what I was supposed to be doing. Student teaching had confined me to someone else's plans and curriculum. Once I was free to make my own lessons, choose my own reading lists, develop my own system, everything clicked."

Caleb took that in, and a comfortable silence lapsed between them.

After a moment, Grace asked, "What about you? Why did you want to be a pilot?"

He ran a hand over his jaw, beard rasping against his fingers. "My dad was a pilot."

A weighted silence followed, and she watched him without saying anything.

Caleb sighed. "He took me up with him all the time. He started teaching me how to fly as soon as I was tall enough to reach the rudder pedals. As far back as I can remember, that's what I wanted to do. It was so amazing—*flying*." He turned to look at her, his expression intent. "We're just humans, and we can *fly*, Grace. That's... that's still amazing to me."

She smiled at the open wonder in his deep voice.

"When I started flying professionally, I was at an age where I wanted to get away from the Valley, without actually leaving. Flying let me do that."

"You never wanted to live somewhere else? Even for a little while?"

He shrugged. "The Valley is my home. There's something about this place. Most of us have a hard time leaving. Flying lets me escape, explore. But then I can come back. Back home."

Home. The way he said the word with such natural

possessiveness made it sound like another world to Grace—like Narnia or Middle Earth. For her, "home" just meant whatever house or apartment she was living in at the time. It had never borne the emotional resonance she heard in Caleb's voice when he talked about the Valley.

Strangely, she could sort of feel it. There was something about the landscape, the lifestyle, the people, that filled her with the same bittersweet yearning she felt when she saw the way Arthur and Natasha looked at each other. Or the way Linnea looked dancing with Roland. Or the way Caleb...

Nothing.

She couldn't stop the wistful sigh that escaped her.

"What?" Caleb asked.

She hesitated for a second, then decided, what the hell. "I wish I had that," she admitted. "I want to have that *here*. I really do."

Caleb's gaze sharpened, his posture tense. "Then choose it, Grace. If you love it here, then choose to be part of it."

Is that was this feeling was? Love? Why did it feel so much like envy and wistfulness? "I'm afraid I want to belong somewhere so badly, I'll shoehorn myself in where I don't belong. And the whole time I'm trying to convince myself that I've done right, I still won't have that *home* feeling."

"So you're planning to leave."

"I really don't have any plans."

"Which means you aren't planning to stay."

She was really just taking it one day at a time. But a lifetime is made of individual days. If she didn't figure something out, she was going to reach her deathbed and still be wondering where she belonged.

Caleb was still tense, waiting for Grace's answer. He shoved away from the table, pacing away from her. He ran his hands through his hair. He paced back, stopping just in front of her. "Make a decision," he snarled. "Either stay here, or don't, but quit jerking the rest of us around."

Grace scowled at him as the last couple hours of camaraderie went up in smoke. "Don't give me orders," she snapped. "I haven't made any promises. I'm not jerking anybody around."

Caleb's expression shifted to frustrated incredulity. "How can you be so oblivious?"

He may as well have called her stupid. She launched out of her chair, closing the distance between them. "Just because I'm not doing what *you* want—" She jabbed a finger into his chest "—doesn't mean I don't know what I'm doing. I'm not obligated—"

"Aren't you?" Caleb demanded, grabbing her shoulders and looking hard into her eyes.

She could tell by his grip that he wanted to shake her. She slapped his hands away. "Is that what you think?" she demanded. "I owe you something?"

"Yes!" he bellowed, moving as if to grab her again, then thinking better of it and running his fingers through his hair. "That's what relationships are! Jesus, Grace. Do you care about anyone? Do you even know how to?"

That one hit right on the mark. Instead of filling her with brittle coldness, she felt a hot wave of self-righteous anger. "Just because I fucked you, you think you own me now?"

"Is that all that was? A fuck?" he demanded.

Grace hesitated. It had felt like more—so much more. But the *more* was terrifying. The last time she gave someone *more*, he ended up being an undead murderer who'd tracked her down even after she fled across a continent to escape him. And now she was staring into the golden, gleaming eyes of another enraged, supernatural predator. But she wasn't scared of Caleb. She was scared of what she felt for him.

When she opened her mouth, her throat closed, and she couldn't get the words out.

With a disgusted sound, Caleb turned away from her, headed for the door.

"Wait—" Grace grabbed his wrist.

Caleb turned back to her with stunning speed. Suddenly, his arms were around her as his mouth met hers in a rough, demanding kiss that silenced her thoughts and lit her body up like a Roman candle. There was no fear here, no questions. There was just heat and hunger and something softer, sweeter, that she didn't have words for. It was just Caleb. The cantankerous but trustworthy man who'd broken apart the ice inside of her, who challenged her and comforted her and wanted her.

But the energy of their fight was still coursing through Grace—coursing through both of them—and the collision of their bodies became a battle. He tore her sweater off and she ripped his shirt open. He grabbed her by the thighs, hoisting her up, trying to hold her in place. But she clambered higher, so that he had to tilt his head up to receive her kisses, so that he had to strain for a taste of her.

Growling, Caleb laid her on the table, bending over her, caging her with his big body. She fisted her hand in his hair, yanking his head back and biting at the tender skin on his neck. He made a choked sound, his hips bucking against her as his hands clenched on her waist hard enough to hurt.

"*Grace*," he growled her name, grinding the rigid length of his erection against her core.

Pleasure lanced through her, making her momentarily

weak. Caleb seized the opportunity, reaching for the zipper on her jeans. He knelt on the floor as he tugged them down her legs. When Grace was left in just her panties, he pulled her legs over his shoulders and pressed his face between her thighs.

"Going to taste you," he told her, lips moving against her slick, swollen flesh. He licked her through her underwear and growled his pleasure. The sound vibrated against her, teasing her clit. Pleasure overwhelmed her, leaving her helpless and arching against him. Vaguely, she had the sense that she'd lost their battle. But how much of a loss was it when the victor's face was pressed between her thighs?

He ripped her underwear—literally just tore them off her body—and flung them away. And then his mouth was directly on her. His tongue swept through her folds and he growled again as he licked and sucked and savored her. He found her clit and lavished it with sloppy, suckling kisses until her back was arched so hard she thought she was going to rise right out of her own body.

Right as she neared the edge of orgasm, Caleb pulled away. Grace let out a wordless cry of frustration, tugging on his hair. He chuckled demonically.

"Demanding," he said with a wicked smile.

"I'll show you demanding." She slid off the table and onto Caleb, letting her weight bear him down to the floor. The quivering tension of her thwarted orgasm made her clumsy, shaky, but she was determined. "Get rid of these," she said, pulling at the waistband of his sweatpants.

Eyes bright, even in the nighttime dimness, Caleb lifted his hips and shoved the sweatpants down in one swift motion. His expression was cool, amused, but his cock was straining up to his belly, the tip weeping with pre-come.

When Grace laid a hand on his hip, his whole body quivered like a racehorse at the starting gate. He licked his lips, eyes meeting hers.

Grace lowered her head and flicked her tongue against the tip of his cock. He made a pained noise, deep in his throat. The cool amusement fell away from his face, revealing raw, desperate hunger. Empowered by his need, she took him in her hand and licked a low, lingering trail along the underside of his shaft. When she reached the head of his cock, she closed her lips over him and sucked.

Caleb let out a strangled groan, head falling back. His body trembled beneath her, but he remained still. The control Grace had over his pleasure, the need in his eyes, was an intoxicating power. She took more of him into her mouth, sinking deep until she felt him at the back of her throat, keeping the rest of him clasped in her hands. Caleb groaned again and again as she slid her mouth up and down his shaft, cheeks hollowed as she sucked and licked. One of his big hands came to rest on Grace's head. There was no attempt to control her—he just needed to touch her. Grace savored the feel of his fingers curling into her hair, the agonized moans being torn from his throat, the subtle flex of his hips as he fought the urge to thrust into her mouth. She worked him until she felt his whole body tense—and then she pulled away.

"Ah, fuck!" Caleb hissed, as if he hadn't known it was coming.

"Turnabout's fair play," Grace told him sweetly, trailing one finger in a featherlight touch over the head of his cock. It pulsed heavily and more pre-come seeped out. Suddenly, she stood up. "Well. Goodnight."

"*What?*"

She started for the ladder, climbing to the lofted bed. "It's late. I'm tired."

"Like fucking hell you are!"

She heard his big body scrambling upright. Biting back wild laughter, she hurried up the ladder. She dove onto the bed—just as Caleb reached the top. He lunged after her and they collided in a hectic tangle of mouths and hands and teeth and claws. He pinned her beneath his big body, licking and biting at her lips and her neck and her shoulders and anywhere he could get his mouth on her. Grace gave as good as she got, clinging to him, rubbing against him like a cat in heat. Caleb reached down and grasped her thighs, spreading them wide. And then he was inside her, big and hard and stuffing her so full, there wasn't room for anything but the awareness of him, the feeling of him, moving in her and on her, harder and faster until she shattered apart as she sobbed his name.

Some time later, when they'd both caught their breath, Caleb rolled off of her. They lay sprawled beside each other on the big bed, staring at the rough timber beams on the ceiling. The same question Grace had been avoiding the last time they had sex was ringing in her ears again, eroding the contented after-glow she should be feeling. But something had changed, just a little. Caleb told her that he wanted her to be part of the pack—got frustrated when she couldn't admit that she belonged. It gave her just enough hope to try and be brave.

"I have a question." There was an embarrassing quaver in her voice, but she wasn't going to let herself chicken out. She needed to do this.

Caleb tilted his head towards her. "And what's that?" His

expression was one of easy self-assurance, but there was something in his eyes that didn't quite sell it.

"Are we just scratching an itch? Or are we... together?" she asked.

In a single blink, Caleb became a stranger. "Well, I guess that depends." Grace found herself facing the silent, taciturn pilot who'd first flown her into Longtooth. Seeing him close off like that filled her with apprehension. But it was time to stop wishing, and start *doing*. She had to be brave and see what came of it.

"*I* want that," she said, her voice fragile. "But I need you to tell me what *you* want."

The warmth came back as if a fire had kindled behind his eyes. His dark irises gleamed with amber heat. "Yes, I want that, Grace. I want *you*." He cupped the back of her head and pulled her towards him, capturing her mouth in a long, deep kiss.

Happiness and relief and disbelief rushed through her, combining with the pleasure of kissing Caleb. She gasped for breath, clinging to his shoulders as she met the possessive hunger in his kiss, matched it with her own. Biting, sucking, licking, the kiss turned hotter and heavier. Caleb's big body pressed hard against hers, his hands gripping her with desperate strength, like she might run away. She felt the urgent press of his erection jutting against her hip.

Grace pulled back from the kiss, eyes wide. "You're ready to go again? Already?"

He smiled rakishly. "Impressed?"

To be honest, yes, she was. She pushed him onto his back and slid astride his hips. "I'm on top this time."

Caleb's hands grasped her hips. His eyes gleamed with golden heat. "I'm yours, any way you want me."

CHAPTER 26

Grace woke to the feel of a big, warm body looming over hers. Caleb pressed his lips to her forehead and she wrapped her arms around his neck, holding him tightly.

"Gracie," he said warmly. "Don't get me revved up. I have to head out and run tracks for a few hours. Jess picked up his scent last night."

"Should I come?"

"No, I'm going to be in my wolf skin. You wouldn't be able to keep up."

"You could use me as bait."

Caleb stiffened. "Not a chance in hell," he growled. "There are too many things that could go wrong."

"So I'm just supposed to hide in this cabin by myself until he's caught?"

"Yes."

Morning light seeped in around the curtains, giving her just enough light to see the ferocity in Caleb's eyes.

"What if you never catch him?" she demanded. "What if he just gives up and leaves?"

Caleb snorted. "He won't leave. They never do. They fixate—and he's fixated on you. Until he gets you, he won't go anywhere."

"Oh." Dread shivered down her spine.

"He's not going to get you, Grace," Caleb told her, totally certain. "We've got his scent and a slight trail. We might be able to find his lair today and take care of him while he's in his daysleep."

"How do you... 'take care' of him?"

Caleb hesitated. "Are you sure you want to know?"

Grace nodded.

"They're not *alive,* so it's not enough to give them the sort of injury that would kill a human. Even severing the head isn't enough—the body can eventually crawl over and hold it back on until it heals."

She felt her face twisting into a grimace, but she couldn't help it.

"Should I stop?" Caleb asked.

"No, tell me the rest." She tried to school her face into something less horrified.

"They have to be utterly destroyed—broken down so far that they have no hope of reassembling. Theoretically, we could just tear them apart with our teeth until the pieces are too small to move on their own. But we've never trusted leaving anything intact. The surest way is to burn them to ash. It's not discreet, but it's easy enough to do out in the wilderness. I've heard of less remote packs using acid to dissolve the bodies."

Grace shuddered again.

"Sorry," Caleb said softly, cupping her face and tracing her cheek with his thumb.

"No, I wanted to know. I'm glad I know."

"Are you going to be okay? I can text Margaret and tell her I can't track today."

"I'm fine," Grace lied. "The sooner you get out there and find him, the sooner life can go back to normal."

"I'll be back well before sundown," he promised. He pressed a long, hard kiss to her lips, and then he was out of bed, disappearing down the ladder.

GRACE HAD PACKED the beautiful blue yarn and all the knitting supplies Caleb had gotten for her, so she spent the day knitting. She'd also packed books, but reading was too sedate for her current state of mind. She needed something to *do*, something to keep both her hands and her mind busy. She started working on a men's sweater, estimating the measurements for Caleb's size. Gifting it to him would be her final act in their yarn war.

It was mid-afternoon when she heard a scratch at the door and a canine whine.

"Just a second!" she called. She quickly wrapped up her project and hid it away in her bag.

When she opened the door, Caleb was waiting in his wolf skin. He was so beautiful, she instinctively reached out to touch him. He leaned into her touch, groaning as she rubbed his ears. His massive tail swished contentedly. A second later, she felt his shape change. His fur receded and he grew broader, taller—taking her hand with him. When he stood before her in human form, her hand was still curled into his hair, and he was still leaning happily into her touch.

"Wow," she said, breathless. She'd never actually seen him shift before. Or felt it. He'd always done it when she was looking away.

Caleb's eyes crinkled as he took in her reaction. His gaze softened, and he touched her cheek. "How are you doing?"

"Fine. Kept busy. How did the search go?"

"Nothing yet. The track we picked up was a false lead—probably laid on purpose. But there are others still searching. We know our land inside and out. There's nowhere he can hide where we won't find him."

The interminable waiting and her inability to do anything about it frustrated Grace. She felt helpless, and it was doubly frustrating, because it was *her* problem, and she wasn't allowed to try to solve it. Instead, she had to sit around and twiddle her thumbs. But it wasn't Caleb's fault. Grace was just human, and too weak and useless compared to what the wolf kin could do. At best, she would only get in the way. At worst, she could get herself killed.

So she simply nodded and turned to the window, looking out at the fading afternoon light. Where was Alex? Somewhere nearby, where he could watch the cabin, waiting for his chance?

"I'll start the stove," Grace said, turning abruptly away from the window. "And heat up the stew." In addition to pierogis, Natasha had sent caribou stew, salmon cakes, some sort of hearty rabbit casserole, and goose soup with dumplings.

"Alright," Caleb said, sounding cautious.

Grace could feel him watching her as she struck a match and lit the old gas burner. She kept her attention on the kitchen, her back turned to Caleb as she put a pot on the stove and dumped the stew into it.

"I'm sorry, Grace." Caleb's voice came from behind her—right behind her. She turned to face him.

"Sorry for what?"

"I'm sorry you're trapped here."

"It's not your fault."

"Doesn't make it fair." He touched her cheek. "It'll be over soon."

"I know." She leaned against him, grateful that she could. She'd been aching to touch him for so long, longer even than she'd been aware of the ache. The fact that she could do so freely, that he would welcome the touch, reciprocate it, filled her with a warm glow that chased away the feelings of helpless frustration.

Caleb wrapped his arms around her. "How long will the stew take to heat up?"

"I don't know. A few minutes?"

"I have an idea for how we can pass the time."

"Pass the time? It's only going to a be few min—*ohhh*, gotcha."

Caleb lifted the hem of her sweater and Grace raised her arms so he could pull it over her head. His hands went to her jeans next, and she smiled lazily, letting him do all the work. He knelt to shuck them down her legs and she leaned on his shoulder as he stepped out of them. His fingers curled into the waistband of her panties next, and she figured she'd be generous and get her bra off for him. It slipped down her arms and she dropped it on her pile of clothes as Caleb slowly peeled her panties down, kissing and licking each inch of bared skin.

This was the first time she'd gotten naked with him in full daylight, but she didn't feel any insecurity. He worshipped her body with his fingers and mouth, and all she could think about was the feel of him, the pleasure of him. There was no room for shyness.

His nose skimmed along her mound, but he didn't put his mouth on her there. Instead, he turned his head, pressing a teasing kiss to her thigh. Then another kiss, and another, working his way inside, closer to the needy spot that was throbbing for his touch. His tongue stroked over the sensitive skin on the crease between her thigh and her sex.

He stopped. Drew back.

"Caleb?"

He hooked one hand behind her knee and lifted her leg, splaying it out. It wasn't a sexy, spreading-her-legs-so-he-could-feast-on-her move. It was an inspection. He stared at her thigh, at a spot she couldn't see.

"No," he said hoarsely.

"That's not the sort of thing a woman likes to hear in this position," Grace said shakily. Her heart was beginning to accelerate, her hands to shake. Something was wrong. Really wrong.

"He *marked* you." He looked up at her, his face a mask of fury and despair. His eyes gleamed gold, the irises gone wolflike. Against her skin, Grace felt human fingernails elongate into claws. "He fucking marked you!" The words escaped as an inhuman snarl. Caleb shoved away from her. Fur burst from his skin and his face elongated into a fanged muzzle. It was nothing like the shift he'd shown her before. This was savage and uncontrolled. It looked broken and... wrong.

He doubled over as he backed away from her, a vicious snarl tearing from his throat.

"Caleb—"

He crashed into the table, sending one of the chairs

flying, and fell to the floor. When he hit the ground, he was fully in wolf form. He lunged to his feet, eyes wild and rolling. He didn't look like Caleb anymore. There was no sign of the man she knew gleaming in those feral eyes. He snarled, and it turned into a shrill, hair-raising howl that seemed to reverberate inside her head like a scream.

Was he still in there? Was he still Caleb?

The big wolf surged towards the door, throwing his body against it so hard the walls rattled. The door didn't budge. He raked his claws over it and then threw himself at it again, and again. He was going to break the door down, and Grace was going to be left here with no heat and no protection. She had to risk getting close to him.

Hugging the wall, she crept to towards the door while Caleb's silver wolf thrashed and snarled. Staying as far away as she could, Grace reached out and twisted the handle. The door popped open, and Caleb shoved through it, disappearing into the woods. She could hear his crazed howling for a long time. Other wolves nearby joined the chorus until she was surrounded by their eerie, ululating cries.

She slammed the door shut and clapped her hands over her ears, sinking to the floor. The coldness that had been slowly fading from her bones snapped back with a vengeance. Curling in on herself, she stayed that way for long minutes, heart pounding, body trembling, sick with fear.

After several minutes—or hours, Grace wasn't sure—she drew her trembling hands away from her ears. Outside, everything was quiet. The sun was getting low, sending long shadows through the forest surrounding the cabin. Letting out a shaky breath, she got to her feet. She went to her bag and dug around until she found her compact mirror. Sitting on a kitchen chair, she propped her leg up and angled the mirror to try and see what Caleb had seen.

There—high on the inside of her thigh—was a stark white scar, shaped like a human bite, with deep punctures where the eyeteeth were. The mirror slipped from her nerveless fingers and fell to the floor. Glass tinkled as it shattered.

CHAPTER 27

When the door opened, the sun had set, and Grace was sitting in the pitch dark, knees drawn to her chest, trembling from the cold.

"Grace?" Caleb's voice was cautious as he stepped inside. Of course it was. She'd been marked by a vampire. Obviously that was really, *really* bad, or Caleb wouldn't have freaked out and run away.

"I'm sorry," she said, her voice like gravel. "I didn't know."

Caleb made a distressed noise. "Gracie, *no*." She sensed his body approaching her, crouching in front of her. "Don't apologize." His hand cupped her cheek and it was so warm she flinched away. Caleb drew in a sharp breath. "You're like ice."

He moved away from her and she heard the ladder creak. A second later, he was back, wrapping the bed's queen size comforter around her. He moved away again, and the heat register made a heavy clunk as he cranked up the thermostat. A second later, a lamp clicked and soft light filled the cabin.

"Have you eaten?" Caleb asked, moving to look at the pot on the stovetop. It'd been simmering the whole time he was gone. How long had he been gone? Was it burnt beyond recognition?

"I'm not hungry," she said. Her voice sounded like a ghost's.

Caleb turned the burner off and came back to her. Something crunched under his foot and he swore. "What the—glass? What happened?" He bent to pick up the shattered compact.

"I was trying to see it…"

Caleb's face clouded. He looked down, staring at the shards of glass.

"I'm sorry I left you alone," he said in a low voice. "I… I haven't lost control to the wolf in a long time." He gathered the broken glass up and brought it to the garbage.

"What's going to happen to me now?" Grace asked, shaking so hard her teeth were chattering.

Caleb came back, flipped the comforter open, and picked her up. His skin burned like fire. Grace hissed and recoiled, but there was no escaping his strength. He wrapped the comforter around them both, and sank into the chair, holding her against his chest.

"The same thing that was always going to happen," he said, tightening his arms around her as she twisted away from the inferno of his touch. "You're going to stay here while we hunt down the strigoi. Once we destroy him, you and I can go back to The Spruce—but I'm hoping that won't be for too long."

Grace's heart seemed to stop. *He wants me to leave.*

"I've been thinking about buying George Prouse's old place," Caleb continued. "It's just outside of Longtooth, upriver a bit. Maybe this is too soon to ask, but whenever you feel ready, I hope you'll move in with me."

Grace blinked. "What?"

Caleb scrubbed a hand over his face. "I knew it was too soon. Forget I asked. I'll wait a normal amount of time and ask you then." He paused thoughtfully. "What would a normal amount of time be, do you think?"

"You don't want me to leave?"

Caleb looked at her as if she'd turned into a tap-dancing frog. "Haven't I been pretty clear about wanting you to stay?"

"I... I'm not turning into a vampire?"

Caleb's face fell. "Is that what you thought? Fuck, Grace, I'm sorry. I'm so sorry I left you." He clutched her tightly to him, dropping his forehead to rest against hers. "No, honey, you're human. You're staying human."

"Why were you so angry then? Why'd you shift? Why'd you run away?"

Caleb cupped her cheek, stroking his hand over her skin. Slowly, his warmth leeched into her, thawing the brittle cold. "I am the wolf, and the wolf is me, but sometimes, we have different ideas about how to handle things. When I saw the mark on you, the wolf got so angry, he needed to find and kill that fucking strigoi. I couldn't hold him back." He let out a weak laugh. "I haven't lost control like that since I was a kid."

"Oh." Warmth flooded her. She relaxed against Caleb's hold. "Is it dangerous when the wolf takes over?" she asked.

"Never to you," Caleb said fervently. "You never need to fear me. Man or wolf, Grace, I would never do anything to hurt you." He let out a heavy sigh. "Except run off like a lunatic, apparently. I must've gone about ten miles before I managed to get control back."

They sat in silence, huddled together, not moving, not speaking. The snapping cold vanished from Grace's bones, her heart steadied, and the trembling eased from her limbs. Her stomach suddenly growled, breaking the contemplative quiet. Caleb lifted his head, a small smile tugging one corner of his mouth.

"I might be hungry now," Grace said.

"Stay here." He set her on the chair and went to fix bowls for them both. He returned to the table and sat across from her, watching intently as she ate.

"What does the mark mean?" Grace asked.

Caleb paused, picking his words. "It's a way of claiming you. It keeps other strigoi from feeding on you. It marks you as... his."

Grace froze, spoon halfway to her mouth.

"They can feed without leaving scars. But the victims they want to feed from exclusively, or to turn, they put a claim mark on them."

"*His*? Like his... wife?"

"In a way. Although, in general, a woman has to consent to marriage before she becomes a wife. With strigoi, they can just take you."

"So he... took me? Am I..." Grace shook her head. She didn't know what she was asking. All she knew was that she was afraid.

"He didn't take you. You're human, and alive. Once we kill him, the mark will go away."

"What happens if he changes me?"

"*He won't*," Caleb snarled. He cleared his throat, relaxed his shoulders. "He won't," he said more gently. "But for people who are marked and then changed, they're bound to their strigoi sire like a slave."

"Are they all evil? If I was turned would I become evil?"

Caleb's hand clenched on his spoon. He clearly had to stop himself from telling her that she was never going to be turned. "There are myths about strigoi who live off animal blood instead of human, but I don't know how much stock can be put in them."

"There are myths about werewolves," Grace said, "And I used to think there was *no* stock in them."

Caleb smiled. "True."

"So if I were turned, there's a chance I wouldn't be evil."

"*You won't turn!*" Caleb's words turned into an inhuman growl. Black claws shot from his fingertips. He closed his eyes, bracing his hand flat on the table. Slowly, the claws receded. He took a steadying breath and opened his eyes. His irises were still wolfish amber. "If I run off again, Grace, it's just to murder a strigoi—not because of anything you did, okay?"

Grace nodded, eyes wide. "Is this normal, or should we call someone for help? Should Anna take a look at you?"

Caleb smiled wryly. "It's not normal, but it's not something a healer can fix. What it is, is embarrassing. A grown man, losing to his wolf..." He shook his head at himself and took another bite of stew.

"So adults never lose control?"

"I wouldn't say *never*. Arthur wolfed out every time Natasha went into labor. Wade famously wolfed in front of tourists when his daughter called to tell him she was pregnant. Happened right in the post office. That took some... creative explaining. Margaret was livid." Caleb chuckled. He thought for a moment, his expression sobering. "After my dad left, my mom was stuck in her wolfskin for nearly a month."

Grace reached out and laid her hand on his, still pressed flat to the table. It wasn't lost on her that each and every one of those cases was over someone they loved. And Caleb's wolf had taken over... for Grace. She lifted her eyes to his. The wolf was still looking out of his eyes, golden and feral. But all that ferocity was not *because of* her. It was *for* her.

She closed her hand around his and stood up, tugging him with her.

"Where are we going?" he asked, dropping his spoon into his bowl as he rose from his chair.

"To bed."

"Are you sure?" he asked gently. "You've had a rough—"

Grace swung back to face him and pulled his head down to hers, silencing him with a kiss. "Let's show your wolf why he needs to leave the man with me." She kissed him again, long and deep and hard.

When they broke apart, Caleb's breath was a little ragged. "*Grace,*" he breathed her name, and she loved the way it came out as reverently as a prayer.

They climbed up to the bed and surged together like a crashing wave. Grace let go of all the fear, all the worry, all the doubt, and lost herself in the feel of Caleb—in the strength of him holding her, in the warmth of him surrounding her, in the pleasure of him touching her. She put her heart into her flesh and gave it over to him. And when they spun into obliterating climax, she never lost the anchor that tethered her to him.

They lay in each other's arms, drowsy and content. She wanted to stay like this forever. She never wanted to leave him.

She loved him.

The realization hit her like a thunderclap. She sat bolt upright.

I love him.

"Grace?" Caleb asked, instantly alert.

How long had she loved him? Since they first slept together? Since the first time he kissed her? Or had it started even before that—when she thought he hated her. Because even then, he was safe and reliable and principled. He'd defended her from his own family—his *pack*—when Isaac had slobbered on her at the Blue Moose. He'd checked on her when he found her crying in her truck, even though he thought she was a nuisance. He'd tried to be kind to her after she confessed why she'd moved to Alaska, even though he still hadn't trusted her. Caleb may not have been the nicest man in the world, but he was a good man. He was steady and kind and he made her laugh, and she even enjoyed bickering with him.

And Caleb wasn't the only one Grace loved. She loved Margaret and Natasha and Jess and Wade. She loved the Valley for its beauty, for its serenity, and she loved the people who lived here. God, she even loved that ornery asshole, Harry Lance.

"Grace?" Caleb leaned over her, worried now, trying to get her to look at him.

Grace lifted her gaze to his. "I love you," she said simply.

The feral golden glow came back into his eyes and his expression turned fierce, but before he could speak, Grace doubled over. Warmth exploded through her chest. It was more than the delicious heat of Caleb's touch. This came from inside her, and it burst outward like a supernova, filling her with glowing contentment, a feeling of total safety. She gasped, disoriented, but Caleb was there, holding onto her. And when the overwhelming headiness cleared, the warm glow remained. She looked up at Caleb in wonder.

"*Grace,*" he said, voice full of wonder. "You're *here.*"

Outside, a chorus of howls filled the air—and with some strange innate sense that she'd never noticed before, Grace knew exactly who they were. Maxim Freeman. Jess Taaltsiyh. Connor Ankkonisdoy. And then that sense expanded outward, and she felt all of them—a warm, comforting presence. Like Caleb had told her, they weren't *in* her head. She couldn't speak to them, feel their feelings, or hear their thoughts. It was more like the subtle awareness of your family's presence in different rooms of the house. Except this family was huge, and the "house" was spread across miles.

The ecstatic howls died away outside, and the awareness of the pack faded to the back of her mind, and then it was just Grace and Caleb, alone in each other's arms.

"I love you," she told him again, just because she could.

He pulled her tightly against him, crushing his mouth against hers. "I love you," he said against her lips. "God, I love you." His mouth moved to her throat, trailing hot kisses to the curve where her shoulder met her neck. "I want to claim you, Grace." He bit down gently. "But there's no going back. Will you take my claim?"

She stiffened. "A bite... to claim?"

Caleb froze. He pulled back carefully. "It's *nothing* like the strigoi. A wolf's claim is about love, not ownership. The mark wouldn't last if you didn't accept it."

She relaxed against him. "Will it leave a permanent mark?"

"Yes. It's very permanent. If I claim you, if you accept my claim, there'll never be anyone else for me."

She let out a small breath. "That's a big risk."

"I want to take it." He held her gaze, searching her eyes for the sign he wanted.

"Not yet," she said softly.

The light dimmed in his eyes. "I understand," he said, rolling onto his back and staring at the ceiling. "It's too much, too soon."

"That's not it," she said, cupping his jaw, making him turn and look her in the eye. "I plan to accept your claim, Caleb Kinoyit."

The gleam rekindled in his eyes.

"But not until Alex is no longer a threat."

Caleb frowned. "Why? Do you still have some kind of feelings—"

"No! No. I stopped having feelings for him long before I left him. And then after I left—when he wouldn't let me leave—the only feelings that remained were hatred and fear. I only have feelings for you." She leaned in and kissed him softly. "But if you take this permanent step with me, and then something happens to me—"

A snarl wrenched from Caleb's throat. His eyes flashed pure gold and fur broke out over his body. He shook his head hard, holding her tight to him. The fur receded back to human skin. He blinked, and his eyes looked mostly human. "*Nothing* is going to happen to you," he said gruffly. "I'll die before—"

Grace pressed her hand over his mouth. "No you won't. If nothing can happen to me, then nothing can happen to you either, understand?"

His gaze burned into hers and he nodded.

"When all of this is over—when we can go back to

normal life without looking over our shoulders all the time —I'll accept your claim."

"And I'll accept yours," Caleb said.

"Mine? I'm not wolf kin."

"You're pack. You can claim your mate."

"How?"

"Same as I do it. With a bite."

Grace stared at him, a slow smile tugging at her lips. The idea of biting him, marking him as hers, had such a primitive appeal. The urge to do it right that instant was almost overwhelming.

"You feel it now?" Caleb asked with a knowing grin.

She nodded, not quite able to speak.

"Still think you can wait?"

"Yes," she whispered.

His grin only widened.

CHAPTER 28

After that, every time they had sex, the compulsion to bite her claim into his skin accompanied every orgasm. Kisses somehow always turned into bites —each one a little harder than the next, until Grace had to step away from him entirely, or lose control and put her mark on him right then and there.

In the mornings, Caleb shifted into his wolfskin and ran tracks with the others while Grace sat in the cabin and knitted or read. In the evenings, she and Caleb ate and talked and made love so often the insides of her thighs were getting chafed. Jess showed up one afternoon with more food sent by Natasha. Caleb and Grace had to hastily dress and when Jess stepped inside the cabin her nose wrinkled and she looked at them both with knowing dismay.

"You could've just told me to leave it outside the door," she said.

Grace flushed bright red, but Caleb just laughed.

Despite the happiness of being with Caleb, the specter of Alex was omnipresent, and his continued evasion was like the winding gear on a jack-in-the-box. Eventually, something had to give, and the tension was becoming unbearable.

They'd been living in the Ranger Station for a little over a week when Margaret called with bad news. "Wade's been attacked."

Caleb put his phone on speaker and they listened grimly as she explained.

"He was following a scent trail along Splinter Creek. The strigoi caught him from behind. Wade's going to be alright. It wasn't nearly as bad as Elena." A few days ago she'd let them know that Elena was fully healed—shifting into her wolfskin with no problem, and running tracks with the rest of the pack. But even so, the memory made Grace's stomach churn.

"How bad exactly?" Grace asked. Wade was in his seventies. A lesser injury for Elena, who was in her twenties, could be much more damaging for Wade.

"He bled a good amount. Anna gave him a transfusion. He's got some deep lacerations down his back, sliced open to the bone in a few places. He can still shift into his wolfskin, but he's not going to be tracking for a few days."

"He shouldn't be tracking at all!" Grace told Caleb after they hung up with Margaret. "Nobody should! He's only here because of me—people I care about are being hurt because of—"

"No," Caleb said firmly. "Stop that. If you'd never come to Longtooth, you'd probably be sucking blood by now. The strigoi is the only one at fault here. Everybody who faces him knows what the risks are."

"They shouldn't have to take the risk," she said, blinking hard to fight tears.

"They don't have to. They *choose* to. Because you're ours, Grace. You're pack. And we love you. I love you."

Grace curled against him, pressing her face into his chest, and holding on to him as tightly as she could. "I love you too," she whispered tearfully.

ANOTHER WEEK PASSED. The tension ratcheted higher and higher. Caleb and Grace tried to exorcise it through each other's bodies, but it never totally worked. After the brief oblivion of sex, they lay in silence, holding onto each other, until they fell into fitful, nightmarish sleep.

The cabin was starting to feel like a prison, especially during the long hours when Caleb was out tracking. Grace rearranged the cupboards three times. She scrubbed the counters and the table and the floors. She finished knitting Caleb's sweater, then unraveled the whole thing and started over. She emptied the box of matches on the table and tried to build a matchstick house like she remembered seeing her grandpa do. She couldn't figure out how to get it to stay together, and ended up striking matches and letting them burn all the way down to her fingers—holding them as long as she could before the pain forced her to drop them.

Eventually, she gave up on trying to do anything. She just stood at the window like a ghost, staring through the trees down to the river. She traced her gaze over the mountain's steep rise, trying to spot any place where Alex could be hiding during the day. He must have been nearby. Jess and Caleb had both picked up his scent in separate spots within sight of the cabin. He knew Grace was here.

He didn't come into her dreams anymore. He didn't speak to her in her mind. Ever since that night when he'd nearly had her—when Grace and Caleb had finally come together—Alex hadn't tried to reach her in that way. Was it because he couldn't? Or was it part of some strategy? Caleb thought he couldn't—because Grace was pack now, and the protection of the pack had severed his control over her. Grace wasn't as sure as Caleb was, and that uncertainty ate at her.

But the pack was a constant presence, like a warm glow at her back at all times, and when she felt the most crazed, she closed her eyes and let that warmth wash over her.

For his part, Caleb didn't ask why there were matchsticks scattered all over the kitchen table, or why the silverware kept moving to different drawers. He often came back from tracking with little surprises—a jigsaw puzzle from The Spruce's lounge, two skeins of pretty red yarn from Lorraine Lance, a half-done book of crossword puzzles from Wade, a stack of essays from Grace's sophomores, and a few different paperback books from a few different people. She appreciated them all, but she couldn't focus on any of them.

It was getting harder and harder to fall asleep at night. Despite the fact that he spent hours every day covering miles upon miles of mountainous terrain, Grace could tell Caleb wasn't sleeping well either. They were both laying sleeplessly in bed, curled into each other, when she felt a sudden emptiness in her chest, like a piece of her heart had been plucked out. She flinched, her hand flying to her sternum. Beside her, Caleb sat bolt upright.

"What is that?" she gasped.

"Daniel," he said, flinging the covers back and surging out of bed. "He's... he's gone."

That's what the emptiness was—a missing pack member. Grace got out of bed too, searching for clothing. "What's happened? Is he okay?"

Caleb caught her in his arms, stopping her from pulling on her jeans. "I'm going to find out, but you have to stay here."

She'd never been alone in the cabin during the night. She glanced at the drawn curtains. "Please, Caleb, let me come with. If you're with me—"

"I can't risk it, Grace. You're safer here than anywhere else—especially outside. I'll call you as soon as I know what's going on. But I have to go to my sister's house and make sure everything's... I have to go see."

Grace nodded, choking back the frantic plea rising in her throat. Already her hands were shaking at the thought of being alone. *Selfish coward*, she scolded herself. Something was drastically wrong with Daniel—now was not the time to be thinking about herself.

"I'll call you as soon as I get there." Caleb pressed a kiss to her forehead. She sat on the bed and watched him disappear down the ladder. The door opened and closed, and then he was gone.

She was alone.

It was the middle of the night, but she couldn't get back to sleep. She pulled on a pair of sweatpants and one of Caleb's t-shirts, then crawled back into bed and listened to the silence.

A few minutes after he'd left, Grace heard Caleb scratch at the door. Had he forgotten something? She climbed down the ladder and pulled the door open, looking down to where his head would be in wolf form. But there was no wolf there.

"Hello, my love."

Alex stood before her, poised on the threshold. In his arms, he held Daniel Gray's limp body.

CHAPTER 29

Fresh, wet blood coated Daniel's throat and stained the front of his shirt. His skin was sickly pale. A scream rose up in Grace's throat.

"You'll be quiet," Alex said softly, "if you care about the boy."

The scream died. She stared helplessly at the horror in front of her.

Alex shifted his arm so that he could close one hand around Daniel's throat. "He's not dead yet, but he is very, very close. If you want him to have any chance of living beyond tonight, you'll invite me inside."

Grace worked her mouth, but sound wouldn't come out. She swallowed, tried again. "Come in." Her voice was the faintest rasp, but it was enough. Alex smiled beatifically and crossed the threshold.

Once inside, he dropped Daniel like a sack of garbage. Grace gasped as the boy's head cracked against the floor and dropped to her knees beside him. Before she could touch him, check for a pulse, a cold hand closed around her throat, jerking her back. His touch burned like dry ice, and she felt that cold pain splintering through her veins.

"Leave the dog," Alex hissed in her ear. "On your feet."

Grace staggered but did as she was told. Alex spun her around to face him, keeping his hand around her throat. She hadn't looked him in the face in a long time. He was even more painfully beautiful than she remembered. His eyes were inhumanly blue. His face was all sharp angles and shadowy contours. His nose was as straight as a blade, and the mouth underneath it was sensuous and full.

He was wearing the sweater she'd knitted for him. It was the first sweater she'd ever knitted after she'd finally moved on from hats and scarves. It was an ugly thing compared to what she was capable of doing now, made from a cheap black acrylic yarn that had been on clearance—because she hadn't wanted to spend too much on something that might not turn out. And it hadn't turned out. Not very well, anyway. It was littered with twisted stitches, one sleeve was several inches longer than the other, and the collar was wide enough for Grace to slip over her entire body. But Alex had treasured it—apparently still treasured it.

"Ah, Grace, I've missed you," he said fervently. His piercing eyes seemed to soften as he gazed over her. "All of this... this disagreement between us is nothing but a misunderstanding. I should've explained things to you sooner. I realize that now. But I didn't want to move too quickly. And I'll be honest, the taste of your blood is *amazing*. I was reluctant to turn you and lose that delicious vintage forever." He smiled fondly. "But if turning you earlier than I intended means having you at my side forever, then I'll happily give it up. Perhaps the two of us, together, can find a replacement who is just as delicious."

"Please," Grace said hoarsely, trying to appeal to the twisted affection he felt for her. "Don't do this. I don't want to be a strig—"

He tightened his hand around her throat, cutting off her air. His beautiful face had turned terrifying, stark with fury. "That is *their* disgusting word. Their *lies*. They told you I'm a monster, didn't they?"

She choked for air, clawing at his hand. He eased it marginally, allowing her to draw in a desperate, thready breath.

"They're jealous. And afraid of what they don't understand. This is an *exalted* life I am offering you. This is immortality. An eternity filled with unstoppable power and infinite pleasure. I am a *god*, Grace, and I will make you my goddess."

"Alex," she pleaded breathlessly. "I don't—"

He tightened his grip just long enough to silence her again. "You'll see," he promised softly. "Once you're turned, you'll understand what a priceless gift I am giving you. I don't have the time to convince you right now. The boy is near enough dead that the other beasts won't be able to sense him, but they won't leave your little hideaway unguarded for long." He sighed. "I wanted this moment to be beautiful. I wanted to shower you with pleasure while I bestowed immortality upon you. I wanted our bond to be sealed in ecstasy. But the time has passed for that." He tilted his head down, regarding her solemnly. "If you accept my gift gracefully, I will make it very good for you. If you fight me, it will hurt. And when it's done, I will make you finish draining the boy for your first meal as an immortal."

Grace's heart stopped. "No—"

"But if you are good, we'll leave the boy to fate. Maybe he'll die, maybe the other dogs will find him in time. The choice is yours, love. Do you want him to have a chance? Or do you want to kill him yourself?"

Tremors wracked her body so violently that, if it hadn't been for Alex's hand around her neck, Grace would have sunk to the ground.

"Time's ticking, love. Will you fight me, or will you be good?"

Her vision blurred with hot, burning tears. "I'll be good," she answered hoarsely.

Alex leaned in, brushing his lips against her ear. "There's a smart girl." He adjusted his hold on her, shifting his grip to the back of her neck, and then his lips were on her throat, colder than ice. She heard the parting of his lips and then the sudden punch of his teeth through her skin. She gasped at the pain.

"Shhh..." Alex soothed. And then his lips sealed around the wound he'd made, and he began to feed. Grace felt her blood siphoning into his mouth. Her stomach churned and cold shivers chased over her skin. He swallowed a hot mouthful, and then his lips were on her again, drawing the life from her veins. Over his shoulder, she could see Daniel laying still and lifeless in front of the open door.

Grace began to grow light-headed and staggered backwards, crashing against the table. Alex moved with her, steadying her as he continued to feed. The wet sounds of his mouth working against her throat filled her ears. The lightheadedness turned into swirling vertigo. Black spots appeared in her vision, prickling and dancing. She put a hand behind her, bracing herself against the table. Her hand skidded over some debris, and she almost fell again. But Alex wrapped an arm around her back, holding her against him as her knees gave out.

The black spots sparked and grew wider. Grace lost sight of Daniel as her head lolled back. Her hands felt cold and numb. She lifted one idly, clumsily, as Alex continued to drain her. Something was stuck to her palm. She squinted. Her vision was fuzzy and dark. It took her a few seconds to figure out what she was looking at.

A matchstick.

She'd left them scattered across the table. Her heart leapt, and her vision seemed to sharpen briefly. With numb, cold fingers, she slowly maneuvered the match so that she was gripping it by the base. Her vision was fading back out again. Everything was getting so dark. And she was so cold. Her arms had no strength. She dragged the match across the edge of the table, but it was too slow to do anything.

Alex shifted his grip on her as he bit into her again, releasing a fresh flood of blood. He cradled the back of her head—bringing Daniel back into her dim view. Grace drew on all of her fading strength and flicked the match head hard along the rough edge of the table. She smelled the sulfur before she saw the flame. With a wobbling, clumsy hand, she pressed the lit match to Alex's sleeve.

It took a second for his sleeve to catch, but once it did, it went up quickly. Alex's lips suctioned wetly as he pulled back from her, making an inarticulate sound of confusion. Without his support, Grace crumpled to the floor. She felt her own blood as a wet gush down her neck. She lay limply, splayed like a rag doll, watching as the flames licked up his sleeve.

"What—what did you do?" Alex gasped, beating at the fire. "No!" He tried to pull the sweater off, but he only succeeded in spreading the flames—cheap acrylic yarn was incredibly flammable. In seconds, his entire torso went up like a late-January Christmas tree. He staggered backwards, letting out an ear-shattering scream that sounded neither human nor animal, but something unearthly and wrong.

He thrashed as he tried to put the flames out, but they only roared hotter and higher as they consumed his body. He stumbled against the kitchen counter. The paint caught fire immediately, and the old dry wood beneath it followed suit. Alex's screams continued to shatter against Grace's eardrums, but she watched it all happen from deep inside her head, lost in some cold, dark, faraway place.

"Grace!" His voice shrieked from within the blazing inferno that had consumed him entirely. "Grace!" he screamed her name, again and again. It echoed in her mind for what seemed like forever.

The world grew darker and colder for Grace, even as the flames grew hotter and higher. Alex's voice finally twisted away into a shrill nothing. His body slumped to the floor, just a big, motionless, burning mass.

In the distance, a howl sounded. Then another. And another. They were so far away.

The world was so dark now. Grace could hardly even see the fire. But she knew it was spreading, knew its heat was raking over her. Dimly, she sensed the glow of flames licking their way along the kitchen cabinets, climbing the wall. They spidered across the floor from Alex's body.

She was so cold. And so tired. Her eyes drifted shut. Or maybe her vision failed entirely. She wasn't sure, and she didn't really care, either.

"Grace!" A new voice—a familiar voice. Why did she know that voice?

She blinked hard against the darkness, but she couldn't

see anything. She could hear other voices, but none of them stood out to her like that one.

"No! No, no, no no, no—Grace! Gracie? Please, honey, wake up." Her heart pinged weakly as she finally recognized that voice. Caleb. "*Please*, Gracie," he begged.

The agony in his voice tore at her soul, but there wasn't enough of her left to try and comfort him. She tried to speak—tried to at least say goodbye—but the world tilted beneath her, and then the darkness ate her up entirely.

CHAPTER 30

The world was empty and white. Grace blinked, and the whiteness resolved into a grid of speckled squares. It took her a few seconds to understand that she was looking up at a drop tile ceiling. She shifted her gaze downward. She was laying in a hospital bed, still in the clothes she'd been wearing at the Ranger Station. They smelled of smoke and blood and body odor. She wrinkled her nose.

Next to her, she heard a low growl.

She turned and found Caleb, sprawled in an ugly armchair, head angled awkwardly, sound asleep. Not growling—snoring. Behind him, bright morning light streamed through the window. Grace shifted, trying to sit up, and found an IV plugged into her hand and taped to her wrist. A drip bag hung from the pole next to her bed, filled with clear fluid. There was another bed in the room—Daniel Gray lay in that one, eyes closed. A russet-colored wolf was curled up in the chair next to his bed, and she stared back at

Grace with eyes that gleamed a familiar gold. Instinctively, Grace recognized pack. She was looking at Daniel's mother —and Caleb's sister.

Grace stared at Daniel for a long moment, until she was satisfied that she could see his chest rising and falling with his breaths. He was alive. He was safe.

And Alex?

Grace gripped the bedrails, trying to sit up. Pain flared in her neck and she let out a little hiss, pressing her hand there. Her palm landed against a thick bandage taped to her skin.

"Grace?" Caleb asked groggily. A split-second later he woke to full alertness, leaping out of his chair and leaning over her in the bed. "Grace," he breathed, his eyes burning with emotion. There was a faint tremor in his hand as he reached out to touch her cheek.

"I'm okay. I think," she said, laying her hand over his and pressing her cheek into his palm.

"God, Grace," he said hoarsely. "I don't—I don't know what to say. 'I'm sorry' isn't enough. If I had just listened to you—if I had just taken you with me..." He closed his eyes, his face a rigid mask of shame.

She didn't need or want apologies. "You were trying to save your nephew," she said, and that was the end of the conversation as far as she was concerned. "But... Alex? Is he...?"

Caleb opened his eyes. They gleamed with feral rage. "He's ash now. You finished him." He leaned down, resting his forehead against hers. "He won't bother you ever again."

"Good."

They stayed like that for a moment, until the sound of a throat clearing in the doorway caught their attention.

Teekkonlit Valley's doctor Anna Daaldinh, a tall, thin woman with steel-gray hair and a lightly-lined face stood in the doorway.

"How are you feeling, Grace?" she asked, stepping into the room. Caleb retreated back to the chair, giving Anna space to examine Grace.

"Alright. My neck hurts."

"I would expect so," Anna said, pressing a stethoscope to Grace's chest. She checked Grace's breathing and her pulse and her blood pressure. She checked her eyes and ears and nose. At last, she removed the IV and declared Grace fit to leave. "You've had quite a few transfusions of wolf blood. Don't be alarmed if your injuries heal much faster than you're used to."

Grace touched her neck, wondering.

Anna seemed to read her thoughts. She smiled, her eyes crinkling. "I doubt you'll be able to shift—but do let me know if it happens. Interesting medical implications, that." She seemed to consider it for a moment. "Anyways, take it easy for a few days. No strenuous activity." She raised her eyebrows, looking at both Caleb and Grace significantly.

It took Grace a moment to catch on. When she did, she felt her face heat. "Right. Got it."

Anna chuckled at her embarrassment.

"What about Daniel?" Grace asked. "Is he going to be okay?"

"He'll be fine. I expect he'll be on his feet by dinner tonight, if not by lunch."

Caleb helped Grace out of bed and bent down to put her boots on for her. "I'm fine, Caleb," she said with a smile.

Caleb simply growled and laced the boots.

Anna smiled at them both and turned to look out the window. She let out a happy sigh. "The days are going to get longer now," she said thoughtfully. "Today's the first day of Spring."

CHAPTER 31

A few days later...

Waiting for Grace to heal well enough for "strenuous activity" was killing them both. Just as Anna had predicted, her throat healed much more rapidly than she ever would have expected. Within a week, the skin was completely knit back together. Faint pink marks were the only indication that she'd been injured, and Anna assured her that those would vanish within a week or so.

The sexual hiatus gave Caleb and Grace time to take care of other things, though. Grace had to get caught back up with her classes. Julie Angwin, a retired history teacher, had taken over her classes while she was away. She'd done a great job, in that fun-substitute kind of way. She'd kept the kids on track with the reading, but she hadn't assigned too much homework. Which wasn't that far off from Grace's own methods, so there wasn't an overwhelming amount of work that needed to be done.

While Grace was getting settled back into classes, Caleb met with George Prouse and bought the house he'd mentioned a few weeks ago. It was just a bit outside of Longtooth, a few minutes north. It was a fairly small two-bedroom house, but it felt like a mansion after living in a single room for so many months.

Caleb had assured Grace that there was no rush to move in—she could stay at The Spruce as long as she wanted. But she didn't want to stay at The Spruce. She wanted to stay with Caleb. So within a single day, all her meagre possessions were moved to his house—*their* house. It took a few more days to get it furnished. They managed to fill most of the space with hand-me-downs from other pack members. Caleb bought a new mattress on one of his supply runs in Fairbanks.

On their official move-in day, Grace woke up next to Caleb in her bed at The Spruce—a bed that had been totally chaste since they'd gotten back from the ranger station. But after school was over, she drove to their new house. Caleb was already there, working on something with one of the ceiling lights, wearing the blue sweater she'd knitted for him.

He was in human form, but Grace would swear his ears pricked when she walked inside. "Gracie," he greeted her in that low growl that seemed to resonate beneath her skin.

"Nice house you got here," she said, hanging her coat on the hook beside the door. "Looking for a roommate?"

He abandoned the light fixture, bare wires and all, to come pull her into his arms.

"How's your neck?"

"Good as new."

"What do you say to a new mark on it? One that won't go away."

Arousal and something sweeter rolled through her. Their mouths met in a crashing kiss and they stumbled to the bedroom, peeling clothes off of each other. Their style of lovemaking was a little combative, but Grace loved that. She loved how he growled when she pulled his hair. She loved how he pinned her when she tried to twist out of his hold. She loved how he became an obedient lapdog when she stroked him just the right way, and she loved how he could do the same to her.

After several minutes of naked wrestling, she had Caleb on his back while she lay on top of him, every inch of her body plastered to every inch of his. She thought she'd gained the upper hand, but he quickly proved her wrong, spreading her thighs and thrusting into her. He sank deep inside, rocking his hips so that he plunged into her with slow, devastating, languorous strokes. Each one stoked the fire inside of her higher and hotter and brighter. Every nerve ending was aglow. Her body was a bowstring being drawn further and further and further.

"Please," she sobbed, clinging to him, rocking back against him.

"Soon," he answered, his lips trailing along the curve where her shoulder joined her neck.

Not soon enough. She slid her hand between their bodies until she found her clit. Caleb let out a satisfied growl as he felt the circling motions of Grace touching herself.

"There you go, sweetheart," he breathed against her skin. "Make us both come."

Those words pushed her over the edge—climax seized her, arching her back, making her legs quake. Her inner muscles clenched desperately around Caleb's cock, and within two strokes, he tipped over into his own release.

Grace couldn't hold back anymore. She buried her face in the crook of Caleb's neck and bit down. Hard. Instinct drove her to break his skin, to bite down deep—so deep he'd never, ever, get rid of her mark. She tasted his blood, coppery and hot. She felt his teeth breaking her own skin, sinking deep into her flesh. But it didn't hurt. It felt nothing like when Alex had bitten her. Instead, Caleb's bite felt like an extension of sex—it ratcheted the pleasure between them.

Something entirely separate from sex was happening inside of her, too. Something warm and steady and familiar filled her chest, like a second heart, beating beside hers.

Grace gasped as her climax finally released her and sagged against Caleb. Sweaty, panting for breath, they lay sprawled together. The new feeling inside of Grace slowly eased into a less startling awareness, a subtle presence warming her own heart. Just as she'd known the pack was with her when she finally joined, she knew now that it was Caleb's heart beating in tandem with hers, anchoring her to him in a way that felt safe and sure and perfect.

Bright morning light spilled through the windows, bathing them both in its golden glow. Grace stroked a finger across the deep bite mark she'd left on Caleb. It should have looked awful—his skin all torn up and smeared with blood —but the sight of it filled her with possessive contentment. *Mine.* The happiness that filled her didn't seem possible, but she was never going to let it go.

"I love you," she whispered, kissing his damaged skin.

He tilted her chin up and kissed her on the mouth, sweet

and hard and long. When they finally broke apart, he met her gaze with burning intensity.

"I love you, Grace."

THE END

A NOTE ON LANGUAGE

The Teekkonlit Valley does not exist in real life, nor do the Teekkonlit First People from whom the present-day pack is descended. However, based on the approximate location of the imaginary Teekkonlit Valley, the original inhabitants would have likely been an Athabaskan-speaking people—more precisely, probably a dialect of the Koyukon language.

To create the fictional people and places in the Teekkonlit Valley, I have borrowed heavily from the Koyukon language. Many of the Teekkonlit place names and surnames are taken from the Central Koyukon dialect. "Teekkonlit" itself is borrowed from a Koyukon word meaning "wolfskin."

My single greatest resource for spellings and word meanings came from *The Junior Dictionary for Central Koyukon Athabaskan* compiled by Eliza Jones of the Alaska Native Language Center (1978).

However, the spellings used in *Cold Hearted* are not totally faithful to Central Koyukon. This is partly because some of the phonetic symbols were impossible for me to replicate. But there are also several narrative reasons. The first is that the fictional Teekkonlit people would have spoken their own dialect, which would have differed from the Central Koyukon. I also wanted to simulate the effect of linguistic drift over time. And finally, related to the phonetic difficulties, I felt it was realistic to represent the influence of colonizer/settler languages on spelling and pronunciation of names.

If you're interested in Koyukon, or other indigenous Alaskan languages, the University of Alaska Fairbanks has a large digital collection of dictionaries.

NEXT IN THE SERIES:
HOT BLOODED

Keep reading for an excerpt from the next book in the *Tooth & Claw* series, *Hot Blooded*...

HOT BLOODED
CHAPTER ONE

For the fifth time, Amos found himself adjusting the floral arrangement on the coffee table, twisting it ninety degrees to the right, frowning, then twisting it back. He clenched his jaw, still dissatisfied. He shouldn't have gone with red. He'd thought the big, scarlet roses looked vibrant and lively on the florist's website, but now that they'd been delivered, he realized they were the exact color of fresh blood.

Blood.

A jolt ran through him, making his spine stiffen and his hands shake. "Stop it," he muttered to himself, curling his hands into fists until the jittery feeling passed. He stared at the flowers, wishing he'd gotten something more cheerful, something colored like daylight and happiness—sunflowers, maybe. Or daisies.

Too late now. The donor from the blood matching agency was due any minute. The sun had set an hour ago, and he'd spent the entirety of that hour fidgeting around his house. God, he wished they'd get here already. The longer he waited, the worse his fangs ached and the higher the hunger rose inside him. He was old enough to control himself, but it'd be a more enjoyable experience if he didn't *have* to control himself. If he could just have a nice, luxurious drink without terrifying the donor.

Amos hadn't had live blood in nearly a century. Not since he was a young vampire, freshly turned. He'd spent a few decades living as a predator, taking victims indiscriminately. He wasn't proud of those days, but at least he hadn't been as bad as some. As far as he knew, he'd never killed any of his victims. Just left them injured and traumatized.

He clenched his fists again.

The donor was a willing participant. They were getting paid. They knew what they were getting into. No harm was being done.

The doorbell rang suddenly, and Amos nearly jumped out of his skin. He leapt up from the settee, smoothed his shirt, his pants, his hair, and then hurried to the door—tripping over the rug on his way and then nearly knocking over a bookshelf as he righted himself. He took a second to breathe, to steady himself.

The doorbell rang again. His fangs throbbed. Saliva pooled in his mouth. He ran a shaking hand through his hair again and went to the door. Feeling as if he might snap the doorknob clean off, he somehow managed to open it smoothly. He put a polite, non-predatory smile on his face to greet his donor. But as the door swung open and his visitor was revealed in the soft glow of the porch light, his stomach dropped.

Oh no.

She was a woman. A very pretty woman, with abundant curling black hair and dark eyes that shone like molasses and warm golden-toned skin that spoke of summer sunshine. She was nearly as tall as Amos, with a lushly curved body that, even beneath the loose cover of pale blue scrubs, looked soft and warm and inviting.

Another shiver ran through him. He stiffened, suppressing it.

"Hi," the woman said, looking wary. She stood with hunched shoulders, her hands knotted together in front of her. Her big, dark eyes regarded him like a rabbit before a hawk. "I'm here from HemoMatch. Are you Amos Hansen?"

Amos couldn't tell how old she was. He'd been turned at forty-two years old and would perpetually look it, but people didn't seem to show their age as quickly nowadays as they had when he'd been mortal. She could've been anywhere from twenty to forty, for all Amos could tell. Whatever her age, there was something about her that made him want to put a blanket around her shoulders and bring her a hot drink. There was a weariness to her, a hunted quality that evoked protective instincts he'd thought long lost.

He made himself relax, trying to look as cheerful and non-threatening as possible. "Yes, that's me. And you are?"

She blinked. "You don't know who I am? Didn't they tell you I was coming?" She shifted slightly, looking as if she wanted to bolt.

Amos nodded slowly, trying not to startle her. "Yes, of course. But they only told me that they'd matched a donor for me and the time you would be here."

"Oh." She gripped the strap of her bag tightly, uneasy. "Okay. That's weird."

He frowned. "Is it?"

"Yeah. I'm a stranger. They didn't tell you anything about me? You're just going to let some rando into your house?"

He laughed. "You couldn't hurt me." Her eyes went wide. Appalled by himself, he quickly tried to backpedal. "Er, I mean, the agency does very thorough background checks."

She arched a skeptical brow at him, but the fear had lessened in her eyes.

"I believe they withhold information about donors to prevent predatory clients from abusing the service as a hunting ground," he added.

And just like that, she blanched again. Christ, he was stupid.

"Look, I promise you don't need to be afraid of me. I have no desire to harm you. But if you're uncomfortable—" he was choked into silence as the breeze shifted, sweeping her scent towards him.

She smelled divine. Like Christmas dinner and birthday cake and the finest pinot noir, but really, like none of those things. Her scent was uniquely *her* and it made his fangs throb and his hands shake. He needed to taste her. It'd been *so* long, and she smelled like the best thing in the world. He swallowed convulsively before he started drooling.

"If you're uncomfortable," he managed to continue, his voice slightly hoarse, "You can leave. I'll understand."

She looked him over, brows drawn together. She seemed to gather herself, inhaling deeply, squaring her shoulders, and meeting his eyes—before wilting back again. "Your eyes changed," she said faintly.

Like a stalking cat, his pupils always dilated wide when

he was about to feed—when he was hunting. He didn't want her to feel like prey, so he looked down, focusing on the welcome mat beneath her feet.

"Yes, they do that."

An uncomfortable silence followed. Finally, she blew out a breath. "Alright, well, are we going to get this over with, or what?"

Amos jerked his head up, meeting her gaze again. Her expression was still wary, her spine stiff. She didn't look afraid so much as resigned. Her obvious reluctance was putting a damper on something he'd been looking forward to for months—ever since he'd enrolled with the blood matching agency, eagerly awaiting a donor. Finally, she was here, and she looked like she'd rather be anywhere else.

"Not if you're unhappy about it," he said. "I can wait for a different match."

At that, her expression hardened. "No. I said I'd do it, and I will."

"Just what a man loves to hear," he muttered.

She scowled. "What's *that* supposed to mean?"

"It means I don't want to feed from a suffering martyr. Sorry you wasted your time coming by." He started to close the door, but her arm shot out, catching it. She was just a mortal, he could've easily overpowered her, but he didn't want to hurt her, so he sighed, and let her hold the door.

"Wait." Her expression softened to something regretful, if not apologetic. "I'm sorry. This is really weird for me, and I won't lie, I'm a little afraid of the pain, but I really need to do this."

Amos frowned at her. "Why?"

"That's my business."

He opened his mouth to object, but she spoke first.

"I promise I'm not trying to be a martyr. I'm just nervous." She held his gaze, a hint of vulnerability shining in hers.

He still planned to send her away, but then the breeze fluttered again, basking him in the unspeakable allure of her scent.

"Alright," he rasped. "Come in." He stepped back, giving her space, repressing the instinct to grab her, immobilize her, drink his fill of her. She stepped into the hallway, giving him a forced smile. He tried to return it, but the slide of his lips over his pulsing fangs was too much and it turned into a grimace.

"My name's Tessa, by the way," she said. "Well, Teresa. But everyone calls me Tessa. Tessa Vargas."

He nodded, pretending he was a civilized creature, as though his thoughts weren't drowning in blood—*her* blood. "A pleasure to meet you."

"Um... where are we going to do this?" She looked down the entryway, still clutching her bag. He wished he knew some way to put her at ease, but he'd already demonstrated his utter incompetence in that regard.

"In the sitting room. If you don't mind removing your shoes first?"

She toed off her sneakers and nudged them over against the wall.

"Thank you. This way."

She followed him silently. He could sense her perusal of his home, feel her gaze tracking over his art and furnishings. He'd had the entire house cleaned, every crevice and cranny from floor to ceiling, in anticipation of hosting a donor, even though he knew she'd only be seeing the entryway and the sitting room. Amos didn't do things halfway. And besides, something could have come up that necessitated using a different part of the house. He liked to be prepared. Guests or no guests, he liked things to be done right.

In the meticulously arranged, spotlessly clean sitting room, he gestured for her to take a seat on the settee. It was a green, velvet-upholstered reproduction of an Edwardian-era piece with carved wooden trim and cabriole legs. Amos wasn't one of those pretentious vampires who had to fill their homes with authentic remnants from their mortal days as a mark of status. But he couldn't help but prefer the aesthetics from his mortal lifetime, especially those that had been beyond his means as a mortal. That said, he drew the line at dressing like a relic. It would have made him just too much of a cliche.

"You want to… feed…" Tessa clearly struggled with the word. "…on this nice couch? Shouldn't we put some towels down, or something?"

His brows drew together. "I'm not a slobbering barbarian." Even in his hunting days, he hadn't left anything more than a rusty little smudge on the throats of his prey.

"Oh." She flushed. "Uh, sorry. No offense intended."

Amos forced himself to relax. Her tension was making him tense. And now that she was in the enclosed space of the sitting room, her scent was becoming overwhelming.

"It's fine," he said stiffly. "Why don't you sit however is comfortable for you, and then I'll arrange myself accordingly."

She nodded, swallowing audibly. She lifted her bag from her shoulder, setting it on the floor beside the settee. She sank down against the curve of the backrest. Her gaze flicked to the blood-red roses before looking up at Amos expectantly. "Where will you bite me?"

Gah. The question went right to his fangs. He had to swallow another mouthful of saliva before he could answer her. "Your neck is easiest."

She nodded tensely. "Okay."

Moving slowly, cautiously, Amos came to stand before her. When Tessa didn't cringe away, only watched him steadily, he bent down over her, bracing one knee on the seat cushions, gripping the top of the backrest for balance. Caging her with his body sent a hunter's thrill across his nerves, but he kept his posture easy, relaxed. Tessa didn't recoil, didn't flinch or grimace, so he leaned closer. With his free hand, he swept her hair aside, baring her throat. He allowed his fingertips to graze gently over that delicate skin, heightening his anticipation. Tessa drew in a stuttering breath, though whether it was from fear or something else, Amos was too far gone to tell. Her scent was filling his head now, the heat of her body pulling him closer. He could see her carotid artery ticking in her throat, a hypnotic beat.

He cupped the back of her head, brought his mouth to her pulse, and bit.

Her flesh parted easily beneath the points of his fangs. Distantly, he heard her gasp again, felt her body tense beneath him. But then the first taste of her blood hit his tongue and he was gone, lost to the ecstasy of Tessa's hot, rich taste flooding his mouth, overwhelming his senses. He groaned, his arms going around her, cradling her body tightly against his as he angled his head to draw more deeply from that rich well.

Amos drank, and drank, and drank—long, languorous draughts that he savored as one would the finest of wines. When he'd drawn enough to sate the sharpest edges of his hunger, he began to regain his senses. He became aware of

Tessa, clinging to him as tightly as he held onto her. Soft little gasps escaped her mouth as her hips rocked against his, grinding against his stiffened cock.

An erection! He hadn't had one in over a century—couldn't get one without live blood. The urge to put it to use was almost as overwhelming as the blood hunger, but despite her gasping, writhing, clinging embrace, Tessa had only consented to share blood. Tamping down the sexual hunger, Amos shifted his hips back so that his cock wouldn't rub against her.

Even if he wouldn't be getting any sexual gratification, he was more than pleased to witness Tessa's. He drew another sip of her blood, and she cried out, arching against him.

What an unexpected pleasure. He could've happily drunk from her all night, listening to her come with each steady pull, but unfortunately, even with the accelerated healing of his venom, she wouldn't replenish her blood supply quickly enough to survive that. Grabbing hold of his self-control, Amos eased his fangs from her throat, licking at the wounds he'd made until the blood stopped welling. She trembled in his arms, gasping for breath. When he eased her back down to the settee, she stared up at him with flushed cheeks and wild eyes.

Energy and vigor like Amos hadn't felt in decades rushed through him, making him feel suddenly lightheaded. He sank down onto the couch next to Tessa, trying not to swoon.

Tessa blinked. She blinked again. Suddenly, she hauled in a ragged gasp, her eyes going wide and stricken. She scrabbled to sit up, pushing away from Amos.

Dismay cut through the wild rush of live blood coursing

through his system. He twisted to look at Tessa. As he met her horrified gaze, his stomach dropped. Something had gone wrong. He'd messed up, but he didn't know how.

"What did you do?" she demanded, staring at him like he was a monster.

CONTINUE READING *HOT BLOODED*...

ALSO BY HEATHER GUERRE

Tooth & Claw series:

Paranormal Shifter and Vampire Romance

Hot Blooded

Once Bitten

—

Hellbound series:

Paranormal Demon Romance

Demon Lover

—

Forbidden Mates series:

Sci-fi Alien Romance

Star Crossed

Moon Struck

Heart Song

ABOUT THE AUTHOR

Heather Guerre writes sexy-sweet fantasy, sci-fi, and contemporary romances. A hopeless romantic and an unapologetic nerd, Heather loves everything to do with romance, aliens, shifters, cyborgs, monsters, and magic.

For more from Heather, you can subscribe to her newsletter at heatherguerre.com/newsletter. Subscribers receive alerts for new releases as well as newsletter-exclusive bonus material.

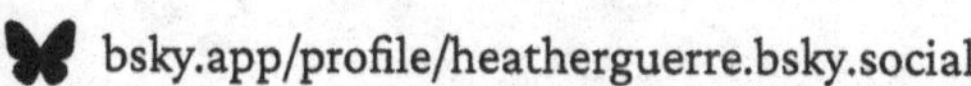

bsky.app/profile/heatherguerre.bsky.social
instagram.com/authorheatherguerre
goodreads.com/heatherguerre
bookbub.com/authors/heather-guerre

THANK YOU

Thank you for reading ***Cold Hearted***! If you enjoyed it (or even if you didn't), please consider reviewing or recommending it on social media and/or the retailer where you purchased it. Word of mouth has a huge impact on an author's success, and it helps other readers find new books to enjoy.

www.ingramcontent.com/pod-product-compliance
Lightning Source LLC
Chambersburg PA
CBHW011129190726
48289CB00012B/2964